MW01440205

This is a work of fiction. All characters, organizations, and events portrayed in this novel are either products of the author's imagination or are used fictitiously. Political and literary quotes are verbatim.

The views expressed in this publication are those of the author and do not necessarily reflect the official policy or position of the Department of Defense or the U.S. Government. The public release clearance of this publication by the Department of Defense does not imply Department of Defense endorsement or factual accuracy of the material.

Copyright 2023 by John T. LaFalce

For Erin Marie

1D343

Attack on the Pentagon

LIST OF ABBREVIATIONS

AGL	Above Ground Level
ASAP	As Soon As Possible
ATF	Bureau of Alcohol, Tobacco, Firearms and Explosives
CAC	Combined Access Card
CDR	Commander
CIA	Central Intelligence Agency
COOP	Continuity of Operations Center
DC	District of Columbia
DIA	Defense Intelligence Agency
DOD	Department of Defense
EAM	Emergency Action Message
EEO	Equal Employment Opportunity
EMP	Electromagnetic Pulse
FBI	Federal Bureau of Investigation
FPCON	Force Protection Condition
HMX-1	Marine Helicopter Squadron One
I-66	U.S. Interstate 66
I-95	U.S. Interstate 95
I-395	U.S. Interstate 395
I-495	U.S. Interstate 495
LTC	Lieutenant Colonel
MAJ	Major
Metro	Washington Metropolitan Area Transit Authority
NMCC	National Military Command Center
NSA	National Security Agency
OPLAN	Operations Plan
OTASCO	Oklahoma Tire and Service Company
P-COOP	Presidential COOP
PFPA	Pentagon Force Protection Agency
POSH	Prevention of Sexual Harassment
POTUS	President of the United States
rad	Radiation Absorbed
RV	Recreational Vehicle
SECDEF	Secretary of Defense
SCIF	Sensitive Compartmented Information Facility
SITRP	Situation Report
SOAR A	Special Operations Aviation Regiment, Airborne
Space Com	U.S. Space Command
TNT	2,4,6-trintrotolune
TSA	Transportation Security Administration
USSR	Union of Soviet Socialist Republics
VC	Viet Cong
XO	Executive Officer

TABLE OF CONTENTS

Chapter 1

Second Action

Tuesday, 31 May, 2017

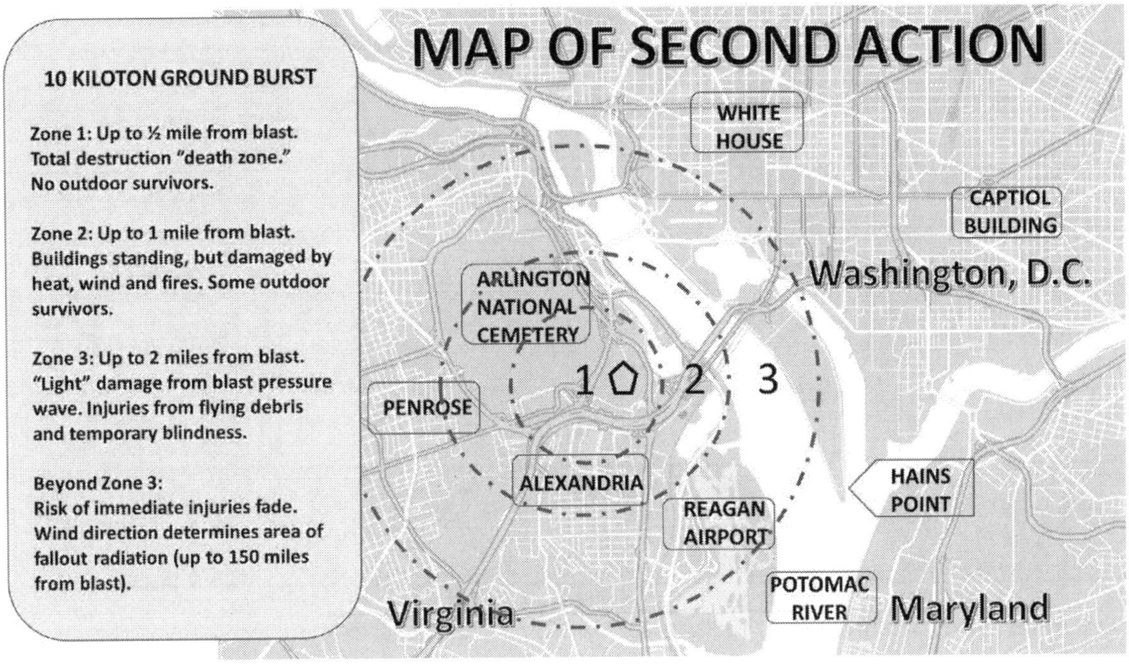

The white panel van parked about fifty yards down the grassy eastern slope of the United States Air Force Memorial in Arlington, VA. The memorial's three spot-lit stainless-steel spires gracefully arched twenty-five stories up and out into Washington, D.C.'s early morning sky. A half-mile away, again to the east, and less than one hundred feet below, the gigantic Pentagon building sat bathed in its own ethereal glow of outdoor lighting.

At 4:00 a.m., a chemical and fission detonator triggered molecular fusion within the highly enriched uranium core of the weapon hidden in the white van. Anyone unfortunate enough to be watching within line-of-sight of the van was instantly blinded by a burst of gamma rays exiting the blast at the speed of light. A tenth of a second later, an over 5,000-degree Fahrenheit fireball would incinerate them.

Radiating outward, the fireball torched everything with sun-like intensity within a circular half-mile of the Air Force Memorial—the death zone. Night turned to the fiercest day, illuminating the progress of the inferno as it scorched outward with dissipating effectiveness for a few more miles. Windows melted or shattered, paint evaporated, and trees exploded into cinders. Uncountable fires ignited as the fireball instantly passed, searing anyone unfortunate to be close enough and outdoors at that early hour.

The bomb's initial gamma radiation burst also produced a high-voltage surge that crackled through the atmosphere. This EMP (electromagnet pulse) fried the local commercial power grid and the microcircuit brains of innumerable electronic devices.

The initial zap of radiation, the fireball, and the burst of EMP all occurred in the first second of the bomb's activation. Next came a catastrophic shock wave produced by blink-fast pressure changes at the heart of the detonation. A fire cracker creates a pressure wave, and a stick of dynamite generates a larger one. The relatively small 10-kiloton weapon in the white van produced a shock wave equivalent to 200 million pounds of 2,4,6—trinitrotoluene, or TNT.

Anything within the death zone around the blast was tossed, bent, toppled, crushed, shredded, and then pulverized. The initial shock wave was over 300 miles per hour, roaring outward and picking up chunks and shards of debris that enhanced its destructiveness. Upon reaching downtown Washington, D.C., several miles away, the intensity of the pressure wave had lessened, but still left a devasting imprint.

An orange-red, fiery globe engulfed the death zone, growing and slowly rising in the cooler pre-dawn air. Airline pilots hundreds of miles away reported seeing "a flashing neon light," sensing the birth of a traumatic event. A grimy reddish-brown cloud arose in a self-illuminating column, casting an eerie glow on the cityscape below. After sucking moisture from the atmosphere, the updraft would slow and cool. The coming dawn would make the deforming mushroom crown visible to the terrified populace below.

The cloud contained debris particles that had been lifted from the moon-like crater formed by the blast below. Later that morning, winds aloft would tug it east-northeast towards Chesapeake Bay and Baltimore. For days, bit by bit, specks and ashes would slowly drift downward like a soiled snowfall, covering everything below with highly radioactive fallout.

Few people in the death zone surrounding the vaporized white van would live to see the sunrise that morning. Tens of thousands of others within a few miles of that spot would also succumb, either quickly or eventually. The bomb and its radioactive fallout would leave a 3,000-square-mile area of long-term devastation, impacting the lives of millions and requiring full or partial evacuation, decontamination, demolition, and eventual rebuilding—or abandonment.

***

Equipment, plans, and procedures were in place to protect the people working in the Pentagon from a myriad of potential threats. Lone assassins and civil unrest would be quelled by the vigilant and well-armed PFPA (Pentagon Force Protection Agency). During emergencies, employees knew to follow luminous signage to building exits and then proceed to outdoor marshalling areas for head counts. If directed, they would bring a personal double-lined "go bag" containing a change of clothes and shoes. Without it, during a chemical event, they would be assigned paper gowns and flip-flops to wear after being decontaminated by pressure washers in the building's parking lot.

By plan or by default, the Pentagon's concentric, interlinked buildings and deep basement make it a redoubtable citadel. To minimize the use of metals needed for early 1940's war production, the buildings' designers relied on continuously poured slabs, beams, and walls of reinforced concrete. A cross-section of any Pentagon building would show it to be a honeycomb of rooms formed by ten-inch-thick concrete dividers. For almost seventy-five years, the building had withstood all natural and manmade threats, save one. The commercial airliner attack of 11 September, 2001 showed that the mighty fortress could be breached—if enough energy were applied.

For the few hundred military, civilian, and contract employees working inside the building at 4:00 a.m. that morning, the first indication of the bomb's detonation was flickering of their computer screens and overhead lights. Those near the building's roof or outside walls may have momentarily sensed the bomb's raging fireball. A second later, the arriving shock wave made it clear to all that a major incident was underway. Resting atop over 41,000 concrete pilings driven down to bedrock, the Pentagon will sway and rumble during minor earthquakes. The bomb in the white van caused its own earthquake, shaking the concrete giant like a toy rattle.

While grabbing hold of anything nearby for support, the sounds of the fracturing building thundered around the quivering employees. Burning smells—rubber, carpet, ceiling tiles, insulation, furniture, paper, electronics, paint, cables, cubicle partitions—if not the fires themselves, soon followed. A cold, wet dousing by the interior fire protection water sprinklers stopped after a quarter-hour due to EMP-induced low water pressure.

Weakened by the bomb's fireball, the ballistic-grade exterior windows that faced the Air Force Memorial were shattered by the shockwave that followed. Their carefully spaced and neat rectangular openings became roaring blowtorches, burning their way into the building on all five floors. House-sized sections of the slate roof were scoured off, allowing more fires to combust in the building's attic and upper floors. Dozens of natural gas pockets accumulated from ruptured service lines, sparking secondary explosions and fires.

To defend against EMP, top-secret areas such as the NMCC (National Military Command Center) had been shielded against the threat at great cost. The true EMP hazard was not inside the building, but outside in neighboring Northern Virginia, the District, and across the Potomac River in central Maryland. This is where the bomb's high-voltage surge knocked out critical generators, transformers, sub-stations, cooling systems, and control centers. This meant no electrical service for millions of local customers, and cascading blackouts in the mid-Atlantic electrical grid. The EMP also brought internet service in North America to a crawl as delicate electronics were frizzled and the flow of electricity ebbed. This was due to the disproportionally high number of government and commercial data centers dotting the landscape around Washington.

In less than five seconds, the bomb had transformed one of the most secure buildings in the United States Department of Defense into the most hazardous. Surviving employees found themselves entombed in a dark, wet, smoldering, and foreboding place. Without phones and internet—classified or not—there was no definitive word on what had just transpired. After peering through existing and newly created building exits, it was obvious that the safer alternative was for them to stay inside rather than venture into the eerie landscape outside.

Instinctively coalescing with other survivors, they surmised that the worst improbability had occurred and began to plan. A large, relatively safe shelter-in-place location would be organized. It would need to be deep within or under the building to shield the survivors from radiation. The wounded would be triaged for medical care. Food, water, lighting, blankets, and medical supplies would be scavenged. Threats of collapsing debris, flooding, fires, and leaking gas would be vigilantly monitored while they patiently waited to be rescued.

Chapter 2

Thirty Minutes

Tuesday, 31 May, 2017

When diplomatic, economic, and humanitarian entreaties fail, the U.S. president can choose among a dizzying array of military options to engage an enemy. If the conflict unlikely escalates to the level of nuclear brinksmanship, a bevy of secret contingency plans will be activated.

Top federal managers and congressional leaders will be evacuated to an underground Government Continuity of Operations site in rural Virginia. This is referred to at the G-COOP and is code named, CLUBHOUSE. Likewise, the President, along with selected civilian and military staff, will relocate to a second below-ground site in rural Pennsylvania. This is the P-COOP and is code named, BUNKER. Panic, fear, apprehension—and possibly anarchy—will grip the country, but Congress and the federal bureaucracy will survive, at least for a while.

For a democracy intentionally designed for deliberative decision-making, the procedure for launching a retaliatory nuclear assault is surprisingly stream-lined. When enemy nuclear missiles are launched towards America, they will be detected by radars and satellites. Space Com (the U.S. Space Command) will alert the NMCC nestled in the Pentagon's basement. An always-present military attaché, and most likely the Secretary of Defense, will assist the president in choosing among a menu of pre-configured strike plans. The president's order will be fast-tracked through the military bureaucracy to aircraft aloft, missile silos, and deployed submarines. At each location, two officers will work in close synchronization (and agreement) to first authenticate their orders, then target, arm, and release their weapons.

The entire process, referred to as the National Command Authority (ordering the attack) and the National Command System (executing the attack), is designed to be completed in less time than it takes to get your car washed. Hostile land-based missiles take half an hour to travel into space and release multiple warheads that shriek down to their pre-set targets. Delivery of enemy sub-launched missiles can take less than half that time, depending on the distance from to the target. Therefore, the allotted time for U.S. detection and the launch of a counterstrike is somewhere between ten and thirty minutes. The faster this can be accomplished, the better.

Almost eleven thousand miles above Washington, a Global Positioning System satellite detected the 4:00 a.m. blast in the white van parked on the grassy slope of the U.S. Air Force Memorial. The satellite transmission triggered alarm bells at multiple Space Com operation centers in Colorado. This was the first official notification that something was amiss in Washington, and many billions of dollars had been invested to make it possible. Just the same, over a million everyday people in the National Capital Region came to the same conclusion by looking out their windows after being awoken by the bomb's shaking, noise, light, and heat.

***

U.S. Marine Corps Colonel Richard Pawlowski was already awake in his Quantico Marine Base quarters, thirty miles south of Washington, D.C. His six-hour shift as Deputy Director for Operations in the Pentagon NMCC would begin at 6:00 a.m. He wanted to get a run in before taking the train and subway to work. He noticed the initial flash from the bomb, like a distant thunderstorm. Stepping outside, he saw an eerie glow above the northeast-facing treetops. A few of his high-ranking neighbors were also outside, and they drifted together, unselfconsciously dressed in whatever their usual sleeping attire was.

"Looks like the lights are out," one observed. "Could be a fire at the Possum Point power station."

"Good thought," another offered. "I'm thinking something industrial, maybe towards Baltimore."

"Too far away," a third chided, "may be a crash at Reagan airport."

"Too much light for plane crash, even a big one," the first one opined. "Now I'm thinking of..."

Col. Pawlowski remained silent, suspecting something worse, yet leery of verbalizing it and appearing hysterical to the others, two of whom outranked him. Out of habit, he had carried his NMCC-issued handheld terminal with him, and it had not buzzed with new messages. He noted that the others were also toting cell phones or devices like his own.

Then the ground vibrated with growing intensity, and a wall of sound roared over the four men and their orderly neighborhood of military housing. He had once viewed a space shuttle launch at Cape Canaveral, feeling the awesome thunder it created while arcing into the night sky. This new sound and shaking were as loud and strong as those of the launching spacecraft. While the group instinctively dropped to one knee on the grass, he viewed his terminal and realized his connectivity to the Pentagon had been severed.

"Gotta go," he announced, springing up, feeling the vibrations ebb as he jogged towards his quarters. In the kitchen, he tested the landline phone and heard the dial tone.

"I'll make you some coffee," his pajama-clad wife softly offered, lighting a candle from a glowing burner on the gas stove. "I think I can pour hot water into a filter and end up with something drinkable."

"Good," he mumbled, sitting at the table, and pulling a three-ring binder from his work backpack. Reading from a laminated card, the colonel dialed the Pentagon NMCC, receiving a busy tone. Next, he called the Marine desk officer at the P-COOP.

A tense, yet tentative voice answered, "Captain Virgil Ivey."

Good! "Captain, this is Colonel Richard Pawlowski, I'm an NMCC ADDO (Assistant Deputy Director for Operations)."

"And you're alive?" Virgil squeaked incredulously.

Better lead him by the hand—and quickly. "Virgil, run my authorization, it's bravo-romeo-five-four-niner, then forward me to the operations chief." Listening to Virgil's deliberate keystrokes, he glanced at the kitchen wall clock—it was about 0410 hours. The red-orange glow outside the window appeared to be brightening, but it was too early for sunrise.

"Sir," Virgil's anxious voice returned, "your authorization is valid, Commander Schiffman, our Operations Chief, is already working three phones...and his terminal."

Pawlowski thanked his wife as she placed a mug of coffee before him and sat down. She silently listened with fascination and growing unease as her husband's secret work world seemed to connect with the odd predawn events. "Virgil, just tell me the current situation—pretend you have to do it in one minute."

"Well, sir, here is what I understand. Space Com reports a nuclear ground burst in the vicinity of Arlington Heights, Virginia around oh-four-hundred hours."

"Got it," the colonel replied, "and the NMCC is off-line?"

"Yes sir, completely. We can't contact them, and neither can Space Com. E-mail and the internet aren't working either."

"Virgil, is anyone in contact with the POTUS (President of the United States), SECDEF (Secretary of Defense) or the Chairman (of the Joint Chiefs of Staff)?"

"Not yet sir, I think that's what Commander Schiffman is working on."

"What the airborne operation centers and Air Force One?"

"Space Com reports two aircraft airborne. One is heading for a holding pattern over Missouri. The other is enroute to Joint-Base Andrews in Maryland from Offutt Air Force Base in Nebraska. We've been trying, but can't contact the Air Force at Andrews, so we don't have status on the president's plane.

Shit, Pawlowski thought, *this is actually happening.* "Virgil, give me a minute here to come up with a plan."

"Yes, sir."

He took a sip of coffee, too deep in thought to notice its weakness or his wife's newfound fascination with him. *The only thing that mattered was securing the POTUS. Andrews was eleven miles from the blast, but was probably getting fallout, or would be soon. The SECDEF and the chairman also needed to be secured. They both lived in historic government quarters on Joint Base Meyers-Henderson Hall...too damn close to the blast to have survived—if they were at home. Consulting his three-ring binder, Pawlowski picked the only OPLAN (operations plan) that made sense. He may be ending his career by acting unilaterally and above his pay grade, but it was logically the right thing to do.*

He could hear Virgil's agitated breath on the line, "Virgil, you there?"

"Yes, sir."

"Write this down carefully and repeat it back to me, I'm ordering OPLAN eight-zero-six-six, appendix delta-three. My authorization is bravo-juliet-lima-one-two-one. Please repeat that back."

"OPLAN eight-zero-six-six, appendix delta-three, authorization bravo-juliet-lima-one-twenty-one.

Pawlowski groaned silently, "one-two-one, Virgil, not one-twenty-one. Run that up to Commander Schiffman, and I'll wait for his response. Watching the kitchen clock, he reached across the table for his wife's hand, sipping some more too-weak coffee. He thought about the "ten-to-thirty minutes" time window the US was supposed to meet when responding to nuclear threats. *He'd already used over half of that sitting at his kitchen table. If they all lived through this clusterfuck, what was happening right now to the National Command Authority would be studied by War College students for the next thirty years. Just the same, if the weapon truly was a ground burst in their own backyard—and not delivered by a missile—then it could be days, weeks, or longer before it was determined who was responsible for the attack.*

Virgil was back at 0426 hours. "Sir?"

"Still here, Virgil."

"Sir, your order has been authenticated and implemented."

"Roger, and good work, Captain."

"Sir, thanks. Sir..."

"Yes?"

In a hushed tone, Virgil asked, "Are we safe?"

"You're safe where you're at, for sure. I would stay there a while," then he hung up. His gaze shifted from the wall clock to his apprehensive wife, "I have to go ASAP, maybe for a few days."

She knew better than to ask questions or to get emotional; that would be worked out later with the other wives and husbands, whose spouses would also be deploying. "Tell me how I can help you get ready," was all she said.

Chapter 3
Talon

Tuesday, 31 May, 2017

The two VH-60N White Hawk helicopters lifted off from Quantico at 0647 hours, not as quickly as Col. Pawlowski would have liked, but they would be landing at the White House in just fifteen minutes. The objective of OPLAN 8066, Appendix D3, was to quickly reestablish the National Command Authority during a national crisis. This would be done by evacuating the president to a backup facility. If the president was found to be incapacitated, the Marines would work through the presidential line of succession, beginning with the vice president.

The sun rose at 5:00 a.m. that morning, dully illuminating the lush Virginia landscape. Clearing the tree line with a northern heading, the White Hawks quickly attained their cruising speed of 149 knots. The aircraft were fully operational, with voice and data links to the Quantico Air Facility and their squadron commander. Land-based navigation aids and regional air traffic control were both offline, so Major Gwynn Elliott, the pilot in command, decided she would visually fly a heading of 033 degrees 28.8 miles to the southern tip of Hains Point. She had flown the route thirty-seven times and knew Interstate 95 would be on the port side and the Potomac River on her starboard. There was zero chance of getting lost. On her approach to Hains Point, she would head 347 degrees for 2.6 miles, slowing and descending to land at the white marker on the South Lawn—if that was even possible on this crazy morning.

Each helicopter was manned by a pilot, co-pilot, crew chief, and two Marine infantrymen. All wore bulky full-cover suits with respirators designed to protect them from chemical, biological, and radiological threats. Another twist on their mission were the M9 Berettas issued to the four pilots and the M27 Infantry Automatic Rifles issued to the aircrews. Theirs' was regarded as a combat mission with the potential for hostile fire from an unidentified opponent. To make things interesting, each aircraft was also supplied with chemical, stun, and sting grenades—should they be needed. Pawlowski rode as a passenger in the second aircraft, receiving blunt guidance from the HMX-1 Marine Helicopter Squadron One Commanding Officer not to inject himself into the mission.

Rising to 800 feet AGL (above ground level), the helicopters passed just east of the Triangle Commuter Lot, where a pickup truck had oddly burned with purple smoke just twenty-five hours earlier. Soon, the dull morning outside the windscreen transitioned to a smoky late afternoon. Stunned by what they were seeing below, and with visibility deteriorating, Maj. Elliott reduced her airspeed. Captain Andrew Stone, the co-pilot, radioed back commentary to the small crowd packed into the Quantico Air Facilities' control center.

"Quantico, Talon One," Capt. Stone called into his respirator microphone.

"Go ahead, Talon One," the com systems operator calmly replied.

"Descending from 800 AGL to stay below falling ceiling. Visibility is five miles and decreasing. We see a wall of dark smoke from one to four o'clock ascending to cloud level. The roads are clogged with outgoing traffic, none of it moving."

"Roger," the radio operator replied, "rad (radiation absorbed) reading?"

"No change," the co-pilot responded, checking the display on a hand-held radiation meter. "Passing Indian Head and approaching Mount Vernon, no damage. Fort Belvoir is ahead now. Route 1 is clogged. We see miles of headlights and tail lights going both ways. The smoke wall ahead is denser, and darker. 540 AGL, vis less than two miles."

"Blackwell to Talon One," the Squadron Commander interjected.

"Talon One," Maj. Elliott responded.

"Get a visual on the Pentagon and call back a SITREP (situation report)."

"Yes,sir," the pilot evenly replied, "Pentagon SITREP."

"Approaching Wilson Bridge, rad now forty-five," Capt. Stone continued his travelog. "475 AGL, vis falling, now about one mile, speed forty-eight knots. Bridge and Interstate 495 packed; we see crashes and civilians on the roadside. Now we see fires ahead, there must be thousands, like a city at night in the smoke. Rad now eighty-three."

"Roger, Talon One."

"Bolling (Joint Base Anacostia-Bolling) now, dozens of fires and visible damage. Rad one-twenty-five—no wait, now one-sixty-five. Reagan Airport on starboard, we see structural damage, fires and aircraft tossed like toys. Pentagon now—oh my god!"

"Talon One, Quantico, report."

"We got low vis, sir, but looks like there is a crater to the south, southwest, about as big as the building. Outer buildings nearest the crater have fallen into it. Many fires, some covering entire buildings. It's a mess. No survivors in sight."

"Rad, Talon One?"

"Two-twelve!"

"Final approach," Maj. Elliott coolly announced, turning right to a heading of 021 degrees. It was time for her co-pilot to stop yacking and start working. "Andy, call out altitude and airspeed. Keep your eyes outside, and watch for the Washington Monument; I don't want to fly into that damn thing—or whatever's left of it."

Each White House approach and departure of HMX-1 aircraft was normally carefully planned, monitored, and choreographed between Quantico, the White House Military Office, and Joint Base Anacostia-Bolling on the eastern shore of the Potomac. Maj. Elliott's mission, call sign Talon, would be more of a smash-and-grab operation. Gamma radiation from heavier fallout particles that had already drifted back to the ground was a significant factor. Two hours of exposure to the current rad level 200 radiation would probably make you vomit. Two hours at rad level 600, which the South Lawn would have been at earlier that morning, would probably kill you. The radiation shielding offered by substantial buildings like the White House ended as soon as an occupant stepped outdoors. One Talon goal was to limit outdoor exposure for all by spending as little time as possible in the hot zone.

Arriving at the South Lawn, the lead copter would onboard the POTUS, the FLOTUS (first lady of the U.S.) and the military attaché carrying the nuclear launch plans, codes, and communications terminal. If, by some fluke, the SECDEF or the chairman of the joint chiefs of staff were there, they would also be evacuated, but nobody else other than non-adult legal dependents of the POTUS. Additionally, no pets or luggage would be allowed on board.

After gently landing, Elliott kept the engines whining at operating speed, with blades chopping at the sooty air. A gaggle of nine people emerged from the White House, all wearing protective suits and respirators. The OPLAN specified three evacuees, with a possibility of a few more. With nine evacuees, the passengers would be sitting atop each other, or on the floor of the small luxury passenger cabin. Exchanging glances, Elliott and Stone silently agreed on what they would do, which was basically nothing. She could stand at the door of the aircraft and argue with whoever was in charge, but that would most likely be her commander in chief, so enforcing the head count would be useless—and prolong everyone's exposure to the deadly radiation.

"Open the door, lower the steps!" She barked into her respirator microphone. "I need confirmation of the nuclear launch biscuit (codes) and the football (terminal). The co-pilot and I will visually identify the POTUS. Remove his mask and bring him forward. If he argues, do it anyway, and make sure everybody else keeps their suits and respirators on. Then close that fucking door!"

The second aircraft, Talon Two, a duplicate of the first, hovered over the Ellipse adjacent to the White House. Its purpose was to be a protective decoy, to provide contingency backup if needed, and to remain relatively uncontaminated on the inside for follow-on leadership extraction missions that day. Onboard, Col. Pawlowski peered through the smoky blizzard outside to monitor the activity on the South Lawn.

Flying at maximum speed, the Talon aircraft would arrive at the P-COOP site in about thirty minutes. Other than the co-pilot's quiet narration back to Quantico, there was no chatter between the pilots, aircrew, or passengers. All were emotionally stunned by that morning's dreadful surprises, and worried about loved ones left behind and about whatever would happen next. Fumbling to remove his mask, the president's chief of staff sought to plot strategy with him. Tiredly raising a hand, the president signaled that now was not the time. With his head tilted back and eyes closed, he needed a short mental respite to prepare for what was ahead.

***

Following the path of the rising sun across America, word of the nuclear attack on the nation's capital spread quickly. Those in the mid-Atlantic region learned something was amiss due to power and internet outages. Most everyone else received the shocking news during whatever their morning routines were that last day of May.

Hurricanes, tornadoes, earthquakes, floods, droughts, pandemics, and wildfires—the American public has become inured to their sporadic reoccurrences. With adequate warning, preparations can be made to reduce lives lost and property damaged. It is understood that local, state, and federal government resources will arrive to help those impacted. Insurance, if bought, will cover material losses. Those carefully groomed understandings and expectations serve to stifle public jitters and squelch potential panic when natural disasters occur.

The IND (improvised nuclear device) detonated outside the Pentagon, turned that logic inside out. There was no warning or chance to prepare. Few people understand what happens during a nuclear attack, or what to do after one. What resources could the government provide if Washington, D.C. had been destroyed? Would more American cities be bombed, or was America bombing other countries? Was this the beginning of World War III...or the Apocalypse?

Naturally, the American public—and the rest of the world—was jittery and panicked. Also, naturally, thoughts turned inward to individual preparation and survival. Families coalesced, taking stock of on-hand water, food, money, and gasoline needed for short-term survival. Just in case the worst should happen, guns were cleaned, loaded, and made ready. Many people reached out to friends, neighbors, and church families for divine and moral support. Humans being what we are, food, tobacco, liquor, and drug stores were inundated along with banks and gas stations. Most were understaffed, or not open at all, but that did not stop some mobs from shopping. Those with habits to feed, legal or otherwise, sought to stock up on their vice of choice.

***

Arriving at the P-COOP, one of the president's first official duties that morning was to mobilize the Army Reserve and encourage a few holdout governors to mobilize their National Guard units. At noon, he gave a nation-wide address on the Emergency Alert System:

> My fellow Americans,
>
> I am speaking to you from a continuity of operations facility in Pennsylvania.
>
> An event we have long prepared for—and feared—has transpired. A nuclear device was detonated in Washington, DC, near the Pentagon building at four-a.m. Eastern Time this morning.
>
> I ask each of you to shelter-in-place at your current location and not to travel. Go to a basement or an interior room if a basement is not available. Additional attacks are not likely, but we should be prepared as if they were.
>
> For your safety and to defend our country, the following actions have been taken:
>
> Our national borders are closed. All commercial air, rail and maritime traffic is suspended. Each state is deploying their Army National Guard units to assist local medical, fire and law enforcement personnel.
>
> For the safety of all of us, citizens venturing away from their shelter-in-place location will be challenged and, if necessary, detained.
>
> Should this morning's civil unrest continue, I will implement martial law in the affected areas. This means, in those locations only, the military will be used to protect both citizens and their property.
>
> Our armed forces are on their highest alert to protect us. This includes sea, land, air, and space-based assets around the world.
>
> We are all enduring something we hoped would never happen. Please pray with me for those lost and injured in today's attack. Be strong and faithful that we can each surpass this challenge with the help of one another. Monitor this station and the Emergency Alert System for further updates and guidance.
>
> May God bless you and the United States of America.

Chapter 4
Lockbox

April, 1980

The key was to keep a slight, but constant, pull on the little knob that opened the small mailbox door. With his face a foot and a half from the brushed aluminum rectangle, Mike swiveled his head side-to-side, monitoring the apartment building's empty lobby. The box had a three-wheel combination lock, offering the false security of one thousand possible combinations. With a fingertip, he rotated the right wheel one notch for each complete revolution of the middle wheel. When the right wheel refused to budge, he repeated the same process with the left and middle wheels. After a minute or so, he slid the little knob a bit, and the door silently swung open. Peering inside the empty container, he sighed, then cursed, sidestepping left towards the next mailbox.

Sensing a threat, Mike pretended not to watch as an older lady shuffled into the lobby, dragging a two-wheeled wire handcart. Gloomily making her way to the elevators, she ignored Mike as he slid along the wall of hundreds of boxes. Opening several more, he stuffed what little he found into a battered leather briefcase, then quickly exited through a rear door to the safety of his car.

"Hold up there, you!" Mike heard from behind him, his stride becoming more purposeful. "Don't make me call the police!" The unseen woman's voice threatened, sending him into an all-out dash towards his '68 Chevy Chevelle. The voice was too intense and authoritative to have been from the old lady he had seen. Someone else, probably an employee, had seen him messing with the boxes. A final, more distant threat came as he clawed car keys from a pocket while leaping over a grass median, "Don't come back here, you little shit! I'm watching you!"

With eight cylinders shooting him through the parking lot, Mike looked for the source of the threats in his rearview mirrors, not seeing the latest person who had almost caught him. Slowing to merge and meld into late afternoon traffic, he headed for his own high-rise apartment building a few miles away. *People up here expect you to be doing something shady. I need to be more careful.*

Staying on the main road, he ebbed and flowed within its eight lanes of traffic hell, a few miles south of downtown Washington, D.C. Watching through the dirty windshield, Mike felt insecure in his new neighborhood. Everything was so crowded—cars, all types of buildings and stores, plus people everywhere. They seemed preoccupied and ignored each other. Judging by what they drove and wore, they also seemed to have a lot of money, which for him meant an opportunity to supplement his miserly government salary.

Slowing down, he watched for the right turn toward his new pad in another complex of tall brick buildings. A short blip from a police siren shifted his thoughts to the blue lights flashing behind him. *Stay cool, keep your yapper shut*, he counseled himself as he pulled over, thinking about the briefcase beside him on the bench seat. Mike waited, growing damp in the warm April afternoon, while searching the glove box for the car's registration form. In a mirror, he could see the cop walking towards him.

"License and registration," the blue-clad officer demanded without preamble, thumbs hooked into the front of his toolbelt. Silently handing over the documents, Mike guessed that he and the cop were about the same age—twenty-two. Sauntering back to his cruiser, the officer spent another twenty hot minutes yacking with somebody on his radio, then returned to the Chevy. "You're from Kansas, Mr. Cap-pi-ello?" he asked, comparing the teenage picture on the license with Mike's current face.

"Yes, sir, a town called, Lawrence."

"I pulled you over because your tag expired three years ago. Who's Joy Cappiello?"

"My mother."

"Do you have her permission to be driving her car?"

Just a traffic stop, Mike realized with relief and a smile. *Play the dumb rube and move on.* "Officer," he earnestly began, "my mother passed and left me this car. I just moved here this week to start a management job at Sears—in household appliances." Pointing through the grimy windshield, he added, "I live down there in Sutton Towers. The DMV said I needed a utility receipt to get a Virginia license and registration."

"Which Sears?"

"Which Sears?" Mike softly repeated. *Is this guy trying to make fuck'n detective in his first year?* With a broad smile, he replied, "Landmark Mall," which he had visited the day before to buy new work clothes with somebody else' store card. Watching as the cop mulled over his options, Mike knew he was out of danger. *The out-of-town license and tag could make the cop do extra paperwork; it might also be harder for the city to collect a quick fine and for him to get credit for that; it would definitely be impossible for him to get credit for adding points to a Virginia driver's license that did not exist.*

As the rush hour traffic pushed a cooling breeze across his sweaty shirt, the cop studied Mike. He saw the leather briefcase, but there was nothing else notable in the car. He could sense that something was "off" about this guy, but he would have to let him go. "Keep this car off the road 'til you get it tagged and inspected," he directed, "if you get stopped again, the car will be impounded."

"Yes sir, will do," Mike quickly replied with a grin and a small salute, signaling to merge into the bumper-to-bumper traffic. *Adios, Motherfucker,* he thought, reminding himself of his own mother, still living in her decaying house in Lawrence. She lived to smoke mentholated Kools, drink vodka, and make a sport of berating her only child. After college, when a government job offered escape, he needed the Chevelle more than she did, so he took it. If he could not coax a signed title out of her, he'd forge a bill of sale and whatever else it took to get a new Virginia title in his own name.

The Chevy's gas gauge was low, so Mike flowed south with the U.S. Route 1 traffic, curious about what he would see while waiting for a Mobil gas station to appear. National Airport was out there somewhere—he saw the exit signs and the big jets approaching to land. *Maybe with his new job, he'd finally ride on one of them.* A no-man's land of trash-strewn lots and public housing was followed by a fancy-looking old-fashioned neighborhood with a lot of walkers.

Seeming to be the only customer, he pulled into a three-pump gas station with a grungy-looking two-bay service garage. "Fill it with regular," he told the kid manning the pump island, "check the oil and get the windshield too." Glancing at the Mobil credit card in his palm, Mike practiced saying the owner's name, "Jacob Wiesner," several times as he walked into the station, placing the card on the glass counter with a slight snap and a smile.

The silent gray-haired owner sat perched on a stool, as worn, and deflated-looking as some of his tires. Using a magnifying glass, he spent the next minute or two peering into a listing of "hot" credit cards, failing to find the number on Mike's card. With binoculars, he read the pump's meters, scratching the data onto a Pop Tart-sized form he placed onto a countertop "knuckle buster" device along with Mike's credit card. With fluid movements born of thousands of mindless repetitions, he forced the top mechanism from one side to the other, then slid the form towards Mike to sign. Without looking up, his only words to the departing customer were an anemic, "Come back soon."

***

Jefferson had been waiting all day; *he would have to get used to that*, Mike thought as the dog manically greeted him at the front door. Checking for accidents in the apartment's two rooms, he saw the dog had used the newspaper on the kitchen floor; Mike rewarded him with dinner and affection. "We'll go out in a little bit," he said while emptying the contents of the briefcase on the dinette table he had found at the local Goodwill store.

With a beer, scissors, trash bin, and shoebox, he carefully examined that day's mail. Anything unsolicited such as sale flyers, political endorsements and letters addressed to "current resident" were trashed. Bills, personal letters, and small packages, if he had any, were opened and reviewed. One tri-folded letter with perforated tear-off edges stood out due to its National Institute of Health return address. Opening it, Mike leaned back, examining the government employee payroll statement while toasting his good fortune with a sip of beer.

In twenty minutes, he had completed a MasterCard credit card application for the NIH employee, whose first name, Gayle, was thankfully gender-neutral. The payroll statement provided the minimal information needed, including her social security number. Mike added his mailing service street address and a bogus telephone number. Assuming Gayle had a good credit history—a safe bet for a well-paid and long-term NIH employee—he figured the new MasterCard would arrive without incident in about three weeks.

Grabbing scissors from the shoebox, he cut the Mobil gas card he had used that afternoon, listening as thick plastic shards dropped into the trash can. His rule was 1-8-1, and it had kept him safe and undetected through four years of college and his first year of government service. It has also enabled him to pass the Federal Government's defense security clearance screening process.

The first "1" meant he would make up to one thousand dollars of ATM withdrawals on Visa and MasterCards before cutting them up. He knew that the big banks did not bother to prosecute small-time fraudsters, so not being greedy also meant being safe. The "8" was the number of weeks he would use a store or gas card before cutting them up. He could probably use them a lot longer, but he knew more time meant more risk. The second "1" meant changing his mail service address at least once a year. He did not want to get nabbed by an FBI agent when he went to open his own mail box. When and if that happened, he would lose his government job and probably go to jail.

"Jefferson!" he called, "go for a walk?" The dog sprang into a manic fit, jumping and pawing at the apartment door, huffing, and barking for Mike to hurry up. Down the hall, down the elevator, then down another hallway, and finally they were outside. The neighborhood was more developed than anywhere Mike had lived before. It seemed to be half commercial and half residential, with a few scattered areas of light industry.

Defense contractors and other white-collar businesses occupied an area called Crystal City for its gleaming façades of low-rise concrete and glass office buildings. Nearby Pentagon City offered expensive high-rise condos, apartments, shopping, and restaurants. Arlington proper, where Mike lived, was a mix of small businesses, affordable apartments, and modest homes built half a century earlier.

Mike let Jefferson take the lead, stopping at anything that needed sniffing or watering. Reaching a park, the dog found a suitable place to take a dump. No one seemed to be watching, so Mike left it there to fertilize the ground, following Jefferson's lead towards an office building bordering the park.

He could walk to the post office, grocery store, and a mom-and-pop drugstore. Between his mom's car, the bus, the subway, and Amtrak, he could get wherever he needed to be, or wanted to go. For now, that meant work and home, because he was basically broke.

Less than a mile to the east was Route 1, also called the Jefferson Davis Highway. You could go south on that road to Richmond, passing a lot of history along the way. John Wilkes Booth was captured nearby. Confederate General Stonewall Jackson died in in the area after being shot by his own troops. Washington National Airport was just on the other side of the highway from where Mike lived. About the same distance to the west and north was fourteen-lane Interstate 395, usually clogged with a combination of local and through traffic. The interstate and Route 1 could both take you south to Florida or north to Maine.

Jefferson led them home, where, on the balcony, Mike sipped a beer. He closed his eyes and listened to grinding traffic interspersed with the sound of jets arriving and departing from the airport. It would take a while to learn to filter out the background static and capture the sounds of the local birds. Kansas was on the big divide between the western plains and the eastern forests. Mike doubted there would be any pheasants or prairie chickens in northern Virginia. Cardinals, doves, woodpeckers, sparrows—the common birds were everywhere. The dropping sun might bring out some goatsuckers, like nightjars and nighthawks. They moved fast, but he had the advantage of being ten stories up. Looking at Jefferson, he wondered if there were some bird-dog instincts in his jumbled bloodline. As he began to drift off, Mike imagined a male bald eagle or osprey soaring by, talons securing a fish just plucked from the Potomac River.

It's Friday, and he had to show up at the Pentagon for work on Monday morning. He needed to find a new doctor for his anxiety pills, as well as get laid. *I could spend the weekend at some bars, but that's too much work, and people are so annoying. I got that Visa—still good for another $400 or so. I'll go up to Atlantic City, get a casino room, and get a chick to do what I want—for a price. Maybe this time I'll get lucky at blackjack.*

The neighbor's adjoining patio door slid open, bringing sounds of the evening news—the announcer yammering about U.S. embassy hostages in Iran. Then Mike heard the unmistakable voice of President Carter:

> Late yesterday, I cancelled a carefully planned operation which was underway in Iran to position our rescue team for later withdrawal of American hostages who have been held captive there since November fourth. The mission on which they were embarked was a humanitarian mission. It was not directed against Iran; it was not directed against the people of Iran; it was not undertaken with any feeling of hostility toward Iran or its people...Thank-you and goodnight.

Chapter 5

Joy

August, 1955 to January, 1963

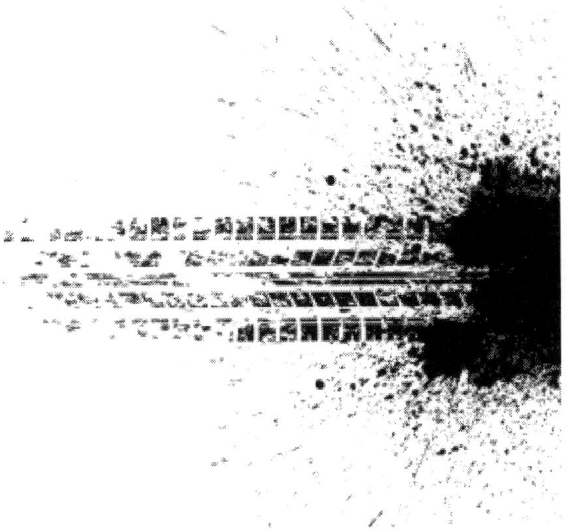

Mike's grandparents met while his grandfather was a student at the state university in Lawrence, Kansas. That was during the tail end of the Roaring 1920s. During the Great Depression, his grandmother's clerical job temporarily kept the young couple fed and sheltered. Eventually, his grandfather landed a teaching position, and a mortgage on a brick bungalow near the university where he was employed.

Strict adherence to the monthly rhythm method of birth control kept the couple childless through the 1930s gloom. Then, just prior to the next Great War, Joy's father sensed a wind of renewal sweeping across the plains. "Let's start a family!" he suddenly proclaimed, ejecting a speck of scrambled eggs across the dinette table onto the lap of her mother's skirt. "We're not getting any younger and things are finally looking up! If we have a boy, he'll be called, 'Junior', and if it's a girl, which I hope not—at least not at first, she'll be called 'Sissy.' Besides, if there is another war, then I won't be drafted if I have you *and* the kids."

"Yes dear," his wife demurred, startled by his abrupt course change. Scanning the cramped kitchen, she imagined where the baby's high chair would sit. Her thoughts expanded to the rest of the tidy three-bedroom house and to the other accommodations she suspected would be needed to raise a modern baby. *Maybe I'll have twins*, she thought—two *birds with one stone*.

The couple imagined a baby that would smile as they cuddled and rocked it to sleep each night. Instead, the daughter they misnamed, Joy, was a colicky, squirming bundle of nocturnal misery. With sleep-deprived eye blemishes, her mother tried to comfort the baby while also tracking her menstrual cycles on a secret calendar, determined to avoid another pregnancy. As a toddler, Joy was content with her own company, sitting alone across a room or at opposite ends of a table or couch from her parents. As a child, she learned ways to avoid her parents altogether, evading their ceaseless pleas and admonishments to "be normal." By her tenth birthday, Joy knew that anything fun and interesting could only be found outside of the house—away from Mom and Dad. By her mid-teens, she had morphed into a nimble shoplifter, a secret truant, and a reliable party girl.

1955

One late July afternoon, Joy spied Mike's future father, Anthony Cappiello, through the dusty plate glass windows of the Oklahoma Tire and Supply store. He was neither tall nor short, a little husky, and probably in his early twenties. From the outside edge of the windows, Joy secretly watched him, the acrid smell of new tires wafting past her from the open door. Tony smiled and nodded earnestly while attending to a lady customer who was towing two small children. Pulling a handkerchief from a pants pocket, he blotted his damp forehead, careful not to disturb his dark, over-Brylcreemed, and carefully side-parted hair. She thought she knew the type, and she was hungry. She would tease and play him, probably getting a dollar or two without any touching. Then she would buy a burger and look for another guy to squeeze for some more money.

Sashaying into the nearly vacant store, the descending sun backlit Joy's lithe and perky silhouette through her thin cotton shrift. Tony gaped and tracked her arrival as she glided across the tile floor, stopping to demurely study a battery cable display. As the mother with kids moved to leave, Joy effortlessly hopped atop a four-stack tire display, coyly watching the lone salesman's measured approach.

"Heads or tails?" he asked, flashing widely gapped front teeth in an otherwise pleasant, yet crooked smile. A quarter sat atop his fist, folded like he was holding a gun, ready to be flipped by a thumb trigger.

"What'll I win?" Joy asked luringly.

"Guess right, and I'll buy you a Coke."

"If'n I lose?"

"Guess heads and you'll aways win," he oily cooed, placing the two-headed coin in her hand without tossing it. "I'm guess'n someone as pretty as you wins a lot."

"Where'd you get that?" she asked in wonderment, closely examining the trick quarter which she held at eye level, rotating it between a thumb and forefinger.

"I found it," he replied dryly, taking back the coin while pulling a dollar from a pocket. "Problem here is I only got this dollar bill and the soda machine takes fifteen cents."

"I've got fifteen cents!" Joy offered eagerly, bounding off the tire stack like the fifteen-year-old she was and reaching into a dress pocket.

He liked her energy and enthusiasm. *Half kid, half woman, and pretty as hell*, he thought. *With any luck, a virgin too*. "Keep your money, lady and I'll show you another trick," he said, motioning her to a stool at the store's register counter. Grabbing a short screwdriver hidden behind a wall calendar, Tony leaned to peek through a rear door, where, Joy assumed, another worker or manager must have been lurking. She watched as he slinked towards a vending machine, kneeling to work the short screwdriver elbow-deep into the dispensing opening. With a slight jerk of his arm, she heard several muted mechanical sounds, followed by Tony's triumphant withdrawal of a purloined bottle of Coke. Like a soda jerk, he gallantly removed the cap and slid the free soda across the countertop towards her.

"I like you," she announced, twisting on the stool's swivel seat while quickly draining the small bottle.

"I like you too," he whispered, returning the tool to its hiding place, and again checking the status of his unseen co-workers. "That's why I'm gonna help you out."

Excited, she sat silently and expectantly, watching him for what would happen next.

"How much money do you have in your pocket?" he wondered, reaching for the rear of his pants.

"A dollar and some change!" she proclaimed, eagerly placing a crumpled bill and a few coins on the Formica countertop.

“Okay, then,” he said, slowly drawing a crisp and new-looking twenty-dollar bill from his wallet, placing it alongside her grungy-looking money. “I’ll trade you *this* for *that*.”

She reminded him of a confused puppy, with her head tilted and her brow furled. “That’s stupid, why’d you do that?”

“Because,” he softly began, “I’ve got a secret.” Leaning in towards her on his elbows, he conspiratorially whispered, “Your money is real, mine’s not, but you can still buy whatever you want with it.” Snatching her dollar, he put it in his wallet, which he slid into his pants pocket with a fluid gunslinger-like motion. Joy bowed her head to closely examine the fake twenty-dollar bill without touching it. “Pick it up,” Tony prodded her. “Rub it, smell it, taste if you want. It looks and feels just like the real thing.”

She did all that, and then her astonished gaze shifted from the bill to the surprising man smiling at her while again wiping his brow. “What’ll I do with this?” she wondered.

“Tell you what Sweety,” Tony began, moving in for the kill with his lop-sided grin. “Go buy whatever you want, then come back here at eight o’clock when I get off. I’ll take you to dinner, and you can show me what you bought.” Then, to improve the odds of her doing that, he added, “I’ve got another one or two of those twenties I might could share with you.”

Joy knew what men wanted and that she would have to do some things to receive any more handouts from the tire salesman. Just the same, this man in his short-sleeved plaid shirt and khakis didn’t look like he’d hurt her. *If she could spend his phony money just like the real thing, then it would be worth it.* “I’ll be back at eight,” she said chipperly, hopping off the stool and quickly exiting, counterfeit bill in hand. As an afterthought, she announced over her shoulder, “I’m Joy.”

“I’ll bet you are!” the bespectacled salesman called after her, eagerly watching her hips and lieth thighs swish out the door into the early evening sun.

1955-1963

They were together for an eight-year peripatetic existence in low-cost hotels across eastern Kansas and western Missouri. Tony was a master of the short con, proposition bets, and other small-time grifts. The double-headed quarter and fake currency, both dependable and reliable moneymakers, were only two of his many scams. Working as a team, they would find marks in taverns, highway rest stops, gas stations, hotels, grocery stores, busy street corners...just about anywhere opportunity presented itself.

In bars, Tony would set up the Triple Turn, betting suckers they could not turn three empty glasses (two at a time) a total of three times and end up with all three mouth up. It could easily be done, but only by a lightning-fast sequence of moves, which Tony would triumphantly demonstrate. He would bet he could toss a peanut over a two-story building—using a nut secretly filled with lead shot. Those and many other simple tricks kept the couple fed, drunk, and never without pocket cash.

Joy's assistance was an integral part of the Badger Game. She would lure a man to his car, where Tony would surprise the dupe *flagrante delicto* with his "wife," demanding a payoff to not call the authorities. Technically, Tony and Joy were not married, but their victims never knew that. When Tony first met Joy at the OTASCO store, he was already married with an infant son. He explained to Joy that she was his "spirit wife" and that was good enough for her.

The Flop and the Mellon Drop were part of their traveling repertoire. Pretending to be jostled, bumped, pushed, or tripped—even by a car—they would proffer previously broken eyeglasses or a smashed wristwatch, wheedling on-the-spot compensation from their victims. They would spend weeks traversing lonely interstate highways, paying their way with fake money, and building a new poker stake for Tony with the change. Highways also offered the best spots for the Stranded Motorist con, where they would pretend to be waylaid travers with emotional hard luck stories—always dutifully jotting down a mark's address and promising to repay their "temporary" loans.

After working in the same town for a few months, the couple would skip out on their hotel bill, which was always purposely kept in arrears. Their travel circuit covered Wichita, Salina, Topeka, Manhattan, Joy's hometown of Lawrence, and their favorite location, Kansas City. Tony had a sixth sense for avoiding troublesome situations, finding the right marks, and knowing when to relocate. This shielded the pair from police attention and kept them away from legal peril.

Their biggest paydays came from the Green Goods game, a longer-duration and riskier scam. Joy or Tony would find a mark willing to pay thousands of dollars for ten times the amount in high-quality counterfeit money. The con was that there never was any phony cash to be bought—the victim was given a "sample" of actual U.S. currency and told it was fake. When a sale was made, the mark ended up with a bundle of cut newsprint, and the grifting couple had a rich payday. They would haul in five to twenty thousand dollars at a time, then immediately head out-of-state for an extended "vacation" to avoid any revenge-minded victims.

Tony was quick to see the potential of credit cards when American Express introduced one late in the Eisenhower administration. Expectant with Mike, Joy spent her pregnancy applying for hundreds of AMEX, department store, and other cards using bogus credentials gleaned from wallets Tony would pickpocket. When new cards arrived, it was his job to quickly bust them up to their credit limits, while Joy was responsible for fencing the merchandise and destroying paper trails of evidence.

Early in the Johnson administration, things started to fall apart for the couple. "When will you be back?" Joy asked softly from the bed of their Wichita hotel room one evening. Tony was dressing to go out, and Mike, who should have been enrolled in kindergarten, was asleep next to his mother.

"Depends," he mumbled, fastening a white belt around his expanding waistline. "Can I get you anything?"

"Another carton of Kools," she whispered through the tobacco haze escaping from her nose and mouth. "Also, go ahead and get a case of vodka liters, we're on the last bottle."

"Sure," he muttered to the floor, one hand on the cold doorknob, "smokes and booze." Hesitating half-way out the door, he took in the depressing summation of his current existence. Inside, his pudgy and alcoholic "wife" lounged in the glow of the TV next to the second kid he never wanted. Outside, in the sleet and snow, his battered and rusting Cadillac sat bathed in neon light, a bald tire reminding him of his own thinning and receding scalp.

"I'll wait up," she offered hopefully through the closing door.

Don't bother, he thought, softly pulling the door shut. *I ain't coming back.*

Chapter 6
Launch, A.M.

April, 1980

For most of us, the first day on a new job is a stressful and worrisome ritual to be endured as few times as possible before the blessed end goal of retirement is achieved. *What will the supervisor be like, and what about the other people that work there? Am I wearing the proper clothes and shoes; Where do we eat lunch, and what are the bathrooms like? Am I smart enough to even be here? Better check my breath and body odor from all this sweating—why did I bring this damned sportscoat anyway?*

Mike had these and other new job jitters bouncing in his thoughts as the municipal bus paced through its stop-and-go route. They had left his leafy apartment neighborhood, wending through the seemingly barren concrete and glass canyons of Pentagon City and the newer Crystal City. With the focused consciousness of a first-time experience, he sensed the bus entering an urban no-man's zone of traffic hell as the Pentagon came into view. In every direction, there were grit-strewn ribbons of worn asphalt and concrete bridges, tunnels, exits, and entry ramps. Unbroken lines of traffic crept along in a confusing, congested, and hectic ballet of twenty-five thousand people reporting for duty in the same building. Two sides of the massive white stone Pentagon building were visible as the bus driver traced a path through manicured grass islands closer to the edifice and complied with traffic cops aggressively directing the continuous flow of pedestrians and traffic.

Mike kept his grip on the seat-top chrome bar to steady himself as the bus made a series of tight turns. Despite a few open windows, the air inside was moist and stagnant from the exhalations and tobacco smoke of the many passengers. He studied them, noting most were dressed as if not quite going to church, at least well enough for a restaurant meal. One lady examined a mini-bible held close to her nose; a man attempted to read a newspaper as his body swayed with the yawing bus. Most seemed resigned to the doldrums of beginning another boring, ritualistic week of work.

After failing a string of corporate job interviews at the university placement center, the U.S. Army made Mike a surprising offer. They would send him to Texarkana, Texas, for nine months to learn how to help manage its vast, global spare parts inventory. Afterwards, he would report to either St. Louis, Detroit, Philadelphia, Rock Island, or Huntsville, Alabama, to manage some of that inventory. All as a federal civil servant—no uniforms, saluting, push-ups, or weapons training required. After acing the Texarkana program, the army surprised him again with a prestigious, and high-visibility posting to the Pentagon with, as they promised, rapid promotion potential.

Mike studied the vast sea of parked sedans, vans, and station wagons, with a few scattered motorcycles and even fewer bicycles. He noted the predominant American car brands along with the vehicles' age and condition, estimating how much money their owners probably earned each year. He wondered where his parking spot would be, figuring he'd be assigned a spot on the outer fringes of the theme park-sized lot. He also wondered how much land the Defense Department owned for its Pentagon reservation, estimating that what he had seen so far took up about half a section, or about 320 acres.

The groaning bus entered a dark portal at the building's base, jerking to a squealing stop among a dozen others. Grabbing a squeeze-to-talk microphone mounted next to his seat, the driver mumbled, "Pentagon," in an anemic whisper. With only a cryptic room number to guide him, Mike followed the flow of other shuffling riders off the bus and through the grimy, soot-tainted cavern to a flight of stone steps leading upwards to the Pentagon Concourse. From the safety of a wooden bench along one wall, he sat with his sportscoat and timeworn leather briefcase on his lap, orienting himself to the building and its occupants.

Brown and tan stone floors, off-white walls, a string of bulky support pillars, and inadequate indirect lighting completed the interior of Mammoth Cave vibe. Uniformed military, primarily officers, from all four services made up about a third of the crowd he saw. The rest of the people were civilians, with a few cops among them. Mike noted the ranks of major, lieutenant colonel, and colonel. He supposed the naval officers had equivalent ranks, although their insignia was a mystery to him. Along one wall, large backlit art deco-style letters were mounted above the entrances to thirty-foot-wide rampways, apparently leading to the offices where all the employees worked.

All of that, he guessed, he had expected to encounter once inside the famous building. What he had not expected to see was a full-sized drugstore, bookstore, barbershop, bakery, bank, credit union, shoe repair, and other service businesses. Two women staffed a long, wooden desk near where Mike sat, a sign announcing "Information" suspended above them. One, a trim, middle-aged woman, was staring at him. She swiveled on her stool towards the heavyset lady perched besides her, "He's a newbie; he'll stop by," she said. "Make him blush?" she offered.

After finishing with a customer, the larger woman spied Mike over her reading glasses. "How much?"

"Five bucks."

"Nah, too rich...he's too young, too green."

"Cup of coffee?"

"You're on, but you gotta do it in less than two minutes and I'll be watch'n, but not watch'n if you know what I mean."

Mike arose, tentatively approaching the information desk and the attractive lady with a welcoming smile. Her blond coif was sprayed to perfection. A sleeveless dress highlighted thin arms, a narrow waist, and, as Mike absentmindedly noted as he peered over the counter, shapely calves capped by red leather pumps matching her painted fingernails. The dress was not cheap polyester, nor was it from Sears or Ward's; this woman was definitely not from Kansas. His assessment took just a few seconds as she put down her thin, brown cigarette while scooting off her seat.

"How can I help you, young man?" She warmly inquired.

"Well, it's my first day here," Mike explained while unfolding and smoothing the creases of a form letter on the countertop. "I'm supposed to report to this room...1D343," he added while pointing to the piece of paper. "And I'm about as lost as yesterday." The heavy-set woman was assisting two young sailors while also monitoring Mike over her left shoulder.

"Let's study this little map," the blonde lady offered suggestively, setting a postcard sized diagram on the counter while leaning on forearms towards Mike, giving him line-of-sight view of her dangling cleavage. Bowing in towards the diagram, Mike sensed an enticing combination of perfume, hairspray, body lotion, tobacco, coffee—and sex. *If she's offering*, he thought, *I'm accepting*.

The map was a top-down drawing of the Pentagon, upon which she etched two small red stars with a ballpoint pen. "This is where we are, Honey," she murmured softly, using the pen to point to one star, "and this is where you need to go," pointing to the second star. "First floor, D ring, third corridor, room number forty-three." She slid the diagram slowly towards Mike, lightly caressing his hand while shooting him an eye-to-eye, come-hither look.

She wanted him to blush, but he turned the tables on her. With his left hand, Mike quickly groped her dangling right breast through the fabric of her dress, maintaining eye contact. While she recoiled in shock, his right hand removed a half-dozen souvenir pens from a cup on the counter, which were now in his pocket. The heavy-set lady watched with her mouth agape.

Mike stood with a triumphant smirk while the would-be seductress became suddenly businesslike and dismissive. Staying out of his reach, she placed a visitor's badge on the counter and pointed towards the gaping entrance to the floor-two walkway. "Go up the ramp and keep going 'til you see the courtyard through the windows," she bluntly recited. "Walk clockwise around the inside of the building 'til you see the apex of corridors three and four—watch for the brown signs on the walls. There will be two stairwells to your right. Take either of them down to the first floor. Walk along corridor three, away from the courtyard, for a while and look for the door with your room number—I believe it's on the left. If you get confused, ask anyone and they'll help you find your way."

Trudging up the wide rampway with other civilian and military workers, he imagined two economy cars racing down it, or a pack of Roller Derby ladies pushing and shoving their opponents as they zipped by. Dodging other people and more support columns, he passed a cafeteria entrance, arriving at what must have been the windows overlooking the courtyard. Turning left, he headed through wide double doors into a very long, twenty-foot-wide hallway full of people obeying the right-hand traffic rule. Glancing at the info lady's map, he guessed this was a segment of the building's "A," or innermost ring.

The same brown and tan tile floor, bare off-white walls, and circular bronze light fixtures as in the concourse continued on and on as he progressed towards his new office. Morning light streamed in from a dozen windows evenly spaced on the right wall. On the left wall were about an equal number of similarly spaced heavy wood doors, some open and some not. All were marked with a standardized placket announcing the door's five-or six-digit room code. He figured there were sixty people in the hallway, but the primary sound was the slipping, clacking, and scraping of leather soles and heels on the tile floor. Looking down, he noted a trail of feather-like black rubber heel marks waiting for the janitors to scrub off the floor.

Mike reached the first apex of his journey and continued moving clockwise around the building, through a second hallway just like the first. Reaching the next apex, he went down one of the stone walkways, noting divots in the edge of the stair treads from almost four decades of continuous use. Hearing a toilet flush, he took time to find and use the bathroom. Returning to the first floor's second apex, he noted an extensive, but aging, museum-quality display covering the life, career, and death of General Douglas MacArthur. *I'll study this later,* he thought. Better *get to work first*. In yet another surprise, corridor three led him out of the building into a five-story open-air canyon between the B and C rings. Pushing on, the hallway narrowed in height and width. Cinderblocks replaced mortar walls, fluorescent fixtures replaced natural light, and everything seemed a bit less grand. Finally, he had reached the metal double door entry to room 1D343.

What did he expect upon opening the grimy doors that needed spray cleaner and a scrubbing? Based on Rock Hudson movies, LIFE magazine articles, and stuff from school, he imagined a curl-and-set secretary rising to greet him by name while guarding a wood-paneled office where an army colonel—his new boss—thoughtfully smoked a pipe and contemplated the Washington, D.C., skyline through venetian blinds. She would guide him through a modern and orderly office with crisp lines of desks and file cabinets. They would stop multiple times as she introduced him to co-workers, carefully annunciating his full name. His preoccupied co-workers would nod and smile, busy typing classified correspondence, consulting large world maps, and urgently talking on phones with multiple blinking lines. In a distant glass-walled conference room, he would watch as men in suits sat at a large table contemplating an army officer flipping butcher paper slides on a stand-up easel while scratching possible courses of action for a critical supply problem on a blackboard.

Pulling open the door to the big shared office space, there was no one to greet his arrival. The rows and avenues of paper and binder-covered metal desks were there; Mike guessed at least 150, maybe more. There were also banks of file cabinets, some with safe-type dials, all doing double duty as repositories of office detritus and scraggly plants piled atop them. The entire room felt as welcoming as a fraternity house basement bar room the morning after a beer bash. Everything was off-white, gray, brown, and grungy-looking. A thin forest of thick pillars held up a drop ceiling woven with fluorescent lights, some working, others not. There were no windows or signs to guide his path, just a well-worn trace in the cheap indoor/outdoor carpet. He tentatively ventured into the big room, nearly bumping into a plump middle-aged lady focused on not spilling her too-full coffee cup.

"Well!" she exclaimed, giving him a quick once-over. "Can I help you find someone?"

Mike stammered, "I'm new...looking for Miss Hunt's office?

"Sandy? well her *desk* is over there," she said pointing to a far corner of the cavernous room, "but I doubt she's in yet. Go over to where that 'Supply' sign is hanging down, and ask for Carl—or Herschel, they're in your area."

"Thanks," was all Mike muttered, wending his way to the gray cardboard sign dangling by links of paperclips from the asbestos ceiling tiles. Two men, one with a gray flat top, and the other with a short afro and tinted aviators, watched his progress.

"You Mike?," the black man called out.

"Yup," was Mike's salutation.

"I'm Carl Ford, as in the car" He announced, reaching to shake Mike's hand, then motioning to the second man, unsteadily arising, and offering his hand, "this is Herschel Utz..."

"As in the pretzel," Herschel grumbled in a deep, too loud voice. "Help us out here, Mike, how do you pronounce your last name?"

"Cap-pi-ello."

"That Spanish?" Carl asked.

"Italian or French I've been told, but the only Cappiellos I know are in Kansas."

"There's no place like home," Herschel added dryly.

"Carry on now wayward son..." Carl began singing the famous song in a strangled falsetto, threatening to reach for an air guitar.

"Spare us," Herschel groused in quick defense, "it's the kid's first day."

"Ever see that band before they hit the big time?" Carl wondered excitedly, making his way to a neighboring gray metal desk with only a telephone on it

Mike had to think for a few seconds, finally connecting the obvious dots between the song and the band, Kansas, "I must've missed it," he murmured, feeling dorky.

"This here's your desk," Carl offered, pulling out a chair with casters. "We cleaned it off for you, so you'd be ready to go. Have a seat and see how it fits."

Mike sat and leaned back in the metal chair, which had well-worn vinyl padding on the seat and arm rests. Testing the five drawers, he found used file folders, a spiral note pad, and a fistful of Skillcraft government-issue ballpoint pens. "This there a requisition form?" he asked.

"For what?" Herschel asked gruffly.

"To get more office supplies," Mike responded as if apologizing for his too obvious answer.

Carl and Herschel exchanged a knowing glance. The kid seemed green, which was understandable, and earnest, which meant he would probably get some work done, but that could just as easily become annoying and bothersome over time. Apparently, his folks did a decent job raising him, but he must have stayed close to mommy's apron strings. "Mike," Carl began, waving an arm towards the cavernous room "we'll get you some supplies from desks that are empty, but we gotta do it quietly. It takes a while to get the lay of the land here and with all the bureaucracy bullshit?" spraying out a Bronx cheer, "forget it."

"Enough with the sermon," Herschel grouched, snuffing out the butt of an unfiltered Camel. "Let's go get some air." Following the worn carpet path, the men pushed through the smudged double doors, turned right into corridor 3, and followed it through rings C, B and A, arriving at the concession stand in the center of the outdoor courtyard. "Grab a bench," he ordered, "I'm buy'n, too early for lunch." He shuffled away, returning to Carl and Mike with three black coffees, dropping heavily onto the bench. "Good weather," he noted, then for Mike's benefit, "soon it will be too damn muggy to sit out here without getting soaked with sweat."

Carl pulled a Doral out of his pack, lit it, and turned to Mike. "You in the Reserves or the Guards, Mike?"

"You mean Army Reserves and National Guard?" Mike wondered.

"Yeah, most people here, at least the men, are either in uniform, or have been. That's how they end up here."

"Or the post office," Herschel muttered.

"I was never in uniform; this recruiter came to school and I signed up...a year in Texarkana and now here."

"And you're a GS-5?" Carl asked.

"GS-7 as of next month," Mike responded.

"Where you live'n?" Herschel wondered?

"Got an efficiency off Route 1 by National Airport."

"What's that run you?" he replied

"Over half of my take home per month."

"Man, that's a bad deal," Carl replied. "Thing is, Mike, the army's got you ass backwards. What you should be doing is working in the field for twenty years, *then* coming here to update some regulations, and then going home. You start off here, in Washington, you can't afford it and you don't know shit...not that you're dumb, but you gotta learn it out there where it's happening, ain't nothing happening here, nothing but *bullshit*."

"Got a wife, kids?" Herschel wondered.

"Just my dog—Jefferson, a mutt I found in Texas."

"Don't listen to him," Herschel advised, waving his foam cup towards Carl. "He's right, but you'll be okay here. Your next three promotions will come like clockwork every year. In time, you'll be a GS-13 and probably top out there. They give you over thirty days off every year for holidays, vacation, and being sick. The retirement's good and so's the health insurance. You could do worse.

"Like the post office?" Mike smirked.

"Or selling insurance," Carl added, "I tried that."

"Me?" Herschel offered, "I've got another fifteen months, then I'm gone."

"Seven years for me, more or less," Carl mumbled, studying the grinds in his cup.

"You were both in the army?" Mike wondered.

"Did two tours at LBJ—Long Binh Post supply base," Carl said proudly, "just a box kicker, never saw any VC (Viet Cong), and didn't want to neither. Herschel, here, he was in the last good war."

"A few months in Dusseldorf, no big deal," Herschel grumbled, rumbling some phlegm lose and launching it into the grass, afterwards blotting his lips with a handkerchief. "Didn't see any action because the Germans were still quivering from the bombs we dropped on e'm. Then the army sent me home and I went back to school...a real war hero."

The conversation hit a natural lull as the courtyard crowd grew and lunchtime approached. Mike observed the parade of uniforms: tan for the Navy and olive drab, with noticeable differences for Marine and Army officers. Two mysterious officers passed by, spiffily starched and animatedly yacking in a foreign tongue. Carl silently eyeballed the passing women like a beauty contest judge, his gaze sprinting from hair, face, tits, hips, and legs. Herschel seemed to be drifting towards a sitting-up nap, snuggly wrapped in his full-length trench coat. Mike felt compelled to break the silence.

"What's going on with those hostages?" he wondered. Herschel and Carl were slow to chime in. "You know, in Iran? I don't understand what they expect to get from us, seems like Iraq is their enemy, not us."

"That's above my pay grade," Carl half-mindedly offered, still on visual skirt patrol. "Maybe if we supported the Shah more, then we wouldn't be having hostages right now."

"Ignore it," Herschel groused, not opening his eyes, "it will fix itself. If you read the Old Testament, that place has been a hot mess for a long time. Back in the day, if you traveled between Europe, Africa, and Asia, you had to go through Persia—aka Iran. They were the world's superpower until Alexander the Great kicked their ass, and that was a long time before Jesus was circumcised. So, what—in the past year, they've swung from a republic to a theocracy and kidnapped some hapless Americans? It'll pass, and those folks will come home. Just give it time."

Wow, Mike thought, *this guy's smart. Why is he working at a desk job buried in the Pentagon? He could be teaching somewhere...I'll let him teach me.*

With a groan, Carl stood up, torquing left and right. "Okay, Mr. Cap-pi-ello," he slowly began, "Mr. Utz and I have work to do. All you've got today is a thirteen-hundred with Sandy."

"If she comes in today," Herschel added, holding up a right fist, thumb pointing down to his lips mimicking a bottle of booze.

"*That* is an issue for management, such as it is," Carl cautioned Mike, "if you want to stay out of trouble, don't narc on your co-workers."

"Not that it matters," Mike began, "but I thought Miss Hunt was management."

"Sandy," Carl explained, "is the supervisor. Keep her happy, and you will get a good rating with a small bonus check every year. Management here starts with Major Black, the Section Chief, who reports to Lieutenant Colonel Moore, the Branch Chief. Then there's Colonel Phillips, he's the Division Chief."

"Is there a general here?" Mike wondered.

"*Brigadier* General Beaulieu is the Deputy Director; his office is on the E Ring. He reports to the director, Major General Parker. That's our management, all the way from your desk to the top."

"How often do you work with Major General Parker?" Mike wondered?

Herschel let out a loud snort, pushing himself up from the bench and looking down at Mike as if he were a puppy chewing his slippers. "Class dismissed, Second Lieutenant Cappiello" he announced. "Go to the information desk in the concourse and get the paperwork for a permanent badge. Then get some lunch. Bring the forms to Miss Hunt's meeting at thirteen-hundred hours and we'll help you fill e'm out. See you then."

Chapter 7
Launch, P.M.

April, 1980

Mike obtained a badge request form from the pretty blonde lady at the information desk. He was disappointed when she did not flash her tits or rub her paws on him. With time to kill, he randomly meandered through the building's levels and labyrinth of hallways. Exploring the outside E ring, he discovered dark wood paneling, deep blue carpet, and gilt-framed life-sized oil portraits of various generals and Secretaries of Defense. Some were over a hundred years old; none were of women, and, as he noted, zero were of black men. The solid-looking doors in the fancy hallway were made of gleaming oak with decorative trim and polished brass hardware. Continuing without stopping, he noted an office placard for the Deputy Assistant Secretary of Defense for Comptrollership. *What the hell was "comptrollerhship",* he wondered, *and how does someone end up in a bigshot office like that?*

Nobody challenged or questioned his presence, so he kept roaming. There were life-like mannequins displayed in tall glass booths. One wore a Revolutionary War uniform, with a heavy-looking flint-lock rifle at his side. Others were dressed and armed for the Civil War, the two world wars, and other eras. Mike wondered if the weapons they held would fire if he loaded the correct ammunition into them. Wandering on, he came upon what must have been the Air Force's domain in the building. Displayed on the blue-trimmed walls were hundreds of cool, original paintings of military aircraft and rockets. In the navy's area, he stopped to admire Smithsonian-quality tributes to Presidents Kennedy, Johnson, Nixon,

Ford, and Carter, all former naval officers. Closer to his own office, Mike came upon a two-hundred-foot, glass-encased homage to the life and career of General Eisenhower.

Hearing someone talking too loudly, almost shouting, he pivoted to see a tall, slim airman wearing what was probably his best uniform. The guide walked backward at a normal forward pace, apparently leading a tour of twenty or so younger women. Like reciting a long-memorized prayer, he rotely recited a script for the tourists. Another spit-and-shine enlisted man, this one a sailor, followed the group at the rear. Mike waited for the group to pass, then tagged along at a respectful distance behind the sailor.

"The size of the War Department expanded to over 24,000 employees during World War II," the Airman was saying, as if for the hundredth time. "These workers were spread over 17 locations, including the Munitions Building on the National Mall that was built during World War I and intended to be a temporary structure. The plan was to build a very large building a mile north of where we are now at the Arlington Experimental Farm. This area was in-between Arlington National Cemetery and the Memorial Bridge, which spans the Potomac River leading into Washington, D.C.

"What did they grow at the experimental farm?" interjected one of the young ladies in the group.

The Airman was ready to quash any threatened back-and-forth repertoire. "Ma'am, we can answer all questions at the end of the tour, time permitting," he said curtly, resuming his monologue," Now, as we were learning, to fit within the terrain of the selected site, the architect, George Edwin Bergstrom, designed a radical pentagonal-shaped building. President Roosevelt wanted the building to have no windows to protect the workforce from enemy bombing raids. The building height was limited to 71 feet due to steel shortages and to not obstruct views in the capitol area. Protests developed over locating a huge office building so close to the hallowed grounds of the cemetery, and potentially obstructing the view from the former Robert E. Lee family mansion within the cemetery.

The same inquisitive lady broke radio silence again, stating "I thought Robert E. Lee owned a cotton plantation in the South."

Maintaining his neutral demeanor, the backward-walking Airman continued, "The building location was moved to a flood-prone open space containing the Washington-Hoover Airport. This included an area known as Hell's Bottom, with homes, pawn shops, factories, a brickyard, and whiskey stills. The Department of War purchased the airport and 287 acres in Hell's Bottom, appointed Colonel Leslie Groves project manager, then began construction 11 September, 1943. The building was dedicated just sixteen months later at a cost of eighty-three million dollars, which is equivalent to three-hundred-ninety-five million dollars in 1980. The original name was the 'New War Department Building in Arlington', but construction workers referred to it as 'the pentagonal building', which stuck and the official name was changed to 'Pentagon Building' in 1942."

Noting the time, Mike broke away from the tour, heading back to room 1D343. Using the postcard-sized map the info lady gave him that morning, he managed to avoid getting lost. Pushing through the double doors of his office, he stopped at Sandy Hunt's desk—and she was not there. "Hey Mike!" Carl called, covering his phone handset, and motioning for him to come over. "Sandy called in sick." Mike waited to see what guidance came next. "You're still going to meet with BG Beaulieu, though."

Surprised, Mike shakily asked, "When?"

"Thirteen-fifteen, so we've gotta go now. Grab your jacket. Bring that spiral notebook and a pen too."

"Break a leg, kid," Herschel offered, sensing Mike's wobble. "Remember: firm handshake, look 'em in the eyes, and keep yer yapper shut unless he asks. You'll be fine."

Carl led Mike out the double doors, turning left past the bathrooms.

"I gotta go," Mike apologized, darting into the men's room. Carl followed, then they continued to the E ring, turning right past another dozen or so closed doors, then turning left into the executive suite, where Mike grew more nervous. A wide-open, knee-deep carpeted area housed the mahogany desks of the executive and administrative officers, along with two secretaries. One wall had several windows and a floor-mounted line of impressive-looking flags—U.S., Army, General Officer, Senior Executive, and others. Back-lit, glass-fronted display cases held presentation gifts from across the army, the federal government, and foreign countries. Quiet as a library, fax and copier machines noisily hummed and whirled while a typewriter pecked out urgent correspondence at sixty words per minute. A tan plastic computer terminal with a glowing green screen silently perched atop one of the officers' desks. Mike wondered what important information it contained.

Carl stopped to face one of the secretaries, who examined him with a doleful gaze over the top of her reading glasses. Consulting a calendar, she used a red-tipped index finger to wordlessly aim the men towards empty couches in a waiting area. Shuffling over, Carl and Mike sat quietly facing each other, ignoring a glass bowl of bridge mix and defense journals on the low table between them. Mike noted *The Washington Post* sitting neatly folded and unread on the tabletop. A bold headline led what apparently was a long investigative story about the Iranian hostage crisis. He could picture Herschel shaking his head in disbelief at the political pressures mounting on President Carter to rescue the captives from the American Embassy.

Mike watched the XO (Executive Officer) saunter to BG Beaulieu's door, exchanging a few inaudible words. Referring to an index card, he padding his way towards Carl and Mike, murmuring, "Where's Miss Hunt?"

Carl jumped to his feet, "She ugh," he muttered, "she had a family emergency today. I am here for her."

"Okay...," the XO replied, looking at his card, then at Mike. Like a hired funeral preacher. "How do you pronounce your last name?" he asked. Mike answered slowly and phonetically. "Okay, is it Michael or Mike?" he wondered, with Mike confirming the latter. "Okay, follow me," he softly directed, "stand in front of the general's desk, do not touch anything, and do not sit down. Do not speak unless to answer a direct question." Mike felt as if he were walking to the plank on a pirate ship, plus he needed to pee again.

Lightly rapping the general's door, the XO led Mike and Carl inside, stopping before a huge mahogany desk where a hulking black man in uniform sat reading something. The view out of the office's two drape-covered windows was of a tan, cinder block wall. A glass-topped conference table with eight chairs and a blackboard occupied half the room. There was also a leather couch, a low table, arm chairs, and floor-mounted flags on the staff. Mike noted a framed and tattered VC flag hanging alongside a small bazooka with a hand grip and folding sight. There was a story to be told between those two artifacts, he was sure. Perched atop a bookcase behind the general was a battered gold football helmet with a single black stripe down the middle. Awards, gifts, mementoes, accolades, diplomas, presentations, souvenirs, remembrances, plaques, and framed heraldry spanning the general's long career were on display throughout the room. A half dozen framed photos sat atop the desktop, all facing the general. Mike would like to have seen their images, if just to gain a glimpse into his personal life. Taking a quick glance at Carl, Mike tried to imitate his ramrod straight military posture.

BG Beaulieu's gaze shifted expectantly to his startled XO.

Placing a manilla folder on the desk the XO explained, "Sir, this is a five-minute meet and greet with Mr. Mike Cappiello, new employee in the Supply Division," then nodding to the folder, "with an appointment affidavit which I recommend you sign, sir."

"Very well," the General boomed in a deep voice, motioning the XO towards the door, "close it on your way out." He inspected Mike while removing his glasses, slowing unfolding to what Carl knew was a height of exactly six and a half feet. His chest was larger than a hundred-pound sack of seed corn, and his neck and legs were sawn from telephone poles. What remained of his salt and pepper hair was trimmed and shaved into a severe high and tight. Tentatively reaching for the general's proffered hand, Mike used his free hand to brace himself against the violent enthusiasm of the general's handshake. "Welcome to the Army Staff!" he thundered, then turning towards Carl he added, "who'd you drag in here with you?"

Stuttering, Carl began, "Su...Sir."

Releasing his grip on Mike, the general swung for Carl's hand, vibrating him as if waiting for a dental filling to be jarred loose. "Just yank'n your chain, Carl!" he roared with a laugh. "Where're you from, Mike?"

Recovering his composure, Mike semi-solidly answered, "Kansas, sir."

"Kansas!" he roared as the room seemed to shake, "I had my brigade command in the Big Red One, and I graduated from the Command and General Staff course at Fort Leavenworth. Kansas is great, Mike! Now tell me, where was your last assignment?"

"Intern Center, Texarkana, Texas, sir."

"Red River Army Depot! I executed a maintenance review of the Multiple Launch Rocket System there while I was an oh-six. Texas is great too!" Picking up the XO's manila folder and shifting to a suddenly solemn tone of voice, he explained, "Okay, Mike, now you need you to take the oath of office." Pointing a tree-trunk sized arm at Mikes left hand, he directed, "Raise your right hand." Confused, Mike lifted his left hand and the General roared in delight, "Ha, gotcha! Works every time!" Shifting back to his judge's demeanor, he explained, "Now, raise your *other* right hand, and repeat after me:"

> *I do solemnly swear that—I will support and defend*
> *the Constitution of the United States against all enemies,*
> *foreign and domestic; that I will bear true faith and*
> *allegiance to the same; that I take this obligation freely,*
> *without any mental reservation or purpose of evasion;*
> *and that I will well and faithfully discharge the duties*
> *of the office on which I am about to enter. So help me God.*

"Good job, Mike!" the General's booming voice returned as he bent over to sign something in the folder, handing it to Carl with a somber, "see that the XO gets that." Looking quizzically at his new employee and suddenly solemn again, he added "Mike, a lot of young people are sour on the military right now—the Army in particular. Not too long ago, this building was surrounded by fifty thousand protesters, some of whom thought they could levitate it out of the ground with psychic powers. The point is, we are coming out of a pretty rough patch, and it's good to see a young man that wants to support the defense of his country."

An economic recession making jobs scarce and the government's low wages look good helps too, Mike thought, quipping, "Thank-you, sir."

***

On the walk back to room 1D343, Mike triumphantly showed Carl the challenge coin he had palmed from the general's desktop during his violent handshake.

"Did you?" Carl asked, responding to his own question with a surprised look and tone of voice.

"He won't be missing it, he had about a hundred of 'em—from all kinds of places."

Carl stopped, holding his hand out and palms up for Mike to give him the coin. It was the size of a silver dollar and almost twice as thick. Viewing one shiny enameled side, he mumbled, "It's from Fort Polk, Directorate of Logistics." Then examining Mike earnestly, he whispered, "Put it back."

"Whoa! What happened to your little speech about 'don't narc on your co-workers?'"

Checking the hall for potential eavesdroppers, Carl stepped closer to Mike, "Look, you like to boost crap? That's none of my business, but as your new friend, I'm telling you not to do that shit at work. There ain't a damn thing you can do with that coin and it's something the General earned...and you took it! Next time you go to the front office, you get yourself another little thrill by putting it right back where it was—and do not be showing that thing to nobody!"

Chapter 8

Lawrence

January, 1962 to January, 1970

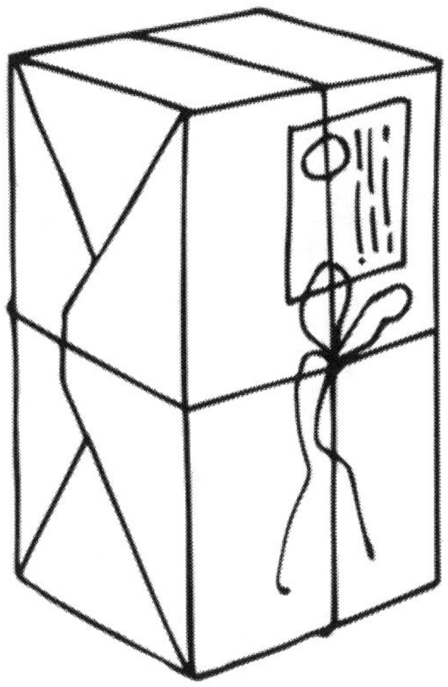

Tony was gone, so Joy returned to her widowed mother's house in Lawrence, less than a half-day's bus ride away. "Hi, Momma," she offered sheepishly when the white-haired lady appeared quizzically at the rear screen door. Joy had not bothered to contact her parents since she had run away with Tony at sixteen, almost six years prior.

"What're you selling?" the homeowner rasped to the woman on her stoop, not recognizing her own daughter. She kept the rickety door latched, gazing down at the unkempt boy standing dutifully at the younger woman's side, their frozen breath captured by the porchlight. The pair had a few suitcases and boxes, but no car in the driveway.

"Momma, its Joy, I've come home!" connivingly adding, "I've missed you so much!"

Alone and lonely, the older woman staggered backwards a step or two, bewildered by an abandoned prayer that had apparently been answered. "My baby came home," she softly muttered, unsteadily reaching to undo the latch and tentatively touch her daughter's snow crusted shoulder.

"This here's, Michael. He's your grandson!" Joy announced, beaming down at the child. Mike held a mittened hand up for the old lady to hold, shake, or whatever she would do with it.

"Please come in, Michael," she softly offered, bending down to him in wonderment. "And tell me, how old are you?"

"My name's Mike," he snarked up towards the woman now grasping at him with both hands. "And I'm four until my birthday, then I'm five!" With Joy's nudging, he remembered to mumble an, "I missed you," postscript.

1970

A few years passed, and moon landings, Vietnam, and social unrest were big items in the news; Mike was twelve and in the seventh grade. He had grown close to his grandmother, but she had retreated into dementia and into her bedroom, rarely emerging from either. Joy remained single, supporting the family with a mail-order business she operated from the dining room. She worked alone, keeping her operations neatly organized in boxes, files, and binders that Mike was forbidden to look at.

Naturally, he snooped when he could, eventually figuring out that her business was tricking men into sending her cash in the mail. She would advertise in the back of weird magazines with naked people in black-and-white pictures and poorly written stories. Sometimes the people in the magazines would be having sex; other times, naked volleyball, barbeques, trampoline jumping, and swimming—even with the kids—seemed to be a big thing.

Joy had cardboard banker's boxes, each filled with blue, red, and yellow file folders. It took a lot of furtive searching sessions for Mike to realize his mom was pretending to be three different people. One was a single school teacher; another was a divorced lady with two kids; and the third was a widow obsessed with stupid ways to have sex. He saw that she kept a folder for each man she hooked into her scam, carefully annotating summaries of their correspondence and payments so that she could keep her lies straight. The letters and cards she received were also neatly organized in the folders and boxes.

As were the pictures—mostly Polaroids with their distinctive chemical smells. Mike figured making your own pictures at home would be quicker and less embarrassing than taking trips to the drugstore to process regular photos. He saw adults doing things in Joy's photos that he wished he could forget. She also kept a small box labeled, "My Pics," that he swore to never open. Finally, he found dozens of bottles of White Shoulders perfume in different shapes and sizes. The powdery floral stench permeated everything in the dining room and faintly seeped its way into the rest of the house.

On Saturday mornings, Mike was required to "go to the city" with his mom, on trips that usually lasted 'til mid-afternoon. Joy would jerkily pilot her tobacco-fouled Chevy Chevelle half an hour east on Interstate 70 towards Kansas City, where she stopped at post offices in the Lenexa, Shawnee, and Prairie Village neighborhoods. Mike divined that she used each post office for her teacher, divorcee, and widow personas, but he was not sure which was which. His job was to go inside, drop off that week's White Shoulders-scented outgoing mail, then empty the rented post office box. He also had to wait in line at the counter for any packages that may have arrived during the week. Like a kid at Christmas, he would shake the boxes to guess what was inside. Lighter boxes, he knew, usually held fancy underwear from her admirers. A box with something solid bouncing around probably contained a sex toy or another bottle of White Shoulders. Joy waited attentively in the car, sipping coffee or vodka, on the alert for postal inspectors and overly amorous clients that might be hanging around and monitoring her postal boxes.

After a hamburger lunch, they would "go shopping" on the drive back to Lawrence, making another three stops on a rotating basis to large chain-type grocery stores. "You got the list?" Joy asked Mike as she navigated the Chevelle through the wintery slush of a Dillon's grocery store parking lot.

"Yeah," Mike mumbled. "Why do you have to ask every time?"

"Don't be sassy, sometimes you forget. What's next?"

Without looking at the never changing and well-worn scrap of paper, he moaned, "Toilet paper, tampons, peanut butter, pot pies and...," sneaking a peak at the list in the dull mid-day light, "...coffee."

"*Tampax*, not tampons, and try to keep it under ten bucks this time, we need to go home with groceries *and* as much cash as we can. Now, what are you gonna do if they catch you?" She challenged him, jabbing in the car's spring-loaded cigarette lighter to heat up.

Like mumbling through an early morning Pledge of Allegiance at school, Mike rattled off their rules for shopping with funny money, "First, cry and lie. Second, drop and dash. Third, meet you one block right."

"Let's see you cry," she challenged him.

He had noted the jab of the lighter knob, he saw "the look" in her eyes, and he heard the slight inflection with a change of tone in her voice. He knew something was coming and instinctively leaned away from her on the vinyl bench seat. But she was quicker; swiftly drawing out the heated chrome knob, she jabbed its glowing end at his face. "Don't!" Mike screamed as he felt the lighter singe on the edge of a balled fist. Gingerly inspecting the fresh half-moon welt, he began sobbing, although he would rather not have given her the satisfaction of knowing that she had hurt him.

"That's how you cry!" Joy howled with laughter, re-plugging the lighter and pulling two fake twenties from an envelope she kept tucked in the driver's sun visor. "Just remember that, 'ya big baby, and you'll squirt tears every time. Now, here's two twenties—and don't be slobbering on 'em. Remember, get four fives for one of 'em and hurry it up too; I want to get going before it starts snowing."

Through welling tears, Mike looked up at his mother, wishing her an instant death. Leaving the car with the counterfeit cash, he wept while slushing his way towards the glowing warmth of the supermarket, ignoring Joy's scream of "No candy and definitely no fuck'n dog food!" Near the store's automatic doors, he huddled in private to ice the fresh burn with some slush while waiting for his sobs to subside, and wiping snot on the sleeves of his coat. *I'll run away*, he willed again, then remembering, *but where'd I go, and who'd take care of Happy?*

Happy was a neglected Labrador mix he had found that lived in the crawlspace under their house. Sundays were always "Happy Days" for Mike and the dog. He would pack a water bowl, blanket, food, and his bird book in a knapsack, then disappear with Happy for as long as he could. They would explore the Lawrence downtown shopping district, then ramble through the university campus, both of which were nearby. The school had a stone campanile surrounded by a park and lake where Happy could roam while Mike watched for birds to look up in the guide book. Ceaseless gritty winds and seasonal weather extremes never caused Mike to miss a Happy Day, even if it meant spending most of it in the crawl space and other shelters he had found over the years.

Sundays were also about trying to understand himself—and his mother. Roaming through the town with Happy, he quietly watched other people, wondering about their private lives. Why were they smiling when they left church on Sunday? What did they do to earn money, and how much were they paid? Did they go on vacations and see other relatives? Did they have grandparents locked in a room and keep their pets in the crawlspace? When their kids wore a bandage, was it because their parents did something to them? Did they do the things he had seen in Joy's boxes and folders, if so, which ones?

Mike was twelve and confused, without anyone to help guide his way. Joy's collection of pornography had a new purpose for him now that he was becoming a man. *Was that right, wrong, or just natural*, he wondered? Adults expected and rewarded "good" behavior in kids, and were always eager to sniff out and discipline "bad" kids. Then there seemed to be a shadowy area between good/bad, right/wrong that both adults and kids liked to dart in and out of. Pot smoking, he knew, was a good example of something that existed in the shadows. It was illegal, but fun; everyone seemed to be smoking it. Gamblers, prostitutes, and tricksters like his mom lived in the shadows, but they either never got caught, or nobody was ever trying to catch them.

The government had rules and laws; they also had police, judges, and prisons. Spend too much time doing bad things, and they eventually force you to live in a cage. Joy did not talk about it much, but he knew that was her number one fear. Then there were the religious people, including their preachers, rabbis, and priests. Out of curiosity, Mike had slinked into the back row, or balcony, of church services on a few of his Sunday explorations with Happy. He understood that churches had commandments and lists of sins to avoid. He also knew that these were conveniently ignored by some of the congregation members in-between their weekly visits to Sunday services. He would watch as the preachers stood up front wearing graduation robes and shouted about everyone being judged by God. Either you would be assigned forever rewards in heaven or just more misery in hell. Mike wondered if he would go to heaven or hell; he knew where his mom was heading. He sat on the hard wooden pew and smirked, just thinking about her screaming in the eternal inferno down below.

Chapter 9
Ascent

January, 1991

Outside, it was another lousy winter day; the last oil-stained remnants of a light snowfall trickled into Potomac River storm drains. Mike and Christine slowly descended into the dank, but warmer Pentagon underground Metro (subway) station. "I'm wiped out," he complained, "spent all day working on one chart for Desert Shield, and still didn't get all the data we needed." Staring ahead, she listened for the sucking sound of inbound and outbound trains to gauge their upcoming wait at the platform. Hearing nothing, she would have to listen to Mike obsess about work until a subway car mercifully arrived. He had arrived early, and they left work late that day. He was all bothered about Saddam Hussein, Kuwait, and whatever supplies the army was moving to the desert for a war that seemed both unnecessary, and inevitable.

"Let's not get the anchovies tonight," she suggested, shoving a paper farecard into the turnstile slot. Momentarily confused, he fell silent, his focus shifting from work to salty fish. "Also, let's get the chianti with the straw bottom on the bottle, like on our first date."

Its three subway stops from the Pentagon station to the Foggy Bottom station on the Metro's Blue Line. The crowded rail car darted above ground, with not much visible in the darkness beyond its large windows. Swaying back into the earth, then under the Potomac, their destination was another eerie cave-like station. Exiting on an escalator into a Georgetown University neighborhood, the bustle of history and wealth was a jolting contrast to the subway gloom and day-long sterility of the Pentagon. What drew them to the area were small restaurants, bookstores, and other funky remnants of the 1970s targeting the student trade.

"Okay," Mike said, sliding into the pizzeria's booth, "no anchovies—and no work talk." That made her smirk. "Let's talk about us," he proposed, erasing her grin as she reached for a menu.

"Chianti, a bottle," she told the waiter. "With a Geppetto's pizza, hold the anchovies, please." A small crowd in the bar seemed to be a mix of graying professor types and grad students. The barkeep switched the TV to what she saw was Gulf War news; she was glad Mike was facing the other way. *Shit*, she realized, he was sliding a small blue box across the tabletop, radiating a look of hopeful anticipation.

"No," he softly cautioned, "it's not *that*, just something I saw and thought you'd like."

With a look somewhere between faux surprise and wonderment, she gave 2:1 odds that the little box held a stupid Claddagh ring. Tell a boy you are Irish, and eventually a department store clerk will steer him to the rings—centuries of mystique, common as potatoes. It would be her third time. At first, his earnest Kansas upbringing was endearing. Then, for her at least, it morphed into an unimaginative, rote frugalness forged by generations of hard-scrabble survival. In short, Mike was boring, small minded, and predictable. He was not going to end up anywhere she wanted to be. Slugging a gulp of wine, Christine opened the little box with a deep sigh that Mike surely misinterpreted.

"It's a *Claddagh* ring," he said proudly, "its *Irish*, like you! The hands represent friendship, the heart represents love..."

"And the crown represents loyalty," she mumbled.

"It's used, but its solid gold—not plated. We can resell it if we need to, but I don't see that happening."

Did he really just say that? Prying the dull ring from the jeweler's box, she motioned for Mike to pour more wine.

"Put in on..." he whispered.

"The right hand, heart pointed towards the wrist..."

"To show you're in a relationship..."

"And someone has captured my heart." Groaning silently, she lamented the ring was a good fit, while once again, the man was not. Rising a few inches on their forearms and leaning inward, they kissed. "Thank-you, Mike, you're thoughtful and sweet." She felt like a mink caught in the jaws of a spring-loaded trap. Tired and hungry, she would free herself by morning, even if she had to gnaw off a paw. The pizza came reeking of broiled anchovies just as the bar crowd erupted in excitement. "Mike," she murmured, "go see what's going on," helping herself to a double slice from the pie.

Desert Shield became Desert Storm as allied aircraft bombed the snot out of Iraqi air defenses, military command locations, and critical infrastructure like bridges and power stations. Mike stepped up to the group at the bar, engrossed by moon-landing-quality images of seemingly millions of tracer rounds arcing into the Baghdad night sky. He knew the Air Force and Navy were launching the bombardment. The next step would be an Army and Marine ground assault to force the Republican Guard out of Kuwait. For all anyone knew, this could be the beginning of World War III.

President George H. W. Bush appeared on TV, and the bar crowd hushed each other. Safely propped behind a desk in front of armored windows, presumably at the White House, the president began:

> As I report to you, air attacks are underway against military targets in Iraq. We are determined to knock out Saddam Hussein's nuclear bomb potential...Initial reports from General Schwarzkopf are that our operations are proceeding according to plan. Our objectives are clear: Saddam Hussein's forces will leave Kuwait. The legitimate government of Kuwait will be restored to its rightful place, and Kuwait will once again be free...May God continue to bless our nation, the United States of America.

"I gotta go," Mike announced after returning to the table.

Christine knew, but asked, "Go where?" adding, "it is after eight."

"To the office, they might need me."

"To update the one briefing slide you worked on all day? Will that change what's the on TV, Mike? What about the poor dog, waiting all day?"

He acquiesced, head hung in defeat, "You're right, let's get this to go. I'll get up and go in early tomorrow."

Silently, they held hands on her one-stop Metro ride to the Rosslyn station. They kissed, and Christine darted through the double-closing doors and out of his life. Alone in the subway car, Mike thought of her and the big step he took that night. *She is the one*, he thought. Maybe this summer they will take annual leave and fly out to Kansas. *She would like that; his mom might even like her. One step at a time,* he counseled himself, exiting at the Crystal City station and surfacing to catch his bus ride home.

***

An hour before normal, he caught his morning bus to work, grabbing a large coffee and newspaper on the meandering journey through the building to his desk. Mike was surprised to find the office half-lit and nearly lifeless. The organizational row and avenue discipline he recalled from his early work years had slowly disintegrated into a sprawl of make-do clutter. The slap-dash construction of the concrete bay housing room 1D343 never foresaw the need for hundreds of computers, monitors, scanners, printers, and copiers. The cables interconnecting all the data processing equipment and power cords needed to run them created aesthetic as well as safety hazards. A wispy forest of floor-to-ceiling metal utility conduits stood at odd angles throughout the big room. To provide privacy, groupings of desks were cordoned off with ratty aluminum-framed cloth dividers that were wildly popular twenty-five years prior. The battered file cabinets were still there, some now used for storage of office supplies, throwaway dinnerware, and Christmas decorations. Personal heaters and fans, binders of regulations and manuals, stacks of computer printouts, and sloppily organized folders cluttered each desk; the worst offenders threatening to slide into mini-avalanches of paper.

Curious, Mike drifted towards the sounds of a TV, observing a purpose-driven swarm of officers manning the twenty-four-hour operations center. They wore camouflaged battle dress uniforms and combat boots. One was shouting into a phone about ethylene glycol, and another was ripping a still-moving printout from a classified printer. Trundling on to his dark corner of the big room, Mike regretted not being more engaged in the lively efforts to support the war.

His first-thing-in-the-morning routine was straightforward and unwavering. First turn on the computer to let it slowly reboot, hang his jacket on the hat/umbrella rack, then study *The Washington*

Post while sipping his coffee. This morning would be different due to the little blue jeweler's box atop an envelope parked in front of his chair. His heart sank. It shattered, wept, and broke in two. Whatever it did, he immediately recognized the undefinable gut punch of being dumped—yet again. He stood, eyes misting, and willed the box to fade away. *Maybe it's a friendship ring for me with a Hallmark missive. But how'd she buy and drop it off so fast? She's giving back her ring, and she must've stayed up past midnight to do it. She was on a mission to get rid of him.* Mike imagined Christine sitting there, smirking while scribbling her poison note, wolfing down the last of the Geppetto with anchovies. She had even left the stained and folded pizza box in the trash.

Retrieving the Claddagh ring, Mike bounced it in his palm, guessing what the scrap value would be. Her note, which he fed to the office shredder without reading. *It's not you, it's me. We've grown apart. I love you as a friend. Someday, we will look back...*he already knew the girl-drivel she'd written, and he didn't keep souvenirs. Sitting at his desk, he unfolded *The Washington Post*, eager to read about the bombing of Baghdad.

Around him, the office slowly came to life. Lenny, one of his deskmates arrived, bringing the odor of a committed smoker with him as well as, Mike suspected, a fresh fart.

"So Mikey," Lenny began, dropping his coat onto a stack of cardboard boxes, "how was the hot date with Kathy? Get any on 'ya?"

Gaze still on the newspaper, Mike reached down to feel the gold ring through the fabric of his pockets, retorting with "Pants are at the cleaners, Lenny. She was Christine, not Kathy."

"Was?"

"Still is."

"I ever tell you 'bout this one gook whore in Saigon..." Lenny began, interrupted by a disapproving look from Alice, their supervisor.

"Division meeting with Colonel Meyer in the conference room," she announced.

Lenny wondered, "When?"

"Right now, and clear your desk for a hot project," she advised.

Mike and Lenny claimed seats in the rear of the conference room, watching and listening as co-workers drifted in. One lady was worried about Scud missiles evading Patriot missiles; another heard about the horrors of anthrax on her drive in that morning. Two guys were debating the merits of the Iraqi Republican Guard; one thought they were fierce, the other a pushover. Then Colonel Meyer entered, the room muting as he stood to face them. Mike had already read in the paper what little the Colonel had to say about the Desert Storm air operations. He explained that any other details were beyond the meeting's classification level and would not be discussed.

Disappointingly, it became clear that the ad-hoc get-together was about the legal-sized spreadsheets stacked in front of the three supervisors. The Colonel was on the hook to provide daily updates to the front office on thousands of critical spare part orders currently on backorder. Translated: Each of them was on the hook to get the updates for him. Looking at the paper stacked in front of Sue, Mike guessed he'd be getting status on about 300 separate "frustrated" parts orders that day, and probably every day for the foreseeable future. Glancing at Lenny to get his read of the situation, he noted the older man was either asleep, or close to it.

Working through lunch and developing stomach cramps, Mike tried to get up-to-date status on the 284 backorders assigned to him. "Status" meant updating the future date that item would be available to the soldier that needed it. The subordinate commands managed the parts were scattered around the country, as were the depots where the parts were stored, repaired, and shipped. Each of those locations had been frantically working, for six months, to support the mobilization of army units to the Middle East. Time permitting, usually after hours and on weekends, their workers stopped to catch their breath and address the nuisance of data calls from multiple layers of management. Using his phone and e-mail to get the required updates, Mike felt he was needlessly harassing people with real jobs doing real work. By the 1400 hours cutoff, he had updated less than thirty items on his spreadsheet.

Lenny, finishing *The Washington Post* Mike bought that morning, tossed it on the pizza box in the trashcan. Discretely probing for a bugger, he pondered Mike beyond the clutter of his desktop. "Get it done, Mikey?" he wondered.

"Mostly, you?"

"I spent some time on it," Lenny said, handing his printout across the desk. "Here, turn mine with yours."

"How many you'd get done?"

"Every damn one of 'em," Lenny bragged, waiting for a response from the visibly shaken Mike that did not come. "Grab your coat, Mikey, I'll buy you some lunch. If you want, we can talk. If not, I ain't offended."

"I'm in," Mike responded, cracking his stiff neck with a jerk to the right, then left.

They grimaced upon entering the courtyard, pulling their coats snug as Lenny made deep drags on a smoke. The limbs of towering oaks branched to the dishwater sky, almost reaching the buildings' fifth level. Hustling through the cold, they reached the small restaurant at the heart of the Pentagon's open space. The crowd inside was thin, and the deep fryer-scented warmth was welcoming. Mike sat with two hotdogs and coffee, wondering what wisdom Lenny was about to dispense that afternoon.

"Mikey," Lenny began, "you need to learn to separate the wheat from the chaff."

Chewing slowly, Mike thought, "You a preacher now?"

"The valuable from the worthless."

"The bullshit from the not bullshit?"

"Exactly!"

Not in any hurry, Mike washed down the first dog with coffee, then started on the second. "So, and I'm guessing here, this morning was something from the bullshit side?"

"Right again!"

With a mouthful, Mike mumbled, "Clue me in."

"Its just common sense," Lenny began, "look at it this way, we are always stuffing a worldwide pipeline with billions of dollars in parts. When things are normal, meaning there is no war going on, stuff moves through that pipeline like cold oatmeal—slowly."

"I like that imagery."

"It's slow and expensive, but it works."

"Then..."

"Then we tell the troops in Georgia, Texas, Colorado, wherever, that they are deploying to the desert. They order every part they can think of, and when it doesn't show up on time, they order it again and then again."

"So, the list we're working has the double and triple duplicate orders on it?"

"Bingo, and the pipeline—containers, trucks, railroads, planes, ships, ports—are all filled to bursting. Some of the stuff being shipped today will arrive in the desert six months from now, probably long after Saddam Hussein has had his ass kicked and said he's sorry. Plus, the army has spent billions on new urgent orders with premium prices on 'em, but that shit takes years to produce—it ain't like going to K-Mart for toothpaste."

Finishing his coffee, Mike re-phrased what he heard, "The pipeline's stuffed to bursting from Kuwait all the way to some mom-and-pop defense contractor in Kalamazoo. So, the likelihood of the day-to-day status changing on any of those backorders, most of which are duplicates anyways, is..."

"Slim to none, the whole drill's a waste of time, but the Colonel wants to get promoted, so he's going to make his boss happy by providing daily updates."

"He could just explain the situation to Brigadier General Nequette, then..."

"Ain't gonna happen, wake up Mikey—wheat and chaff. Ya' gotta smell the bullshit and walk around it. Ya' gotta be omnipotent."

"Now you're God?"

"I meant omnipresent."

"That means God is everywhere."

"Okay, smartass...omniscient. Ya' gotta be omniscient—like me."

"All understanding, took you awhile, but good point. Now, what if Sue looks at your omniscient status updates and smells bullshit all over them?"

"Won't happen. They're too many backorders and management's hair is on fire with other war-related problems. Right now, as you eat, someone is rolling-up all those spreadsheets into one pretty chart. That chart will get stuffed in a stack of other charts Colonel Meyer will have five minutes to brief before BG Nequette moves on to the next topic. It's the omnipo...omniscient thing, ya' gotta understand what's actually going on."

"You probably understand better when you're retiring in fifteen months, too."

"Fourteen and seventeen days."

***

Craving a drink and sleep, Mike threaded his usual path through the building towards his afternoon bus. Always peering ahead for obstacles in the corridors, he would duck into a staircase or utility passage to avoid them. These included promotion ceremonies, the construction of new displays, celebrity visits and booths peddling employee health insurance, charitable donations, and union membership. He figured he would also have to start keeping an eye out for Christine—along with Susan and Anne—but the building was so damn big, it was easy to dodge the girls he had dated when they came into sight. Ruminating on lost loves while turning to pass through a wide-open junction, he had to dodge a backward-walking tour guide spouting Pentagon factoids:

> "...5.5 million cubic yards of fill dirt, 41,492 concrete pilings,
> 680 thousand tons of sand dredged from the Potomac River,
> 13 thousand workers laboring day and night, 6.6 million
> square feet of floor space, 3.7 million used for offices,
> 13 freight elevators, plus one for the Secretary of Defense.

"...131 stairways," Mike mumbled in unison with the fading guide, "284 bathrooms, 4,200 clocks, 691 water fountains, 16,250 light fixtures..." He smirked, imagining more interesting facts like how many foreign spies, office romances, and generals were caught with secretaries bent over their office desks.

***

Mike's new dog, Milford, a youngish beagle mix, went berserk as he noisily plugged his key into the apartment door. The dog's over the top greetings were the highlight of Mike's day, but apparently not for the neighbors. The manager had put another note in his mailbox warning him about Milford's baleful howling. "Just a minute, buddy," Mike said soothingly, pouring food into one bowl, water into another. "One for you, one for me," Mike added, shooting back a shot of whiskey with a chaser of two prescription pills. "No master's degree work tonight," he explained to the dog, "too damn tired." Also in that day's mail was a statement for his federal employee savings plan, which he opened and beamed at. He was probably the first Cappiello from Kansas to have money in the bank since the Roaring Twenties.

His mother had warned him not to trust the stock market, but so far, other than a short downturn in 1987, Mike's stock fund account had grown steadily. "Okay, Milford," he said, "it's your turn."

Bundled against the January cold, Mike let the dog pull him on the leash towards the small local park. Glancing skyward, he sighed. Too much city light to see stars; not enough light to see birds—not that he expected any on a January night. He noted another man with a dog headed the same way. Howling and yanking Mike along, Milford completed his usual circuit of tree trunks, bench legs, and fresh finds in the frozen grass only he could detect.

"Good evening, sir," the other dog walker offered in a relaxed, yet formal way.

Startled, Mike wondered if the man was going to ask for money, or worse, start proselytizing for God or Amway. "Hey," was his lame response, intended more for escape than in greeting.

"We are همسایه ها , that means neighbors," the man continued, "in the Sutton Towers, no?"

"Oh yeah," Mike stumbled, "Sutton Towers. You live there too?" There seemed to be all kinds of foreigners living above, below, and around him, but in eleven years, Mike had managed to avoid them with a quick nod or forced smile. The man had dark hair, dark clothes, and even a darker little dog. Mike had not noticed either of them before. The man reminded him of his friend, Ahmed, from college. Maybe he was also from Iran.

"I am Kazim, my dog, he is called دوستانه, which means friendly."

"He looks friendly to me," Mike bumbled, his breath visible in the dim streetlight. "I'm Mike, I don't know what that would be where you're from."

"In Arabic, your name is Mikel, not so different from the English. What do you call your beagle?"

"He's Milford, it doesn't mean anything, just a small town in Kansas."

"Mikel, and Milford, I am honored to meet you. Perhaps we can meet again, hopefully when it is warmer."

Mike considered asking Kazim about Desert Storm; it would be interesting to hear the perspective of someone from the other side. But then, maybe the stranger would get all excited, spouting off about America, the Great Satan, western imperialism, and all that. He instinctively knew to keep the stranger at arm's length, and avoid the trite standby of offering to have a beer sometime. "Well, Kazim," he said woodenly, "it's good to meet you too," then turned to let Milford lead him back to his apartment for more whiskey, some TV war news, then bed.

Chapter 10
Apogee

September, 2003

Something woke him up—probably his own thoughts. Mike lay in the darkness, peering through the motionless window box fan, listening for anything beyond the familiar sounds of his boring life. Today was the day, at 0900 hours in the Colonel's office, when they would congratulate him on being promoted to GS-14 supervisor. He remembered Herschel, his best mentor ever, warning him against becoming a manager. In his usual economy of words, the older man had gruffly laid out, "A twenty percent pay raise was not worth twice the amount of work."

Mike was twenty-two when he started at the Pentagon in 1980. He smirked in the darkness, recalling what he imagined that would be like, versus the disheartening reality of first walking into room 1D343. Sue, his first supervisor, came to mind. One morning, the military police quietly escorted her to the infirmary, trembling with the DTs. Then she was gone. Twenty-three-years later, there had been five other supervisors, and Mike wanted to be the sixth.

They announced the opening five months ago, so he updated his information in the personnel system and applied for the job. He had made it through all the selection hoops to the final interview six weeks ago. He thought of the small interview room, the factory-fresh smell of his suit, and trying not to appear nervous. Four army lieutenant colonels arose from behind a folding table, eyeing him for defects. Mike offered each of them his sweaty hand, answered four simple questions, and was back at his desk after just twelve minutes.

"Do we gotta genuflect to you now, your highness?" Paul, his current cubicle mate, asked after the interview.

"Better start practicing," Mike retorted, hanging up his suit jacket.

"How many rejection lettehs you got now in your collection? Betta make room for another."

Mike pulled a stack of ragged rubber-banded envelopes from a desk drawer, wagging them in the air for Paul's benefit. Most were for jobs within the building and the D.C. area; some were for jobs in other states and overseas. "Thirty-two, but I'm not counting. If I get picked, I'm going to put all of these into the shredder."

"They use one interviewer or a panel?" Paul asked.

The question jarred Mike a little, "A panel—four lieutenant colonels."

"Let me guess, two men and two women with at least two minorities?"

Reflecting back, Mike answered, "...white man...black man...white woman...then I guess a Mexican woman."

"Mike, look, I know yah want this, but tha tide's against yah, buddy. If I were picking, I'd select you in a heartbeat, but there's nobody ask'n me, know what I mean?

Mike lay in bed, listening as the highway traffic slowly increased and a big jet departed from Reagan National. Out of habit, he lay still, not wanting to wake the dog that was no longer there. Maybe with the promotion, he would get another dog. Then he recalled the smell of day-old piss on wet newspaper, harvesting turds from the carpet, hair everywhere, and stepping into surprises on the floor. Having a dog also meant ten thousand trips on the elevator, plus vet bills. The dog could wait.

Five o'clock and time to get up; Mike stayed in bed. What if he did not get promoted? Maybe it was time to move on...to what? Back to Kansas, maybe being an assistant manager at Tac-O-Rama? What would Kazim say? Mike's mother had moved to Arizona, so he could not live cheaply with her. Everybody always talked about retirement...I've got X years, Y months, and Z days. Mike was forty-five; retirement was fifty-seven. Twelve more years doing regulatory and audit staff work that made the generals yawn while their eyes glazed over.

He could be dead. The September 11 attack two years ago killed 169 people in the building, army military, and civilians among them. The engineers had picked the Army's "wedge" of the building to work on first in a multi-decade update to the sixty-year-old Pentagon. All five floors and the two basement levels of the wedge were stripped to the concrete floors, pillars, and walls. New plumbing, electrical, fiber optics, escalators, blast-resistant windows, and fire sprinklers were installed. Each employee was assigned to a brand-new beige cubicle with access to an office-wide kitchenette and conference room.

As luck, or fate would have it, the newly renovated wedge was where the terrorists hit the outside of the building with their high-jacked jetliner. Most of the completed office space had yet to be reoccupied, with the workers in off-site rented space. The engineers had included enhanced structural supports as part of their upgrade. Without the empty desks and re-enforced pillars, the fatalities in the building would have been in the thousands. Mike figured he would have been one of them, burning in the jet fuel fire that scorched the D Ring.

***

Climbing down from his morning bus, Mike flowed with the crowd toward the row of ten-foot wood doors guarding the Pentagon's main entrance. The smoggy internal bus terminal he remembered from his early days closed in the early 1980s after the truck bombing of the Beirut Embassy. Uniformed PFPA (Pentagon Force Protection Agency) officers stood at their posts, gloved hands cradling fully-automatic machine guns. The flow of workers slowed to a crawl at the doors, where they surrendered their bags and satchels for random checks and x-rays. Once inside, Mike swiped his badge at a turnstile and began his trip through the rat maze, towards the coffee kiosk, then on to his desk. Everywhere he went, excluding bathrooms and inside his office, he would be monitored on surveillance cameras—not personally, like he was someone important, but in general, along with everybody else.

"'Bout time," Paul said wryly, as Mike bent to turn on his computer, doffing his bookbag and jacket. "Yha' know, you ain't gonna be sipp'n java and gawking at *The Washington Post* every morning if they make you the boss."

"I'll worry about that if it happens," Mike replied, settling into his chair.

"When they drop'n the guillotine on you?"

"Oh nine hundred, in the Colonel's office."

"Where's your fancy suit? You ain't weah'n it to see Colonel Hagadorn?"

"Keeping it fresh—for weddings and funerals."

"Mike, no joking now, I'll take yah to lunch today. We can celebrate, or well, whatever. I know a good place downtown. You in?"

Startled by Paul's offer, Mike glanced at him wondering what he was thinking, replying with, "Yeah, sure."

***

The other three promotion candidates were already seated around the conference table, silently judging each other, when Mike walked in.

"Mike, good, close the door and have a seat," Colonel Hagadorn directed. "This will not take long. I want to commend all four of you for the outstanding work you do for the Army. I have directed that this selection be conducted in an unbiased and objective manner, as should all personnel selections. All of you have outstanding performance records and future potential, but only one person can be selected and today, that is Mr. Robert King." Rising, Colonel Hagadorn extended a hand and congratulations to Bob King, who nonchalantly stood to thank him in return. "You other three should keep applying and not be discouraged by this little setback. Moving to open the door, the other three quickly filed out, but Mike stayed.

"Sir," he began, tamping down his shredded emotions, "can you spare five minutes?"

"Go ahead," the Colonel said, neither surprised nor eager to have the coming conversation.

"Sir," Mike began in a quivering voice, "I've been on the supply team for twenty-three years. I've earned a master's degree in logistics. I've completed two Excellence in Management programs. I've been acting supervisor five times for a total of eight months. Why...," he stopped, halted by an eruption of emotions he felt welling up.

"Mike, as I said, it was an unbiased and objective selection, which I directed, but I personally do not have the details. I recommend you go the G-1 Personnel Office and have them explain it to you." Rising, he recalled something, "Oh yes! I have something for you," reaching towards his desk he offered Mike a stiff sheet of manilla paper with a large gold-embossed seal on it. "Your twentieth anniversary certificate, congratulations!"

Rising to shake hands, Mike replied with a weak, "Thank-you, sir," while edging towards the door.

"Ugh, also, Mike, your security clearance is under review, as it is every ten years. The investigator needs to meet with you—just a few questions, she said. I forwarded her message to you and Lieutenant Colonel...I mean, *Mr.* King. Be sure to let him know how that progresses."

Could this day get any shittier? "Will do,sir," Mike muttered, leaving the office, and wondering what witty things Paul would be slinging his way.

"Don't even sit down!" Paul ordered. "Grab your jacket and follow me." Scoping the twenty-year certificate, he grabbed it from Mike's hand, tearing it into small pieces. "Let's go!"

***

They rode the Metro yellow line to the gargantuan L'Enfant Plaza station. Mike closely followed Paul up several escalators into the cloudless and warmish day. "Do you like buffalo?", Paul wondered.

"What for?"

"For eating! We are having buffalo steak for lunch."

"Where at?"

"The Smithsonian! Museum ah tha American Indian, they got buffalo in tha cafeteria." Paul led them through a confusing landscape of government buildings, microparks, and endless cars. The museum was a modern sandstone-clad structure on the National Mall, less than half a mile from the awe-inspiring Capitol Building. Paul had been there a few times and knew his way to the buffalo grill. "Too early for lunch?" he asked the white-hatted cook at the counter.

"Were open," the cook replied.

"Perfect! Two prairie specials, cook mine medium and for my friend..." he swiveled towards Mike.

"Medium's good," Mike replied over his shoulder as he headed towards the coffee urn.

They claimed a table by a wall-sized window. "Looks like a London broil," Mike remarked on the meat. "The wild rice with berries looks good too. Before I forget, Paul—and I will, thanks for taking me here."

"Whatever, let's eat while it's hot, then we'll talk shop."

Outside the window were displays of what Mike guessed were Native American dwellings and some type of woven bins for crops or something. The structures were made of mud, just big enough for one person to stand inside, if he were crouching. He thought of the Potawatomi Indians in Kansas, who lived on their own tribal lands and were not exactly welcome when they ventured into town. His mother had a handful of anecdotal Indian stories, always ending with the edict to "stay the hell away from those brown fuckers." He sighed, recalling teachers at school who were even less enlightened. Maybe he would take leave and spend the rest of the day wandering through the museum, before he met with Kazim. If it was boring, he could cross the street to the Air and Space Museum to see what was new in the early space program displays.

"You're bump'n up against what I call tha 'green glass ceiling,' Mike," Paul began, waiting for a response he knew was probably not forthcoming. Mike was usually eager to listen and slow to speak, which Paul admired. "You—me and most any civilian cannot compete with retired officers. They guy Colonel Hagadorn selected, our new supervisor?"

"Robert King."

"Yup that's right, he's a retired lieutenant colonel. That means he has probably had a command, which means he's supervised a lot of people and managed large budgets. Plus, he has been in leadership development classes for the past twenty yeahs. He may be a monster jagoff for all we know, but on papeh, he's on top."

"You've got more to say," Mike observed.

"There used to be a law against 'double dipping.'"

"Getting military retirement pay and active civilian pay at the same time."

"Right, so when yah retired from the military, the best place to work was at a defense contractor."

"Two paychecks."

"Right as rain, but they changed tha law and now you can retire from tha military on Friday to do the same damn job on Monday as a civilian—still getting two paychecks."

"Plus, disability pay."

"Look, Mike, that's just tha way it is. We have got good jobs and good benefits, but we ain't moving up from where we are now. Yah can keep trying, but that list of rejection letters in your desk drawer will just be getting fatter."

Mike had heard all this before, and Paul was spot on. Being a first-line civilian supervisor in the military bureaucracy was a grinding job, so maybe he would be better off without it. On the one hand, you have imperious, impatient, and impertinent bosses in uniform passing taskers to you. On the other hand, you have got a crew of less-than-stellar people to work them. Over the years, Mike watched carefully as each of his successive supervisors frantically tried to bridge that chasm. It was a no-win situation that was not likely to improve. Slowly replacing mid-level civilian supervisors with mid-level retired officers, in his opinion, only made the situation more frustrating for everyone.

Paul pushed himself away from the table, his chair screeching against the concrete floor. "Yah ready, Mike?" he asked.

"Tell Mr. King I'm sick today—and turn off my computer for me.

"Yah got it, see yah tomorrow! Ugh, Mike, just forget about this morning, it ain't worth it."

***

Washington sits within the mid-Atlantic tidewater region. a gentile way of saying they built the city on a seaside swamp. By the late 1800s, municipal sewage festered on Potomac River tidal flats, waiting for the next orbit of the moon to carry it away. The Army Corps of Engineers solved this problem, as well as the issue of periodic floods, by dredging a deep channel in the famous river. The muck they removed became a mile-long island that is today called East Potomac Park. The Thomas Jefferson Memorial marks the northern tip of the park. A picnic area shrouded by mature poplars and willows marks the southern tip, called Hains Point. This is where Mike and Kazim would meet.

Mike strolled along the breezy eastern seawall walkway with the Washington Channel over his left shoulder. Fort McNair and the National War College were a half-mile away across the gleaming water. Straight ahead, two miles beyond the confluence of the Anacostia and Potomac Rivers, he could see

Joint Base Anacostia-Bolling and the headquarters of the Defense Intelligence Agency. The White House, he knew, was a mile away (behind him) as was the Pentagon (in Virginia, at his one o'clock). Bicyclists zipped past as joggers treaded by on the perimeter roadway to his right. Probably fifty yards away, he heard the grating sound of golf shoe cleats on concrete, followed by the thwack of a wood driver in the distance. Someone had nailed carefully spaced bluebird boxes on utility poles, but none seemed occupied. With the open space and miles of waterfront, Mike was hoping to see a raptor or two, but so far, it was just rock doves and various gulls.

Reaching the southern tip of the park, Kazim rose to greet him, a big white smile buried in his dark beard. "درود بر شما (Peace be upon you!)" he offered in welcome, shaking Mike's hand.

"And unto you, peace, my friend," Mike retorted, examining the small dog Kazim guarded atop the picnic table. It had a thick brown, black, and white coat; sitting motionless, it examined Mike in return.

"You two are a good pair," Kazim noted while sitting down.

Weirdly, the two men were suddenly mute, Mike massaging the dog where its ears and neck met, Kazim admiring the overwater postcard view toward Maryland. Finally, a large jet departed from Reagan National, a mile south of them, and Mike began talking in short declarative bursts while Kazim nodded his understanding.

"Afghanistan is on the back burner...they're going into Iraq...the port will be Shuaiba...the logistics base will be at Arifjan." Kazim nodded, his gaze returning to the waterway while they waited a few minutes for the next plane. "They're working on an acoustic version of the artillery fire finder...this one will be fully automatic...they're setting up a joint program office," he halted while the departing plane gained altitude. Patiently waiting for the next plane, he finished with "...to build a heavy wheeled vehicle...that can survive road bombs."

Kazim watched a couple energetically rollerblade past, while Mike moved the dog onto his lap. "If you take revenge, then do so only in proportion to the wrong done to you. But if you bear it patiently, that is indeed best for those who are patient," Kazim softly intoned, "that is from our holy book."

Not sure what to say in return, Mike concentrated on the dog, lifting it back to the tabletop.

Ignoring the lack of covering jet noise, Kazim grinned, asking, "What will you name your dog?"

Startled, and trying not to show it, Mike announced "I'll call him Potawatomi...maybe just Potawa."

"He is a reclaim dog, from my country." Mike looked puzzled. "A find dog."

"A rescue dog?"

"Yes, a rescue dog! And he is a tangle, we know you like that." Mike knew he meant mixed breed—just a mutt from the street, like himself. Pulling a large manilla envelope from his backpack, he slid it across the table to Kazim, who nonchalantly stowed it within his suit jacket. "There are new funds in your account," Kazim said, "do not be a fool how you spend them."

Mike understood that meant to avoid loose talk at work along with stupid displays of wealth like fancy clothes, cars, jewelry, and vacations. Outwardly, Mike was still the stolid middle-class government bureaucrat living a dullard's life. Inwardly, he was an international spy with a growing appetite for solo adventures to Atlantic City and Las Vegas for gambling and paid sex. When Kazim stood to leave, Mike sought to impress him, "تا اینکه دوباره همدیگر را ببینیم (Until we meet again)," he struggled to pronounce in Persian.

"تا زمانی که دوباره همدیگر را ملاقات کنیم، دوست من (Until we meet again, my friend,)" Kazim returned, smiling as he walked off. The two men would never meet again.

***

Potawa sniffed the newspaper Mike had placed on the kitchen floor, then peed on the side of the refrigerator. His first bath and walk to the park were even more problematic. Eventually he'd adapt, and the two would meld into one as they always did. *What a crazy day: kicked in the balls at work—again; free buffalo steak for lunch; another dog; ten grand more in the secret account.* Mike congratulated himself with a bottle of brandy, which he drank on ice with his medications serving as *hors d'oeuvres.* Watching TV with Potawa asleep beside him, he came upon the end of Secretary of State, Colin Powell's presentation to the United Nations that afternoon:

> For more than 20 years, by word and by deed, Saddam Hussein has pursued his ambition to dominate Iraq and the broader Middle East using the only means he knows, intimidation, coercion, and annihilation of all those who might stand in his way. For Saddam Hussein, possession of the world's most deadly weapons is the ultimate trump card, the one he must hold to fulfill his ambition...The United States will not and cannot run that risk to the American people. Leaving Saddam Hussein in possession of weapons of mass destruction

for a few more months or years is not an option, not in a post-September 11th world.

Chapter 11

Jayhawks

October, 1979

Mike grew up while Happy slowly grew gray, stiff, and lethargic, choosing to spend more time lounging in his crawlspace nest than not. Living at home while working part-time, Mike breezed through community college classes, transferring to the local university after three semesters and receiving a reduced tuition benefit from the grandfather he had never met and of whom Joy never spoke.

Working part time in a university cafeteria, he met the best friend he would ever have. Ahmed was from Iran, and looked it. He did not wear robes and a headdress, but his skin was darker, and his thick, short-cropped hair and beard were jet black. He also had an intense way of looking at someone new, as if searching for defects or weaknesses. Initially unsure of the foreigner, Mike kept his distance, arranging racks of used dishware on square plastic trays and then sliding them across the wet countertop towards the short and trim Iranian operating the aluminum dish washer.

They were opposites. Where Ahmed was pleasantly witty, hopeful, and energetic, Mike was moody, sarcastic, and doubtful. Ahmed saw potential for future improvements in most people and situations. Mike focused on identifying and evading obstacles to his near-term survival. Their personal and cultural differences should have inhibited their bonding. Ahmed was a Shia Muslim whose native tongue was Persian. If Mike had to peg his own faith, he would have chosen agnosticism and was quick to ridicule others' religious beliefs and practices. Toiling side by side, Mike swallowed the insulting zingers that naturally occurred to him, while Ahmed maintained his *shahada*, or profession of faith, without being annoyingly sensitive about defending it. Over time, they grew to understand and respect each other.

Ahmed had no shortage of friends in Iran. Had his choices and timing been better, he would have made dozens of American friends during the four years he spent studying chemical engineering abroad. His first oversight was picking a relatively conservative school with a fairly homogenous student body of white Kansans. There just were not many foreign students in Lawrence, especially from the Middle East, at that time. "At that time" was also the second obstacle to Ahmed's social stature at the school. The '73 Arab oil embargo with its resulting "energy crisis" and inflation were not forgotten. Nor was the Yom Kippur War between the "A-rabs" and Israel. During college, Ahmed wisely chose to maintain a low profile to avoid confrontations with the few openly hostile students he encountered.

During lulls in their cafeteria work, Mike liked to probe Ahmed with moral and ethical dilemmas. The cheerful Iranian would provide a logical, and usually faith-based, response quicker than the noisily splashing washer could process a rack of dirty drinking glasses. "Do people cheat each other in Iran?" Mike wondered, while using a hanging sprayer to rinse a tray of silverware.

"Of course, they do!" Ahmed replied, adding, "but the holy book tells us to 'give full measure, and be not among those who cause loss.'"

"What's that mean?"

"It means, dummy," Ahmed continued while raising the square side of the washer and releasing a cloud of steam, "that you should not cheat."

"What about stealing? Do people steal things over there?"

"In my country, when you see someone missing fingers or a hand, that man has probably been caught stealing. People steal all the time, but The Prophet, درود بر او (peace be upon him), made it clear that 'whoever claims something that does not belong to him; he is not one of us.'"

"Do you lose a foot if you get caught lying?" Mike sardonically retorted.

Ahmed's shoulders drooped in slight exasperation, "No, Mikel, you do not lose a foot—you can lie all you want in my country. Not a problem."

"Really?"

"No, idiot. Why would it be any different in Iran than it is here? Lying, cheating, stealing, and deceiving—they are all *haram*—forbidden. It is simple," Ahmed began, wiping his brow. "The holy book says, 'whenever you give your word, say the truth.' Always do that, and you will not be troubled by these questions. Americans make things complicated—keep things simple and you will not be confused."

***

One Sunday in the fall of their senior year, Ahmed met Mike and Happy near the university's one-hundred twenty-foot stone campanile. Lounging on Mike's blanket in the warmth of the autumn afternoon sun, they shared a six-pack of Grain Belt beer and their thoughts. "At home, I could receive forty lashes for drinking this beer," Ahmed reflected after gulping half of his first can. "But I feel I should understand why alcohol is forbidden, and the only way to do that is to test the effect." Mike ignored him, lying on his back with his eyes closed, an arm crooked behind his head. "Are you sleeping?" Ahmed asked.

"Listening to the birds."

"What do you hear?"

"So far, woodpeckers, mourning doves and rock pigeons—nothing special."

"Mikel, when you earn your degree, what do you plan to do?"

Mike rolled towards his friend, pretending to be earnest and replying, "Move to Iran, convert to Islam."

Ahmed gazed across the park and its lake, then past the red-tiled limestone campus buildings and into the brown fall grasslands beyond Lawrence. "I am not joking; what will you do?"

Mike sat up to open a second can of beer, checking on Happy, sniffing and pawing at something in the ground. "When I graduate," he slowly began, "I'll leave my mother, leave Kansas, and work at an honest job just like everyone else...and I'll drink beer better than Grain Belt," he quipped, guzzling from the can then examining it while slowly belching. "I know what you'll do."

"Go back to Iran?"

"Yup."

"Get a job?"

"Basically."

"I pray every day for Allah to guide me.

"Better not pray again 'til that beer wears off," Mike quipped, adding, "I guide myself."

"That is what I do not understand about Americans...how do you pick which choice to follow when there are so many—too many; it's confusing."

"I'm following my bladder right now," Mike announced, twisting his gaze to the park bathroom in the distance. "Let's do this...I'll take a leak, then you explain what's confusing—deal?"

"Yes, of course, and I will leak also."

In the small stone building, Mike bent to fill Happy's water bowl at a spigot while thinking about Ahmed's probing question, which he knew was a veiled challenge to his lack of faith. Returning to the blanket and the last two unopened beers, Mike fell heavily on his back, sighing with his eyes closed. After waiting for the fifty-three-bell carillon to finish its hourly chimes, he announced, "Okay, Ahmed, what's wrong with guiding myself and having too many choices?"

"Imagine this," Ahmed began, "you need an oven for your home, so you get in your car. Is your car made in America, or overseas? Is it big or small, gas or diesel, expensive or cheap? If you need fuel, what gas station do you go to and do you pay cash or use a credit card?"

"Maybe you don't have a car, like me, so you either take a bus, or taxi or walk."

"Yes, exactly! More choices. Which store do you drive to; Is it downtown, in the country, or in a mall? What color oven do you buy? Does it sit on the floor or on the counter? Do you prefer one manufacturer or another; should it be electric or gas?"

Interrupting him, Mike held up both palms and professed, "Beats me Ahmed, I don't need an oven."

"It is an allegory."

"The parable of the oven?"

"It explains the problem of Americans having too many choices."

"Why's that a problem?"

"First off, its inefficient and wasteful."

"Actually, it's the opposite because a free market rewards the efficient and forces the wasteful out of business. Capitalism 101, ...but I'm suspecting you're going to toss in a religious grenade pretty soon."

"I am, but only metaphorically. In Islam, humans are Allah's representatives on earth and are to be *amanah*."

"Amana, that's an oven brand I have heard of, probably on a game show."

Ahmed glanced sideways, lightly shaking his head at Mike's total secular and commercial indoctrination. "*Amanah*, Mikel," Ahmed sighed, "basically means we are trustees of the planet, should keep nature in balance, and use resources to benefit everyone."

"Now," Mike added while rubbing Happy's belly, "would be a good time to yack about *human* nature, which seems to me is rarely in balance and never benefits everyone."

Ahmed sat staring at the noticeably dimming sky, wondering how to follow Mike's erratic train of thought. Opening his last beer, he challenged his friend, "I explained choices and amanah, you explain human nature—and try not to be too depressing."

Mike ignored the jibe, taking a moment to prepare his response. "Imagine," he began, "you put one thousand random people from around the world in a very large windowless room for one year."

"Men and women? Food, water, toilet paper? No escaping?"

"An equal number of adult men and women with all the supplies they'd need and no way out."

"All Muslims?"

"From many faiths, including no faith, and speaking many tongues. What do you think would happen?" Mike closed his eyes and thought of the stench that would pour out when the door was finally opened, revealing the world's biggest crime scene.

"Okay, I have it. The parable of the room. Sounds good—keep going."

"What do you think would happen?"

"In the room, with the people, after a year?"

"Yes."

Ahmed laughed, falling backwards onto the blanket. "Maybe they would all come out singing, laughing and holding hands."

"Right," Mike began derisively, "and maybe they would be waving governance documents that could be the blueprints for world peace. I think the door would be opened and there would be one survivor left gnawing meat off a bone from the second-to-last survivor."

"A cannibal!" Ahmed chuckled at his friend's imagination. "Maybe he would be someone they picked from a jungle. What is the point of your little story?"

"It's that human nature is a shitshow. It's unpredictable and flawed—that's why no amount of spiritual guidance and direction will keep it in balance." They both lay on their backs, feeling the sun's warmth ebbing and slightly buzzed from having drunk three Grain Belts each. Mike added, "I don't know why we're yack'n about religion, choices and human nature, but I do know we're out of beer.

Ahmed sighed, zippering his coat against the late afternoon chill. "Do not be so gloomy, Mikel. Where I am from, there are few choices; to you, they may seem rigid and unforgiving. Maybe with human nature as you see it, that is what is needed. Just the same, I believe ethics, morals, and beliefs are flexible—within limits and for a good reason—like testing beer. Things are never as they seem, and for you, they are not as bad as they seem."

"Let's get going before it gets dark, but first, Ahmed, I've got my own little speech—just a reminder I tell myself now and then. It not fancy like yours, just what I guess is true."

"متشکرم دوست من (Thank-you, my friend)!"

"ماقی مشلیا (No problem), Mike casually returned in halting Persian.

"You've been studying!"

"A little," Mike modestly replied. "Here it is: I think people want to know why they were born and what happens when they croak."

"Croak? Like a frog?"

"Croak as in pass away—die."

"Existentialism!"

"I don't even know what that word means, but I do know that those two questions can't be answered. Religions claim to have the answers and they promise bright, shiny futures—if you follow their detailed programs. You want to know why there are so many confusing faiths to choose from? I guess because that's what people want—along with too many choices for cars, gas stations, and ovens. None of the spiritual choices is more right or wrong than the other, although most seem to insist they're the only true option.

Stunned by Mike's reasoning and self-assurance, Ahmed studied his friend in the dusky light, "Wow, Mikel, is that what you *really* believe?"

"آیوا (Yes), but I think I understand your faith, and in a way, I envy it. It just not for me."

Staring again into the darkening distance, Ahmed struggled for an apt reply but found none.

***

"What're you bust'n your balls for?" Joy rasped one night while he was studying, leaning on a door jamb for support in her alcoholic stupor. "Those books won't teach you noth'n 'bout how to make money. You're waste'n your time when you could be out earning and helping me pay for things around here," she said, hoisting a saggy and wiggly upper arm through the dimly-lit upstairs hallway, momentarily losing her balance.

"I'm not a thief," Mike sighed righteously, rubbing a yellow highlighter across an open textbook, while purposely avoiding her gaze.

"Here we go again," she squawked derisively, toasting her tumbler of vodka towards him, "Mr. Too Good for his Family." Padding into the room, she stopped to admire an unusually large textbook, "*The*

History of Art," she haughtily read from its cover, watching for a reaction from her son. "Wonder what this big fuck'n book's for, Mr. 'I'm not a thief?'" Like a cat, she swiftly flicked the heavy volume from atop the bookcase onto the rag rug, where its opened spine revealed drawings of medieval cathedrals.

Silently watching over a shoulder, Mike knew he had been busted. *Damn it!* With her, especially at that time of night, withdrawal and avoidance were his only options. Soon, she would pass out in her favorite stuffed chair, raggedly snoring while she slept. "Go'n out," was all he said, standing and grabbing his winter coat. "See you tomorrow," he added, brushing past her to nimbly tread down the well-worn staircase of his grandparents' home. He would return and nudge her awake after midnight, when she might, or might not, get more to drink, then stumble to her bed. *One more semester*, he thought, then he would be gone and she'd be alone—and forgotten.

The History of Art book was a scam he thought he had successfully hidden, not just from his mom, but from everyone. Tuition may have been reduced for Mike, but textbooks were expensive. Each semester required a new batch of books, most of which could be resold to the university bookstore four months later for ten cents on the dollar. The bookstore, in turn, would resell the used books to another student. The more expensive the book, such as The History of Art, the greater the refund. Always on the lookout for unattended textbooks, Mike would slowly accumulate an eclectic collection of titles in his room each fall or spring. When the bookstore was swamped with end-of-semester buybacks, he would anonymously enter the line multiple times to sell back the books he'd stolen, using the refunds to pay for his next semester's books, and then some.

He cursed himself for letting Joy learn about the book scam. She had snooped and figured him out, just as he'd done many times with her. Now his veneer of moral purity was sullied, and she would enjoy verbally piercing him over and over with that knowledge. *Look out for yourself*, she liked to say, *'cause nobody else will; the whole world will stand in line to fuck you if you let it*. He didn't know what the world was waiting to do to him after college, but he suspected it wouldn't be as bad as the way she'd raised him. With his business degree in hand, he would work at a real job and pay for everything with real money. That's what normal people did, not the lying, cheating and stealing she'd taught him. His grandfather had worked at an honest job; maybe he would be proud if his grandson did the same.

His first stop that Halloween night was to check on Happy in the crawlspace. As spartan as it was, Happy's living space was tolerably warmer in the winter and cooler in the summer than the ambient temperature. Mike offered the sleeping dog a slice of baloney, which he sniffed without raising his head, then ignored. Slowly stroking Happy's rough coat, he noted it felt more like a carpet than the fur of a living animal.

Sensing the dreaded end was near, he softly choked, "I love you," to the dog. Mike recalled the previously unknown warmth and affection his grandmother had given him before she became senile. Surprisingly, the dog, in his endearing ways, had done the same. In hindsight, both had offered him much-needed respite during the miserable upbringing he longed to escape from. "I'll come back later," he promised softly, adding, "I'll miss you, Happy." Bent at the waist like a coal miner, with cold tears running down his cheeks, Mike carefully edged through the dim light towards the foundation opening and the cold beyond. I'll go to Ahmed's, he thought, as if he had other friends he could visit unannounced late at night.

***

Through a soft drizzle, with his head bowed and hands kept warm in his coat, Mike quickened his pace towards Ahmed's rooming house. He passed a few jack-o-lanterns still aglow with sputtering candles, beckoning to younger visitors who were most likely asleep.

Ahmed lived in a rattletrap rooming house; his third-floor hallway was accessible by an infirm metal staircase bolted to the rear of the building. Greeting his surprise visitor with a vigorous, "من به شما سلام می کنم (I salute you), Mikel," he bowed just slightly, waving Mike to enter the cluttered room.

" درود بر شما (peace be upon you)" Mike returned in beginner's Persian, adding, "trick or treat!" while waggling a six pack of Grain Belt for Ahmed's inspection.

"Ah, Mikel, you know that is حرام (forbidden)! But just for tonight, because you have traveled all this way to visit my home, we will make this one-time exception."

Mike did not want the tea he knew Ahmed would offer; he also knew to quickly divide the six pack equally to prevent his friend from drinking more than his share.

Before Mike could plop into his usual spot upon Ahmed's ragged loveseat, the Iranian was excitedly pacing the room while rattling off political developments in his homeland. Mike's role, he knew, was to be a sympathetic listener while non-judgmentally sipping beer. He would nod when he sensed he should, stifle any yawns that crept up, and avoid making non-supportive interjections.

Mike understood the basics of the on-going Iranian civil war. There was a king, called Shah, who was corrupt and, according to Ahmed, depraved. On the other side, there was a clerical leader called an Ayatollah who wanted to lead an Islamic cultural revolution. The Shah was being treated for cancer in the States, so his prospects were dim at best. Europeans and Americans were the bad guys due to past ham-fisted colonialism and imperialism focused on vast oil deposits under Iran. Then there was, not surprisingly, a bloody schism in Ahmed's otherwise peaceful faith, which reminded Mike of the Catholics and Protestants that were busy killing each other in Northern Ireland.

Checking his watch while draining his last beer, Mike noted his friend seemed to be nearing the end of his diatribe. "Iran seems to be the biggest thing in the news these days," Mike offered sympathetically, "along with Cambodia, South America, Korea, the price of silver and high interest rates. There is a lot going on out there," he added, aiming to calm his friend. "When're you going home, Ahmed?"

"I will grab my diploma in May and go straight to the airport! انشاالله (God willing), I will join in the struggle to create the new republic."

"Maybe I'll visit you over there someday."

"Mikel, a friend in need is a friend indeed."

"Am I 'in need'?"

"Yes, as am I. We are friends for life wherever we are."

***

Arriving at his grandfather's house, Mike ducked into the crawlspace opening, stooping and edging towards Happy's spot. In the bleakness, he could see that the dog's heavy-lidded eyes were dull and lifeless, while his tongue hung listlessly from the mouth. Happy was dead. Mike was crushed inside like he'd never been before and probably never would be again. Pulling a ragged, moving blanket over Happy, he lay under several more, unwilling to leave the only past he cared to remember. Eventually, he fell asleep in the damp cold, dreaming of an unknown future.

Chapter 12
Descent

2009 to August, 2015

She usually sat alone in the same spot, reading a novel while eating a home-packed lunch. One day, Mike found the courage to sit at the adjoining table in the Pentagon cafeteria. She was heavy with thick calves, Mike noted, yet he was weighing in at the quarter-century mark himself. Smiling warily as he stumbled through a self-introduction, she returned the next day, and a romance neither of them expected slowly blossomed.

Surreptitiously, she probed him for every shortcoming of her ex-husbands. Mike drank, but not too much. He did not watch sports, much less bet on them. There were no ex-girlfriends that "needed his help," and he was not in debt. Mike was lost spiritually, and he did not seem to have any family, but she could help him with both of those problems. For his part, Mike was worried he would scare her away like every other woman he had tried to date. But she did not leave, and she liked his dog. Best of all, there was no drama. She didn't cry, scream, throw things, or hit him like his mother had. Her family in rural South Georgia had plenty of drama, but they were a day's away and seemed to welcome him like an old friend.

The wedding was in Georgia; her brother was his best man, and Joy sent her regrets. Afterward, Mike and Potawa moved into the Woodbridge, Virginia, townhouse she had clawed out of her second marriage. The furniture was too small, the colors looked like an 80's sitcom, and 437 Hummel figurines stared out with glazed smiles from ceiling-high curio cabinets.

She should have worked for Amtrak, as everything in her world ran on a time schedule. Sunday at 9:30 a.m. was bible study at her stadium-sized Baptist church. 11:00 a.m. was worship service, ending with her elbowing him to go down to the pulpit while the congregation pleadingly sang *Jesus is Calling...calling for you, and for me*. He resisted being born again, insisting he was Catholic and citing his long-dead grandparents, who would not understand. Grocery shopping was a mandatory attendance event at 6:30 p.m. each Wednesday. Dental and doctor visits were planned six months ahead; they vacationed at the exact same Maryland beachfront time share every third week of August. Sex was weekly at 7:00 p.m. on Saturday, but only after one bottle of the same brand of Chablis served in champaign flutes on ice. Surprisingly, she was uninhibited and skilled in bed, but by his mid-fifties, he found his own prowess waning.

Just the same, he loved her and loved being with her. If there was perfection in life or marriage, he never expected to encounter it. When she sometimes seemed robotic, he smiled, knowing that she was programmed to make him happy. When he brooded on her lack of spontaneity, she would surprise him with warmth and affection that he had never experienced before.

After four years together, something was wrong. Pheochromocytoma, the doctors said. She had a two-in-a-million tumor on an adrenal gland. They removed it and irradiated her, prognosing a 50 percent survival rate over five years. The required deviations from their weekly schedule confused her. Mike held her close and said the right things to console her. A year later, she passed.

He buried her in Georgia, surrounded above ground by inconsolable family members above ground and by her ancestors beneath it. She left him the free and clear townhouse, its contents, and an older four-door Dodge. An antiques dealer took the Hummels and their coffins. What her family did not claim, he donated or trashed. Even the dog died, severing the final link to his last friend, Kazim. After a few years, contact with his former in-laws was lost as the townhome became haphazardly junked on the inside and screamed for maintenance on the outside.

Alone and ensconced in his basement den, Mike spent his non-working hours in a fog of Islandic Vodka, which he sipped while watching TV. Arrayed on the coffee table in front of him were variously shaped prescription bottles for blood fat, cholesterol, depression, anxiety, and sleeping, plus another two for his blood pressure. The doctors were also warning him about being "pre-diabetic," which he ignored.

Drifting into sleep one night, the TV showed President Barack Obama making a statement sometime that day that Mike would never remember hearing:

> After two years of negotiations, we have achieved a detailed arrangement that permanently prohibits Iran from obtaining a nuclear weapon...Under this deal, Iran cannot acquire the plutonium needed for a bomb. Iran will also not be able to acquire the enriched uranium that could be used for a bomb... Thank you very much.

***

With bloodshot eyeballs peering from his puffy face, Mike climbed out of the Dodge while grabbing his backpack. Still not rating an assigned parking spot after 36 years of government service, he parked at an overflow lot a half-mile from the building. If it was full, he would use a commercial parking garage another quarter mile away. A concrete-lined hexagonal tunnel under fifteen lanes of highway traffic connected the remote parking site to the outer perimeter of the sprawling Pentagon lot. Mike made sure to tread close to the tunnel's walls, ready to reach out for support in case vertigo struck him.

Congress is recessed in August, and the presidential family goes on vacation. That's because the city, built on the swamp, was an unbearable sauna that month. By the time Mike reached the building, he had sweated through his golf shirt. He carried that day's underwear and work shirts in his backpack to keep them fresh and dry. Past the wood entry doors, but before the turnstiles, two PFPA ask him to step aside for a random search. Still sensing the remnants of the previous night's drunkenness, Mike stayed silent and followed their commands. One wanded him, with legs spreadeagle and arms outstretched. The other probed his backpack, and then they released him. Continuing, he stared ahead, thinking of nothing other than coffee and that morning's edition of *The Washington Post*.

Mike detected a large group clapping in unison ahead of him. It was too early in the season for the Army-Navy game, so it probably was not the annual group of cheerleading Annapolis Midshipmen or West Point Cadets. Getting closer, he found his path blocked, annoyed that he had not managed to dodge this unknown obstacle. Random civilian and military personnel lined each side of the corridor as far as he could see. Younger people, mostly men, slowly made their way down the hallways, as the onlookers energetically applauded them. Some visitors smiled in gratitude, while others were more stoic.

Peering from a recessed doorway, Mike realized these were wounded veterans from the distant battlefields of Afghanistan and possibly other places. The Veteran's Administration must have bussed them over. The least-wounded led the private parade, with some seemingly unscathed. Then came those on crutches and missing limbs, followed by the more grievously damaged in wheel chairs, with a few on gurneys. Family members accompanied some of the wounded military. A few of the overseas veterans were stone-faced; some smiled meekly, others broadly. Many shed tears, while one of the last in the parade seemed overwhelmed with gratitude and reversed thanks. It was obvious this ad-hoc and hidden tribute had a deep impact on these brave men and women wounded while serving their country.

For Mike, the war in Afghanistan was conceptual, like one of Einstein's theories. Yes, it was true and important, but it was not something that impacted him, unlike the wounded souls parading past. Iraq ended nearly four years ago. Afghanistan was dragging into its fourteenth, and seemingly never-ending year. Military families were tired of being separated by multiple deployments. Politicians and the press had lost interest in the War on Terrorism after Saddam Hussein and Osama bin Laden had been killed. Interest had waned so much that "We Are at War" reminders were posted in conference and break rooms to remind the Pentagon workforce.

The Wounded Warrior procession reminded Mike of Kazim, whom he had not heard from in a dozen years. In Las Vegas, the money he gave him had slowly been squandered. He knew he should sense guilt and shame for betraying his country, but he did not. Kazim had sought him out, slowly reeling him in with flattery and ever larger deposits of cash. It felt good to be appreciated, and he regretted that it had stopped. Just the same, the supportive applause and tears of appreciation he observed in the hallway veteran's parade made him uneasy. He wondered if, in some unlikely and indirect way, the information he sold to Kazim contributed to any of the injuries he saw passing by. *Nah,* he told himself, leaving to find a bathroom where he could change his shirt.

His current deskmate was a twenty-three-year-old black woman just a year out of intern training in Texarkana. Arriving at his desk, he found her stifling tears and avoiding his gaze.

"Let's go," he softly directed, dropping his newspaper and bookbag without sitting down, "I'll buy you coffee."

"Okay," Ruby blubbered.

Mike took a box of Kleenex with them to the cafeteria, where he patiently waited for Ruby to recover her composure. She was single, without kids, and from rural Mississippi. The Army recruited her out of a small state college, and she seemed to be alone without family or a support network. Clearly, she reminded Mike of himself over three decades ago.

"What happened?" he asked gently.

"He snapped at me at the copier," she began, "said I was wast'n paper."

"Who?" he asked, wondering if she was over her head leaving home and trying to survive in Washington alone on a small salary. Maybe she should do what he never did and find another job somewhere—anywhere away from where they were. *Should he gently push her out, or keep helping her to understand and adapt? He had never figured it out for himself, so it was probably best to let her make her own choices. He would listen and try to be neutral.*

"LTC (Lieutenant Colonel) Cordivari," she quivered, "said I should be doing my work on-line and not making him wait. Made me feel I was in the way of him doing someth'n more important."

Mike sighed. She could make it if she wanted to, but he knew her bags were already mentally packed. They'd sip coffee for an hour or so; he'd help her settle down; then he'd go rip LTC Cordivari a new asshole—in private. Past the minimum retirement age, Mike had nothing to lose. Plus, the LTC was not in their chain of command, so he was way out of bounds getting snippy with someone as impressionable as Ruby. After thirty-five years in 1D343, he had learned how to play the game.

***

Mike considered his options during the car drive home. *He could catch the Redeye flight to Vegas, but it was too late to get a cheap deal on a plane, car, and hotel package. He could drive to the Charlestown, West Virginia, or Baltimore casinos, but he had four days off, so why not go to Atlantic City? The shuttle bus left from downtown at 8:00 a.m. He could drive himself, but getting through Baltimore and Philly was a hassle. He could fly direct to Newark, but that still meant getting a rental, and overall, it was still slower than the bus. He would pack, take the Metro downtown in the morning and be at his favorite black jack table at Harrah's Atlantic City by early afternoon.*

Arriving home, Mike noted a dark car parked at the curb. The front door to his townhome was also unlocked, but Mike entered through the garage and did not notice. With a cold glass of vodka, he went upstairs to pack for his Atlantic City trip. Rummaging through the closet, he grabbed a couple gaming shirts and spun to stuff them, still on hangers, into the bag on his bed. The dark outline of a man in his bedroom doorway made him freeze physically, figuratively, and mentally. *Fuck.*

"درود بر شما! (Peace be upon you!)," the small man said in a calm, soothing voice.

Mike staggered to sit on the bed, his shirts still folded over an arm. "And unto you, peace, my friend," he croaked, surprised he could talk, much less remember the Arabic response greeting.

"*Mikel*, do not be afraid," he said, "you have a job to do."

Reaching for his glass, Mike stayed silent, pulling a long sip of ice-cold vodka.

He led the stranger down two flights of stairs, growing increasingly embarrassed by the bleakness of his home as they descended. The man was his first visitor since his wife's family stopped visiting several years before. In the TV den, Mike cleared clutter from a soiled recliner for his guest, silently claiming his usual spot on the couch. Remembering that alcohol was *haram*, he had left his drink in the bedroom, which he now regretted. While the visitor took in the room, Mike made mental notes to replace a bulb in the ceiling fixture and to find the dehumidifier his bride had left him.

Like Kazim, this new stranger had a penchant for black. Black shoes with soft soles, black pants and belt, black shiny shirt, and leather jacket. All were new and expensive-looking. With his black eyes, he turned to probe Mike. "You will call me Arif," he said, "that means 'knowledgeable.'"

Well, it sure don't mean 'modest', Mike thought, wondering if the man wore black underwear.

"Kazim is in بهشت (paradise)," Arif explained.

"He's dead," Mike bluntly added, knowing better than to pry any deeper than one declarative statement. Just the same, he wondered what Kazim's name meant in Arabic. If he had ever told him, Mike had forgotten.

"Yes, and the تقلا (struggle) will continue."

The men blankly stared at each other in an edgy silence. Arif had expected that Mike would blabber aimlessly, as most کافر (infidels) seemed to do. This one, however, was content to quietly listen while his guest eventually got around to explaining what he needed.

"We have a job," Arif began, "it will require planning and time and صبر—patience."

Mike zeroed in on the word "time." He was thinking of retiring and moving to Las Vegas. The bursting of the home mortgage bubble six years ago made Clark County, Nevada, the epicenter of the home foreclosure crisis. He wanted to move there and claim a cheap repo home in the desert before the housing market rebounded back to normal. Arif's word "planning" also stood out. Instead of just providing them scattershot information from inside the building, they apparently wanted him to help do something—which sounded risky on his part. He knew that getting convicted of sedition was the one surefire way to lose his pension—and was also a guaranteed ticket to prison.

"There is half a million dollars in your account," Arif said, pausing for an expected response that Mike failed to produce. "One half for your pay, one half for your job," he waited, but Mike remained silent. "Only withdraw from your account. We will watch the numbers. No other banks, no help, no paper, no phones, and no internet. You will work at the Pentagon and be hiding."

Mike leaned back onto the couch, cursing himself for not bringing the glass of vodka with him. *What the fuck did these crazy bastards want? A quarter million, and for what, a year? He just tripled his salary, and two-thirds of it was tax-free! They wanted—no needed—him, he could ask for more...ten percent would be twenty-five grand, twenty percent would bring it up to three-hundred thousand!"*

Arif watched Mikel closely and knew he was thinking about the money and how to get more. *These Americans,* he thought, *their enemies are in the mirror.*

"What's 'my job'?" Mike calmly wondered.

"Buy a place of business—no more than one-point-five kilometers from the Pentagon."

"Buy a business?"

"No, a place for business, to make things."

"A factory?"

"No, no, to keep things."

"A warehouse?"

"Yes, a place to keep things—a warehouse."

"How big—what size?"

Arif hesitated to think, "As big as a house."

"A big or small house?"

"In the middle."

"And buy it with the cash?"

"No," Arif struggled for the English words, "to have for a time."

"To rent?"

"Yes, to rent."

"I got it," Mike interjected. "I'll rent a warehouse—within one and a half kilometers of the Pentagon, the size of a medium house. No banks, no help, no paper, no phones, and no internet."

"Also," Arif remembered, "do not spend ten thousand dollars at one time."

Mike knew this was the dollar threshold for reporting cash transactions to the federal government. To fight drug lords, tax cheats, and terrorists like Arif and Mike, Internal Revenue Service Form 8300 was supposed to be submitted for any cash transaction of ten thousand dollars or more. Apparently, working at this next and higher level of espionage was going to be cryptic, but for the money, he would adapt. It felt good to be wanted and important.

"We will contact you," Arif explained, "when we are ready. Do you have questions?"

"I'll show you out," was Mike's reply.

At the door, Arif bid him, "تا اینکه دوباره همدیگر را ببینیم (Until we meet again)," as he trod off to the dark car parked at the curb.

Chapter 13

Impact

August, 2015 to July, 2016

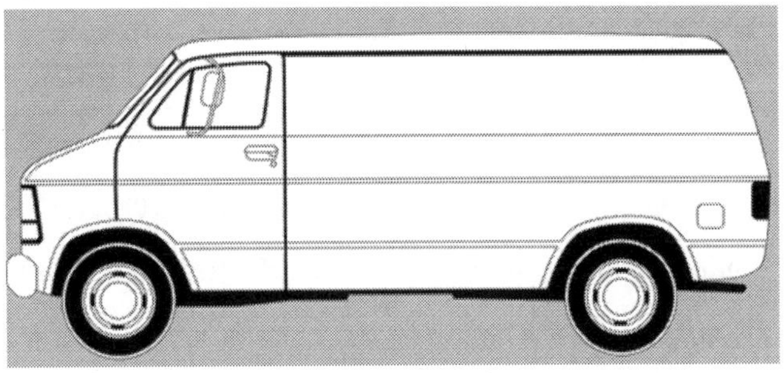

Mike drew a one-mile circle around the Pentagon on his map. The nine o'clock to four o'clock area was off limits as a potential warehouse location. That section included Arlington National Cemetery, and West Potomac Park, home of the Martin Luther King, Jr. Memorial. South of that was Hains Point, where he'd last met with Kazim. The four-to-eight o'clock area included more of the Potomac River, a slice of Reagan National Airport, the northern edge of Pentagon City, and a lot of Interstate 395 traffic hell. He wondered if Arif had spent much time in the area to expect to find a low-key commercial building so close to the beating heart of the U.S. Department of Defense.

Mike would focus on the narrow eight-to-nine o'clock slice that was west of the building and south of the cemetery—just beyond the U.S. Air Force Memorial. In Foxcroft Heights, he found three streets of small, utilitarian brick colonials. He guessed the neighborhood was the remnants of housing for Pentagon construction workers from the early 1940's era. Disturbingly, he also encountered a well-manned and heavily barricaded gate to Joint Base Henderson-Myers Hall, as well as a Virginia State Police building. Eventually, he found a miniscule commercial area that held promise. There was an independent auto repair shop and an odd combination Ethiopian restaurant and bakery, but that was it, so he continued west on Columbia Pike.

The Penrose section of Arlington was the next possibility, but it was half a mile beyond Arif's stated limits. The Army Navy Country Club was to the south, and a naval aviation facility was to the north. The primary thing in Penrose, Mike noted, was low-rise brick apartment buildings and single-family homes, some dating back to the early 1900s. The two living modes were sandwiched together on leafy, dress-right-dress streets. He slowed as a window tinting business caught his attention and stopped in front of a commercial "for lease" sign. The single-story brick structure housed a Halal butcher, a beauty supply wholesaler, and a payday/car title loan business. There did not seem to be any vacant space, but Mike jotted down the realtor's address and drove off to find him or her. It would have been easier to just call on his cell phone, but Arif had said, "no phones." Just the same, he did use the online map to save time getting from point A to point B in the crazy Washington traffic.

"It's in the basement," Suzy Wilson, the realtor said. Her narrow office was sandwiched between a bagel shop and a weight loss franchise in a midcentury shopping center. She was trim and well-dressed, but with a craggy smoker's face and phlegmy baritone voice. "There's a ramp in the back with a regular door and a roll-up door," she continued, sucking hard on her smoke. "That's the only way in and out, and there ain't no windows. If you want it, honey, its more for storage than a real business, if you know what I mean. The last guy was an undertaker—stocked his coffins, chemicals, and whatnot down there. If you want creepy, that's it. It's got rats too and the lease don't cover pest control."

"I want it," Mike said, not hesitating.

"Don't 'ya wanna see it first? Whada 'bout costs, n' square foots, 'n bathroom, 'n restrictions? Don't 'ya need to see all that, Hon?"

"How 'bout today?"

"Today, for what?" she asked, smoke snorting in angry puffs from her mouth and nose. "'To go'n see it? Right now, like, I don't got noth'n better to do but show you that dingy basement?

"I can wait," Mike replied, looking around the vacant and still office, "I've got all day. Maybe I can fill out some forms while I wait?"

Suzy sighed, leaning forward to inspect her blank daily calendar. The physical motion induced a gurgle deep within her chest. "I gotta see a client for lunch," she explained, "then I'll meet you there in an hour." She spun in the chair, her left arm reaching for multiple cubby holes, yanking forms almost without looking. "Here's the particulars for the basement," she said, placing a flyer atop the thin stack of papers. "You can stay here and start on this if you want, or I'll just meet you there."

***

The flat-roofed building had parking for about twenty cars in front, and a dozen in the rear. A row of poplars lined the rear of the lot, beyond which Mike could see more apartment buildings. The ramp to the basement was at the rear, towards one end of the building. Disfigured and formerly yellow metal beams poked out of the asphalt, marking the entrance to the ramp. Warily descending the concrete slope while wearing red leather pumps, Suzy brushed one hand along the retaining wall for support, while the other delicately held her cigarette holder and a lit smoke.

You can squeeze a van in here," she explained, "that's what the grave digger did. But there ain't enough headroom for a box truck. You do get five spaces in the back lot though."

She opened a normal-sized gray metal door, groping for a light switch in the gloom. Mike followed her inside as a long row of haphazardly positioned fluorescent lights slowly hummed and crackled to life. The unpainted cinderblock room ran the length of the building and most of its width. A row of evenly spaced metal beams supported the floor above. The unfinished ceiling was a maze of steel and copper pipes, cloth-covered wires, and heavy-duty air ducts. A stench somewhere between mold and sewage made Mike's eyes water, and he sensed a queasiness beginning, worried that he might hurl in front of Suzy.

"It ain't much," she apologized. "If want to leave, I ain't offended. Most folks don't make it past where you're standing right now."

"Let's open the big door," Mike gasped, pulling the rusty chain loop, first the wrong way, then the other. The balky door was damaged on the bottom, probably from a car strike, and resisted Mike's efforts. As it was lifted, the full tragedy of the basement room came to light. Moisture-stained walls hosted patches of flaky white and wispy-looking black mold. The concrete floor was stained with various hues and littered with left-behind debris from one end to the other. Moving to inspect a walled-off area mid-room, Mike recognized rat droppings on the floor.

"That's a bathroom," Suzy explained. "There's a shower, a shitter and a sink. You also got that utility sink over there."

Probably before he was born, Mike thought, someone bought some plywood and made the cheapest bathroom in Washington. Stepping inside, he pulled the string on a bare bulb, scurrying a nest of cockroaches. Trying the sink faucet, there was no hot water, and the cold ran rusty brown. The same color stained the toilet bowl and shower basin.

"It's $4,200 a month and thirty-two hundred square feet. That's a buck thirty-one a square foot, and you ain't gonna find that nowhere else in Penrose."

"I doubt if I could," Mike murmured.

"First and last at signing, rent due first of the month, ten percent penalty if you're over a week late or bounce a check.

"I'll be paying in cash each month. What about garbage?"

"You're gonna need to rent your own dumpster."

"Utilities?"

"Included."

"Restrictions?"

"Noth'n illegal or outside the zoning. Inspections are at the owner's discretion. You've got to show proof of insurance for whatever it is you'll be do'n down here. Any improvements belong to the lessor—it's all in the contract."

"I'll take it!"

"Hon, you bring that paperwork and your money to my office tomorrow and we'll get you the keys."

***

The lease for the basement warehouse was effective 1 September, 2015. Mike hired foundation specialists, plumbers, carpenters, electricians, and an automatic door company, careful to keep all jobs under Arif's $10,000 ceiling. The cinderblock walls were waterproofed and painted, the bathroom gutted and rebuilt, and the cement floor shined with a coat of gray epoxy. A remote control opened and closed a replacement big door with a higher threshold than the old one. Mike even had a kitchen nook installed with cabinets, a hot plate, and a small refrigerator.

He figured a warehouse needed a forklift, so he bought a mini-electric version. Staying under the spending cap, he also procured a panel van, then spent the same amount again having it repaired. The last task was the installation of commercial-grade shelving units that lined the long back wall, along with a half dozen workbench tables that he could scoot around on lockable casters. Whenever Arif chose to reappear, Mike hoped that he would approve of the warehouse.

The holiday season, New Year's, and the Super Bowl had all passed. Now it was Valentine's Day, always a downer at the office for someone unlucky in love—like Mike. He would play hooky from work and hang out in the Penrose basement for a while, maybe taking a nap on the cot he kept there. Stopping for coffee, pastry, and *The Washington Post*, he threaded the white van over dark, wet roads through aggressive morning traffic to the Penrose warehouse.

Entering the steel door, Mike shook the rain off his coat, subconsciously listening for whatever faint tune was playing in the dim room. He figured an 80's boombox did not violate Arif's disdain for technology, so he kept one always turned on and tuned to an AM oldie's station with a DJ named, Doctor Dust. Psychedelic, funk, punk, disco, metal, and especially rap, were not for him. Most anything else from the mid-50s through the mid-80s would do: doo-wop, folk, Motown, rhythm and blues, beach, pop, and soft rock—even some country. That morning, he was welcomed by Dr. Dust spinning Mr. Tambourine Man by the Byrds, and he smiled as he hung the wet coat on a hook. Halfway through his coffee and the paper, he heard three rapid thuds, figuring it was the butcher cutting meat upstairs. When he heard them again, he realized someone was banging on his door.

The stocky man stood in the rain, holding out a silver badge for Mike to inspect. "I'm Detective Rodriguez, Alexandria P.D.," he announced, rain dripping in a rivulet off his hat. "It's kinda wet out here, you mind if I come in?"

Mike had seen enough police procedurals on TV to recognize a cop fishing for information, but what choice did he have? "Sure! Come on in," he replied.

"Artro Rodriguez," the detective said, extending a hand.

"Yeah, well um, Mike Cappiello."

"With two 'p's?"

"And two 'l's." Mike retorted, watching Rodriguez slowly scan the room and its contents.

"Mind if I look around?"

"Go ahead, not much to see yet, I'm still setting up shop."

"What kind'a shop?" Rodriguez wondered, stopping at the folding table and chair where Mike had been reading the paper.

"I'm going to package kits for the military...tools, food, electronics, depends on the small business contracts I win."

"Ain't that a cart and horse type deal? Don't the factory come after the orders?"

"It's a *facility*, and you have to have one to bid on the contracts, but I gotta retire first."

"Retire from where?"

"The Pentagon; current employees can't bid, but I'm planning ahead."

"Way ahead, looks to me. Tell me Mike, do you have insurance?"

Looking at the van by the big door with a rainwater puddle under it, Mike said "I've got car insurance."

Rodriguez had moved on to inspecting the kitchen area cabinets and drawers, "I mean business insurance."

"Liability, theft, fire?"

"Business disruption, Mike. Small businesses like yours need to be protected from unplanned events."

There it was—just a shakedown, Mike realized. He wondered if the butcher, beauty supplier, and loan shark above them kept Rodriguez on retainer. *The path ahead was obvious, and there was no shortage of cash to pay off the extortionist with a badge. Rodriguez would be useful. He could quietly tamp down problems as they arose and head off too much outside scrutiny.* "What's the going rate for that kind of insurance?"

"Somebody told me a policy like that could cost twenty grand a year. I think they said payments were quarterly."

Making his way to the smaller door, Mike called over his shoulder, "Tonight, in the mailbox by the door. Don't let the mailman find it tomorrow."

Trailing behind, Rodriguez pulled a card from his wallet, handing it to Mike, "If you need to make a claim," he said, shaking Mike's hand limply while lightly snorting as he walked back into the rain.

Mike lay on the cot, Detective Rodriguez's stiff card in his hands. Recalling Arif's "no paper" imperative, he realized it had prevented clues that otherwise would have been lying about for the detective to discover. *I should have been more nervous,* he thought. *What's wrong with me?* Mike wondered if he was so depressed that he just did not give a damn what happened to him with Arif and whoever, or whatever, he represented.

***

By mid-summer, 2016, Mike had returned to his old life: marking time at work, drinking 'til he slept, and visiting Vegas and Atlantic City when he could. The retirement windfall, and a cheap house in the Nevada desert he had envisioned when Arif first appeared would have to wait. In just ten months, he had blown through his entire quarter-million payday, learning to play craps with the big boys. He'd also lost some of the "for your job" funds and desperately hoped Arif and his people would not notice.

His routine was to stop by the Penrose warehouse weekly, mainly to trash the junk mail that piled up. The butcher upstairs had seen the basement improvements and talked to the landlord about evicting Mike so he could take over the space. One call to Detective Rodriguez, and that minor issue was resolved.

***

Early in the evening on a late July Saturday, Mike was in the basement with the big door open and fans blowing the warm, moist air. Vacuuming spider webs, dust, and whatever else needed it, he watched as the little man in dark clothes appeared in the gaping doorway, silently gazing across the basement's contents. Furtively, Mike pushed his near-empty bottle of vodka behind a box and out of sight.

"من به شما سلام می کنم (I salute you!)," Arif said excitedly, quickly pacing through the room towards Mike.

"درود بر شما (Peace be upon you!)," Mike returned with a warm, but wary smile. Turning off the vacuum with his foot, Mike wondered what was about to transpire. Would Arif ask about the money he had blown through, or not approve of his "place to keep things" being more than a one-and-a-half kilometers from the Pentagon?

Holding his arms out wide, Arif spun in a circle, admiring the basement warehouse. "You chose well!"

Relieved, Mike motioned his visitor to the folding table and chairs. He knew this was a time for *sabr* (patience) and listening carefully. "Water?" he offered, pushing an unopened bottle across the tabletop.

"The struggle continues," Arif quickly began, ignoring the water. "We are making progress on our job as you are."

Mike took a long sip of water and waited.

"You should plan for your action," Arif advised.

Mike waited and thought. His "job" had been upgraded to "an action."

"You will have an action one day before our action."

"Tell me about my action," Mike cautiously inquired.

"You will build a fog, a fog to hide the second action."

Fuck'n metaphors, Mike thought. He hated crossword puzzles. Then he got it. "The first action won't be the real one."

"Exactly!"

"The first action will hide the second action."

"Yes," Arif nodded solemnly.

"When?"

Arif paused to reflect, choosing his words carefully. "There are many factors and with good progress. You will plan your action for early morning. The number two action will take place early the next morning. You will be told six months before the time it is to happen. Be careful, as you have been. You have more funds in your account, point six million; half for you and half for the first action. Also, Mikel, never forget: no banks..."

"...No help, no paper, no phones and no internet," Mike chimed in.

"Yes, you do not know how important that will be."

"You didn't say it, but I was assuming that meant no computers either."

"Most of all, no computers! If you need things, we will help." Satisfied he had conveyed his message, Arif stood to leave, but hesitated, looking down at Mike sitting opposite him, both men obviously in deep thought. They had stealthily monitored Mike at home and during his efficient, lone wolf efforts to establish the Penrose warehouse. Three other assets they had groomed over the years were picked to progress towards this final task. Only one had prevailed, but she was now faltering and would probably be terminated. The weapon would soon be in-transit to the Canadian port, then slowly make its way to this very room. Breaking protocol, Arif sat back down. "Mikel, he began purposely and solemnly, we have a parable that says, 'Wisdom consists of ten parts: nine parts silence, and one part a few words.' You and this parable are one."

Wow, Mike thought, *a compliment*; Remaining silent, he tried to conceal a grin of self-satisfaction.

"Now I will be unwise and tell you what I should not, do you understand?"

Unsure what to say, Mike rubbed the back of his neck with one hand, responding with an unconvincing, "Probably."

"After your action, you will leave the past and start again."

Mike pondered that one, doubting it was another Arabic parable or bit of scripture. Arif was being literal, as in "you will pick your sorry ass up and move" to somewhere yet to be disclosed. Clueless people paid tens of thousands of dollars to life coaches like Tony Robbins to tell them what to do; he was getting it for free from the smallish mystery man sitting across from him. Now was the time for specific questions he had been politely avoiding, "Start again in Iran?" Mike asked.

Arif smiled and nodded placidly, adding cryptically, "It has not been decided." Not surprisingly, Mike had divined his and Kazim's nationality despite their careful efforts to conceal it over the years. "You will not be safe here after the actions."

"Safe as in my government will be looking for me, or safe as in staying away from the Pentagon?"

"Yes, both," Arif murmured, concerned he was revealing too much too soon. "Mikel," he began, rising from his seat, "you have done well, we are pleased. We will meet here in four weeks. You will tell us your plans for your fog and what you need from us. I will tell you more of our plans, but I warn you, do not betray your friends."

Standing, Mike offered his usual "I'll show you to the door," good bye as, over the sound of the droning fans, Carol King mutely belted out, *It's Too Late* on the radio.

Chapter 14
Fortress

July, 2016

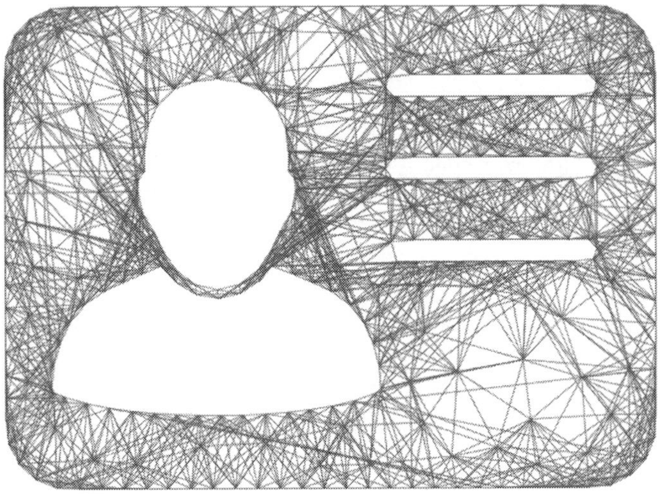

Mike thought about the various types, levels, and layers of security protecting his humble inventory analyst job in room 1D343. The Army had trained him to carefully assemble notes, first into draft text, then into formal documents with salient points colorfully illustrated on PowerPoint charts. Arif's "no paper" dictum turned all that on its head. It was a challenge adapting to the undocumented process, but he had begun to respect the mental discipline, clarity, and conciseness it required.

The beginning, he reasoned, seemed like a good place to start his analysis. Mike recalled the SF 171 Application for Federal Employment he had carefully completed with a typewriter and mailed to the Army intern recruiter back in 1979. If you were a convicted felon or had been court-martialed out of military service, you were not eligible for DOD (Department of Defense) civilian service. The SF 171 had blocks for reporting DUIs, psychiatric visits, and any interactions with local cops after the age of eighteen. "Forget" to mention some unpleasantness in your past and it would bite you in the ass after you were hired and the data you provided was thoroughly vetted. All the forms, college transcripts, recommendation letters, and other documents Mike submitted in his 1979 application package were stored in his official personnel file. As his career progressed, the file grew like an accordion with promotion, reassignment, annual rating, awards, and other paperwork.

To an outsider, the swelling personnel file may seem like innocuous overkill, but Mike understood it was the bedrock upon which DOD built an extensive, interwoven network of personnel, physical, and data security measures. When and if Arif and his friends completed their "second action," eventually DOD would figure out and carefully study Mike's role. The goal would be to understand his motivations and methods to thwart future versions of his disgruntled self. The personnel file would be part of that analysis.

Once hired, Mike was issued an employee identification badge with his picture and vital stats. The students and employees of the intern school in Texarkana wore their badges dangling from a lanyard around their necks. A detailed background investigation was begun for his security clearance, which included ten years of personal information and face-to-face interviews with three people he recommended. Mike was granted a CONFIDENTIAL-level security clearance, which meant, if required, he could view and carry (in double envelopes) data and documents marked with that security level.

After his permanent change of station to the Pentagon in 1980, his security clearance level was upgraded to SECRET, which was required for his new job. The new building access badge dangling from his lanyard was upgraded to a color, indicating his higher level of security clearance. This provided a visual signal that he was "cleared" to handle CONFIDENTIAL and SECRET documents which were stored in either a locked safe or a secure room that was, in effect, a safe itself. He could also attend briefings, meetings, and seminars classified as CONFIDENTIAL or SECRET, but not TOP SECRET.

There was no e-mail, internet, or even personal computers in government offices when Mike began his career. There were "mainframe" computers that spit out paper reports by the ton. Database changes were scrawled on stiff 80-column cards and submitted to a room full of deaf girls operating desk-sized keypunch machines. Leap forward three decades, and Mike was doing ninety percent of his job on a government-issued laptop. He was assigned a microchip-bearing CAC (common access card) that, along with multiple passwords, was required to access his computer and authorized databases.

There was a "high" side for classified data and a "low" side for work on unclassified e-mails, spreadsheets, documents, and endless web browsing. Eventually, non-work-related web access was restricted, and employee computer usage was monitored by a shadowy IT staff sequestered in half-lit secure rooms. Each employee was required to complete annual information security and security awareness training sessions. Thumb drives, DVD disks, and wireless devices were banned from the office. Post office box-sized lockers in the corridors outside of room 1D343 were assigned for employees to stash their cellphones and other personal electronics before entering the office.

Maintaining a SECRET security clearance was required for Mike to retain his job in the Pentagon. A new background investigation was performed for all employees every ten years. He got a jolt when an investigator asked him about Kazim back in 2003. *How the hell did they piece that together,* he wondered. They should have nailed him and made his sorry ass a cautionary tale in future security awareness training presentations. Instead, Mike calmly agreed that he knew Kazim from the neighborhood dog park, but no more than that. Amazingly, instead of being arrested for selling classified information, he was greenlighted for another ten years of SECRET-level work.

Over the years, Mike quietly observed as other employees screwed up their personal lives, lost their security clearances, and then lost their jobs. Personal sloth, office romances, and controllable drinking problems were discouraged, but tolerated. Robbing a fast-food joint, selling pot from your house, or bribing small Latin American governments trying to do business with the Army were not. One manager with gambling issues hit up subordinates for five thousand dollar "loans." He was encouraged to retire. Another manager had an internet porn problem; they took away his computer and responsibilities for a year, then he retired "early." Get convicted of a DUI, fraud, theft, or assault, and you will lose your clearance forever. Then you would either be fired or, if somebody powerful liked you, reassigned to do menial work that did not require a clearance.

Other than the security level color identifier on employee identification badges, the multiple integrated layers of security measures utilized by the Pentagon are not visible to the layman observer. The physical security measures are the most obvious. A barbed eight-foot perimeter fence surrounds the 280-acre Pentagon reservation, which is under continuous video surveillance. Dozens of PFPA police on foot and in cars patrol, control, and direct vehicle and pedestrian traffic while vigilantly surveilling for anything unusual. Stone staircases, curbs, interior fences, jersey barriers, car-sized planters, and rows of bollards keep all traffic, and potential bombs, at least thirty yards away from the building. Hundreds of exterior Pentagon windows have been upgraded to thick, ballistic, and shatter-resistance glass.

Parking is by assigned space only. Each car must be registered with the PFPA and have paper parking permits prominently displayed. Random sweeps of the parking lots are made with drug- and bomb-sniffing dogs. Parking close to the building is limited to top executives and general officers, who are provided with a secured, private lot next to the north-facing side of the building. As in the balance of the federal government, the most important people, such as the secretary of defense and the chairman of the joint chiefs of staff, are transported in one-to-three vehicle caravans of black Chevy Suburbans and Tahoes with heavily tinted windows. Mike had watched many times as these vehicles entered the building courtyard and suit-clad security details climbed out sporting dark glasses and coiled wires, leading to speakers in their ears. He wondered what weapon caches the vehicles contained, as well as which had been upgraded with armored plating and bullet-resistant windows. For executives, generals, and foreign dignitaries in a hurry, the building also has a steadily utilized pentagon-shaped helipad outside its north-facing side.

Barriers are used to funnel the daily influx of more than twenty thousand employees into security checkpoints at two entrances. The smaller, south parking lot entrance requires passing through a bank of clear glass exterior revolving doors activated by CAC identification badges. Between the first checkpoint and the building, a PFPA guard visually inspects you and your building pass. The main commuter station entrance receives a much heavier volume of bus, auto, and Metro commuters. As commuters weave their way through steel barricades to one of seven ten-foot wooden double doors, PFPA cops visually check their building passes. The doors open to a three-story vestibule the size of an auditorium. The side walls are made of large, roughly surfaced limestone blocks supporting enormous quilt-type memorials to the 9-11 attacks. One is an artistic American flag, that, on closer inspection, has embedded images of each victim from the Pennsylvania, Pentagon, and New York City plane crashes. Employees silently swipe their CAC badges at a long row of waist-high glass and steel turnstiles, then proceed quietly on gleaming stainless-steel escalators to the second floor and their day of work.

At both entrances, everyone is monitored by dozens of uniformed PFPA police positioned outside and inside the building. All are armed, some with fully-loaded machine guns; some are standing guard behind bullet-proof barriers. The last two items were added after separate instances of anti-government lunatics popping out of the subway station and bus terminal with guns blazing. The PFPA suffered fatalities, but quickly picked off the protestors like shooting gallery targets.

Anyone wanting to enter without valid building access identification is shunted to a separate gymnasium-sized facility at the main entrance for x-raying and online vetting. As a final building entrance security measure, random visual and x-ray bag checks are used at both entrances. Mike chuckled, remembering the contract worker in his office who "forgot" he had a loaded handgun in his gym bag while trying to pass through the main entrance. When a random bag check uncovered the gun, he was quietly reassigned to another job away from the building, never to return.

For Mike, all the layers of personnel, information, and physical security were facts of life and minor annoyances required to be endured daily—and to get paid every other week. For the average, non-defense-employed American, they probably seem excessive at least, and frightful at worst. But, Mike thought, while lying in the Penrose basement and smirking to himself, the worst news was yet to come. The DOD uses a five-level FPCON (Force Protection Condition) system at all its installations. The standard security processes he had mentally considered so far were used during FPCON levels Normal and Alpha, which are assigned when there is no, or just a possible threat of terrorist activity.

When he eventually figured out what his "fog" action would be and executed it, Mike would need to avoid knocking up FPCON level up to Bravo. That level indicated an "increased and predictable" terrorism threat and would put the PFPA on high alert. It would also turn the heat up on Arif when he they tried to execute his "second action" the day after Mike unleashed his "fog." The last two, and highest FPCON levels were Charlie (imminent threat) and Delta (specific terrorist threat). Mike assumed the Pentagon FPCON level would be a glowing Delta after Arif's stunt—whatever it was. That thought made him smile and chuckle in the silent gloom of his hideaway. He got up to pour another cold vodka from the fridge.

Mike suspected there was a well-stocked arms room within the building that would supply weapons needed to defend against Bravo, Charlie, and Delta level attacks. When someone was taking recurring nighttime pop shots at the building from a nearby highway, a series of sophisticated microphones were set up outside to triangulate the shooter's location. On the battlefield, these would be connected to chain guns or mortars that would automatically unleash return fire. While that was not possible to do adjacent to fourteen-lane I-395 in Virginia, it did tell him that the military would freely dip into its awesome arsenal to defend its headquarters citadel. He had also noted CBRN (chemical, biological, radiological, and nuclear) monitoring stations outside of the building and a large RV-type CBRN command post the PFPA kept stashed somewhere in the building.

The military personnel working in the Pentagon were another less obvious threat to budding terrorists that should not be discounted. They were physically in the prime of their lives, schooled in hand-to-hand combat, and trained to operate and maintain a multitude of weapons and munitions. There were thousands of these men and women; they would all be hyper-vigilant during higher FPCON levels. Many of them would not blush at the opportunity to become an overnight hero by interrupting an in-process terrorist action. There were also thousands of ex-military personnel that, while not in combat-ready shape, would be just as eager to protect the building from external threats.

There are a dozen or so large military installations within a thirty-mile perimeter of the Pentagon. They provide the pageantry of formally attired bands, colorful honor guards, ceremonial remains transfers, and impressive presidential aircraft as seen on TV and in movies. Mike knew they would also provide extensive first response support in defense of a serious terrorist event at the Pentagon. As during the 9-11 attack, F-16 fighter jets and Vietnam-era UH-1N Huey helicopters would quickly be sortied from nearby Joint-Base Andrews in Prince George's County, Maryland. The JTF-NCR (Joint Task Force-National Capital Region) would get busy coordinating the deployment of Army, Navy, Marine, and other Air Force surface, air, and space assets. Boots on the ground would be provided by the USAMDW (U.S. Army Military District of Washington) and the DCNG (District of Columbia National Guard) including its WMDCST (Weapons of Mass Destruction Civil Support Team). To defend against the worst threats, tactical and combat vehicles, uniforms, food, medical supplies, tents, communications gear, weapons, ammunition, and all the other materiel needed to fight a war would be authorized for release from pre-positioned contingency stockpiles stashed in regional warehouses.

Mike laughed out loud at the lunacy of anyone contemplating lighting a firecracker, or worse, anywhere near the Pentagon. It was a fool's errand, and he had been enticed to be the clown. The alcohol was kicking in, so he stumbled back to his cot. Not bothering to undress or take off his shoes, he drifted into sleep while Dr. Dust played *Betcha by Golly Wow* by the Stylistics.

The song reminded him of high school, where he transformed into an ugly turkey vulture. He was flapping his way north, high above the Potomac River, at night. Sutton Towers were below, the tenth-floor windows of his former apartment glowing warmly inviting him inside. The riverways' moonlit branches shimmered below. To the right, downtown Washington, D.C., radiated its luminous majesty in the cold night air. The Pentagon was a darker area to the left, and Arlington Cemetery was even more opaque. An incredibly loud whop-whop and thunderous rush of air sent him tumbling. He struggled to right himself and regain level flight. The helicopter dashed at him again to keep him away from the mammoth building, so he flew west and higher to avoid it.

Circling, Mike the Vulture could see Prince George's County, Maryland, where the dispossessed of D.C. gentrification lived. Following the George Washington Parkway north, he flew over McLean, home of wealthy lobbyists and the Central Intelligence Agency. The weird confluence of Virginia, Maryland, and West Virginia was visible, as was the Gettysburg battlefield, where he viewed the lunacy of Pickett's ill-fated charge; cannon and musket fire angrily flashing in the darkness. Drifting south, he flew over the working stiffs of Prince William County, glancing down at his own miserable little townhouse in Woodbridge. It looked even less impressive from high above. The long, dark backbone of the Blue Ridge Mountains squatted to the west, beyond the Shenandoah Valley hunt clubs and gentlemen's farms of the truly rich. He chose a perch atop a cabin in a Spotsylvania Civil War battlefield, thinking of John Wilkes Booth cornered in a burning barn and Stonewall Jackson having his arm sawn off.

Mike awoke feeling nauseous, so he sat on the edge of the cot, draining his vodka glass. With eyes closed and his head hanging, he fuzzily recalled the bird flying, the helicopter, and maybe some civil war stuff. He tried to grasp more of it, but it all faded like steam. A vision remained of never-ending red and white snakes on the ground wherever Mike the Vulture flew. He got up to pee, cursing because he had dreamt of traffic—it was bad enough when he was awake.

Mike did not appreciate how burdensome the D.C. area traffic was until he married and left the convenience of his Arlington apartment. After moving into her Woodbridge townhouse, twenty miles south of the building, they would take her Dodge to work, never leaving home later than 6:00 a.m. Doing otherwise guarantees a miserable hour-plus commute each way in stop-and-go highway hell. On workdays immediately before and after major holidays, they stayed home and used vacation time just to avoid the extended commute times. Want to go to the grocery store or home improvement store on the weekend? Better do it before 10:00 a.m. to avoid traffic delays. You need to see the doctor or dentist, and you work in the Pentagon? Better schedule at least half a day off to get that done. Same for visits to the DMV, car repairs, and other services not open on the weekend.

The National Capital Region is one of the country's worst commuter nightmares. Millions endure multi-hour round-trips from their homes in Pennsylvania, Maryland, West Virginia, Virginia, and Washington, D.C. Some ride on trains, buses, in carpools, and on the Metro, but most drive single-occupant cars. The roads are barely adequate to handle local traffic volumes, yet there is also heavy interstate traffic passing through. Radio traffic reporters sound bored, giving repetitive reports of aircraft crashes, truck rollovers, fatalities, fires, Metro derailments, hit-and-runs, injured pedestrians, political protests, spilled chemicals, road rage, and multi-county police pursuits.

Exactly what out-of-the-ordinary commuter traffic event will happen on any given day is unknown, but a handful of them occur daily. When they do, the "normal" flow of traffic noticeably slows and then usually stops as police, ambulance, fire, and tow vehicles slowly creep their way to the incident. Experienced commuters will detect something amiss and avoid entering highways and being trapped for hours in traffic jams that can stretch for miles.

Stumbling to his chest-high fridge, Mike opened the door to choose between a water bottle and a nearly empty fifth of vodka. Slaking his thirst, he wondered if he would recall the flight of Mike the Vulture in the morning. Probably not. Closing the door on the brightly lit interior, he reached out to send a message to his tomorrow self. In the thick dust atop the fridge, he used his thumb to write a one-word message: CARS. Then he tottered back to the cot for a deep sleep.

Chapter 15
Head Slap

August, 2016

Mike awoke, briefly wondering where he was. Mentally shifting gears, he wondered where the bottle of vodka was and how much he had left in it before passing out. Groaning in distress, he could hear the hum of the fans and an annoying pest control ad on the radio. With eyelids shut, he divined that he had left the basement lights on, as well as his clothes and shoes. He needed to find that bottle.

Suzy Wilson once again beat the smaller basement door with her umbrella's hard handle. Annoyed at having to wait in the morning's light drizzle, she shouted, "I know you're in there, Mike, open the damn door!" She gave the metal door another rapid drubbing, which Mike could not avoid hearing from his fetal position on the cot. Finally, she heard the deadbolt lock click open, and prepared to bust Mike for violating his lease by living in the basement. As his disheveled head with puffy eyes peered into the morning air, she slumped slightly forward, abandoning thoughts of a confrontation. "Hon, you don't look so good," she said.

"I feel worse, c'mon in, Suzy," Mike offered, staggering to the folding table and chairs.

Following him, she surveilled the mostly empty room. It had not changed much since she had last been there a few months prior. Mike had his old van and new forklift, lots of empty industrial shelving, and a few heavy-duty tables. He had created a little nest area by the bathroom where, apparently, he liked to drink alone and sleep. He kept the rental orderly and clean, but overall, it was a melancholy place for anyone to be living alone.

"Water?" Mike offered her, pushing a fresh bottle across the table where they sat, just as he and Arif had a few weeks prior. She noticed his hand tremble as it reached for and withdrew from the bottle. "Baby, where's your drink?" she asked softly and empathetically. "You need some." Mike nodded to the fridge, where Suzy retrieved an over-half-empty fifth of expensive vodka, handing it to Mike. Without preamble, or nod to social graces, he screwed off the top, swallowing two greedy gulps of the clear, cold liquid. "That's, enough," she said, reaching for the bottle. "That'll settle you long enough so's we can talk."

"'Bout what?" Mike queried with a small burp, annoyed that she had taken the booze. He would make sure this visit was short so he could drop back into his cot with the bottle and go back to sleep.

"Two things, the first is your lease."

"I'm paid up."

"You are."

"You approved the improvements."

"I did, and it looks much better."

"I ain't putting anything together in here, so what's to talk 'bout?"

"You're *living* in here. That's not allowed by the lease."

His head hurt, and he felt nauseous; he would cut to the chase. "Suzy, the rent is $4,200 a month. I'll give you another $3,000 a month, cash money—starting right now, to be my rental advocate." She watched as he stiffly made his way to a cabinet, where he found a wad of cash, snapping thirty crisp hundred-dollar bills on the counter. Shuffling back to Suzy, he dropped the $3,000 in her lap, knowing she would not bother him with pesky questions.

Glancing up toward him, she looked like she had just won something big, but dangerous.

"Being an advocate," Mike began, plopping down in his chair, "means you look the other way when I violate the lease by sleeping here and quietly do other things without bothering the people upstairs. It means you approve any additional changes I might need to make to the building. Most importantly, it means you make sure the lease continues without any issues or hassles." He could sense the moral and professional calculus Suzy was struggling to perform in her head. He knew she was on board when she quickly placed the money in her purse.

"You won't do anything stupid that sends me to jail, will you?" She asked warily.

"If, for some reason, we need help from the police, I have got another advocate there that can help us out. How's that?"

"Sounds better, I'm just..."

"I don't think I'll be here for more than another fifteen months or so. When I do leave, you'll get a $5,000 cash bonus, then we'll part ways. Right now, I just wanna violate my lease by going back to bed."

"Mike," Suzy confided softly, searching her purse for a business card and pen, "I've been where you are now, and I don't miss it." She scratched a location and time on the back of the card, handing it to him. "Call me and we will visit this place together, if you want. I don't like seeing you hurting like I was."

He figured she was off to church as he watched her walk away in her Sunday dress, leather loafers clicking on the hard floor. Pulling out his thirty-year-old leather wallet, he inserted her card next to Detective Rodriguez's, but not before examining what she had written on the backside: Tuesday, 7pm, Mt. Sterling Methodist. *Probably an Alcoholics Anonymous séance*, Mike figured. *I like to drink, but I don't have a problem.*

After Suzy left, he lay on the cot for an hour. The wet morning outside made the basement feel muggy. Too many thoughts kept him awake, most of them negative. *Prioritize your problems and work on them one-by-one,* his grandmother had counseled him years ago. With the pop of a knee, he shambled to the card table, grabbing Suzy's pen and a scrap of cardboard. Starting with an underlined heading of "Problems," he paused to reflect, then wrote: *Escape*. With additional consideration while draining a bottle of water, he added: *Work* and *Money*. *Good start*, he thought, distracted by four fingers of fluid remaining in the vodka bottle. Returning to the list, he added: *Iran* and *Fog*, the letters slightly deformed by the tremor in his hand. *Maybe he did have a drinking issue, or maybe it was just stress getting to him. Either way, better slow down on the booze*, he told himself.

A quick shower, a change of cargo shorts, a t-shirt, and white socks, then Mike was ready to go out for the day. He needed coffee, he needed to ponder his list, and he needed to prepare for Arif's visit the following Saturday. Leaving the radio on, he killed the basement lights on the way out, grabbing Suzy's left-behind umbrella, a folding lawn chair, a baseball cap, and his credit card-sized cardboard list.

***

The deli was close, but crowded that Sunday morning. With coffee and a lox bagel in-hand, Mike drove half a mile to the U.S. Air Force Memorial. He wanted inspiration while thinking about the five items on his list, hopefully lifting the growing unease and dread he sensed. Slowly edging past a bus disgorging elderly tourists at the memorial, he nearly nudged their leader with his car. She was waving a red flag on a stick, shouting orders while ignoring the only other vehicle in the parking lot that morning.

Grabbing his chair and breakfast, Mike skulked away from the memorial's small visitor's center and solemn displays. Above him, three triangular stainless-steel spires curled hundreds of feet into the air, like an *avant-garde* rendition of the Saint Louis Gateway Arch. It was not the grand architecture that held Mike's attention in the grayish sky, but a pair of swallows diving like circus acrobats. Those and the phoebes working diligently around the overflowing trash bins to clean up the droppings left by humans. Raptors, especially eagles, he knew, would be soaring on the less-developed Maryland side of the Potomac—too far away to see without a birding scope.

The rainy drizzle had stopped, the sun could be felt more than seen, and another sauna-like D.C. August day was underway. Mike knew where to set his chair, far from the tourists and maximizing his panoramic view of the Pentagon. A half-mile away, the Air Force Memorial perched atop a grassy hillside, just seventy-two feet above the monumental building. In pancake-flat Washington, that slight elevation change is a mountain. Looking down, he could see the entire building like an architect's drawing. A spider web-like maze of steep gray tiled rooftops interconnected the five concentric rings of five-sided buildings. All the west and south-facing facades were visible, along with the acreage of parking lots and highways surrounding the building. Even after working there for three regrettable decades, he had to admit the colossal scale of the building was still captivating.

Over his left shoulder, Mike could see parts of Arlington National Cemetery, its manicured grasslands crisscrossed with endless rows and avenues of white marble tombstones. Beyond the graveyard stood the Netherlands Carilion and the commercial buildings of Roslyn, Virginia. To the right, he looked down on the Crystal City section of Arlington, with Reagan Airport in the distance. Sutton Towers, where he wistfully remembered living, was just beyond his field of view. Straight ahead, and beyond the Pentagon, the Potomac River broadly flowed from his left to his right. With the low-ceilinged clouds lifting, he could easily pick out the National Cathedral, White House, Washington Monument, and Capitol Building in the distant Washington cityscape.

Munching his bagel, Mike glommed at the concrete structure below, trying to summon the optimism and naivety that had motivated him long ago. Like a rat, he decided, he had spent thirty-six years silently padding along the baseboard edges of its endless corridors; always seeking, but never finding the cheese. He wanted to *belong*, to *contribute,* and to *be somebody important*. Instead, he ended up being excluded and minimalized—basically, a nobody surrounded by untold thousands of other nobodies.

Then, a decade into his career, Kazim showed up. "Will you watch my dog?" he had asked. "Need to borrow my car? Come to dinner, you are welcome in our home!" Over several years, many small and pleasant interactions morphed into their swapping of Pentagon information for cash. Mike never gave him much more than could be gleaned from the press and defense periodicals, but he was always satisfied, and the size of the payments always grew. With Kazim, he did *belong*, he did *contribute,* and he was *important*. With mournful lament, Mike realized that after nearly thirteen years, he still missed Kazim's friendship, and wondered if he truly was in *Jannah*, like Arif had said, or someplace lesser than paradise.

It was 9:30 a.m. Glancing up, he could see the fog dissipating along with the chance of a relatively cool and wet day. Folding the chair, Mike headed for the old Dodge, tossing the paper cup and uneaten bagel into a trashcan. Pulling out the cardboard list he had made an hour ago, he realized he had memorized it, so he also trashed that on his way to the ex-wife's former wheels.

Needing a new compressor, the aging cars' air conditioning was slowly dying. Mike had the cash to fix it, or to buy any car he desired, but years of frugal practicality by necessity were an ingrained way of life for him. *Summer was almost over, so why fix it now, just to lay fallow for over half a year?* Also, Arif could give his "six months" warning at any time, and destroying the Dodge was part of his "action" plan. If nothing had changed by next April, he counseled himself, he would get the compressor fixed in time for next year's heatwave.

Just for fun, Mike imagined the leather-bound scent of artic-cold air breezing past him from the ergonomically positioned vents of a brand-new BMW, Mercedes, or Jaguar. He had never ridden in, much less driven, any of those cars, but he had the cash to buy one of each. Instead, he sat sweating in the hot Dodge because he knew not to spend the Iranians' money on anything visibly obvious. He also never mentioned his gambling habits to anyone. During mandatory annual Security Awareness training, the Pentagon reminded its workforce that looking meek was an important part of remaining undetected as a "foreign agent." The message was the opposite—to squeal on coworkers who flaunted bling above their humble civil service means. That included clothing, jewelry, cars, vacations, foreign travel, and craggy teeth that suddenly became Hollywood perfect.

Mike thought about his escape problem. He could skip town and avoid getting involved with whatever Arif was planning to do at the Pentagon. The secret account held about $690,000 that he could drain, disappearing into the desert sprawl around Vegas. He was fifty-eight with thirty-seven years of federal service; there was almost $900,000 in his 401(k) and his monthly pension would be worth about the same—if he lived another thirty years to collect all of it. He could bolt tomorrow morning, as soon as the bank opened; point the piece-of-shit car west, and never look back. He would do the retirement paperwork online, and the world could kiss his hairy ass goodbye.

Except his life expectancy would be a lot less than thirty years if he double-crossed the Iranians. "Do not betray your friends," Arif had warned him. Mike knew that was a threat with teeth. Their hackers would find him virtually, and then they would send another dark little man to quietly settle the score. Also, they could barter his identity with the CIA, FBI, DIA, State Department, and Woodbridge Police—whomever. Maybe they would exchange him for the release of one of their own by the Americans, or another country. Maybe they would get minor concessions to American or other sanctions burdening the Iranian economy.

Most likely, though, his insignificant deeds would not warrant any high-level foreign policy attention or consideration. That could quickly change based on the second ominous tidbit from Arif, "You will not be safe here after the actions." That clearly meant the Iranians were planning something big on the morning of their action. Did it mean he would not be safe, as in the feds would eventually find and end him? Or did it mean he would not be safe as in breathing and doing other essential things among those currently living in Washington?

Jesus, what had he gotten himself into? Good thing his family had not lived to see this. His wife would have silently hung her head in shame—then divorced him. His grandmother would have slapped his left cheek raw, immediately gouging the other side of his face with a savage backhand, rings, and all. He wasn't sure what Joy, who was still alive, would think or do if she found out.

She had distracted him, he decided—not his mother, but his wife. Maybe he should never have gotten married. At that point in his life, Kazim's friendship, and payments, were a fading memory. The probability of the government catching and prosecuting him for selling defense information was lessening every year. *That* would have been the perfect time for him to have retired and moved on to something else—anything else, and somewhere else. But then he stumbled into love, and he realized, momentary happiness. They had talked about leaving the government and moving to live among her family in southern Georgia, but then she had decided they would keep working to maximize their retirement benefits.

Again, he tried to summon the feeling of work being interesting and challenging—back when the future promised to be something better and not just more of the same. Paul, with that Boston accent, was the last guy that it felt good to work with. Lenny, before him, was always ragging about something, but he was generous with good advice. Then those two cats way back at the beginning—Carl the crazy black guy, and the older smart guy, Herschel Utz—*like the pretzel*. He was gruff and wore crooked horn-rimmed glasses with black lace-up shoes, white socks, and floodwater pants, but he was brilliant and the best mentor ever. Without asking, and annoyingly too often, all four of them would let you know how many years, months, and days until they retired. With crystal clear hindsight and a gentle head slap, Mike finally realized what they were telling him: *get the fuck out of here as soon as you can*. They had practically chiseled it on the side of the building, but he was too stupid to listen.

"You will leave the past and start again," was another breadcrumb Arif had tossed out, semi-confirming that he meant living in Iran. Relocating from a democracy to an Islamic theocracy had about as much appeal as the daily tablespoon of cod liver oil his grandmother had forced on him. Would he just hide in his brick hut all day, eating on Persian rugs with his fingers instead of a fork? Would he drink tea with his buddies in casbah cafes, all of them wearing white robes and Yasser Arafat headdresses? Maybe he could find a blonde bride online from eastern Europe with straight teeth and a thigh gap. They would share his hut and she would wear her burqa when they went out to the local mosque.

Helping Arif with his two upcoming "actions," Mike realized, was not something he wanted to do anymore. He could keep his money, and Mike would give up on trying to belong, to contribute, and to be someone important. Too late, he realized, he had stupidly screwed himself while trying to screw the Army, which had royally screwed him. There would be no escaping. He would try to appear unchanged to Arif, and he'd have to make do with whatever the outcomes were to be. He would make sure to talk money—real money—with Arif when he visited on Saturday. If he had to leave everything behind, and his action was truly important, he should be well compensated.

Chapter 16
Planning Factors

August, 2016

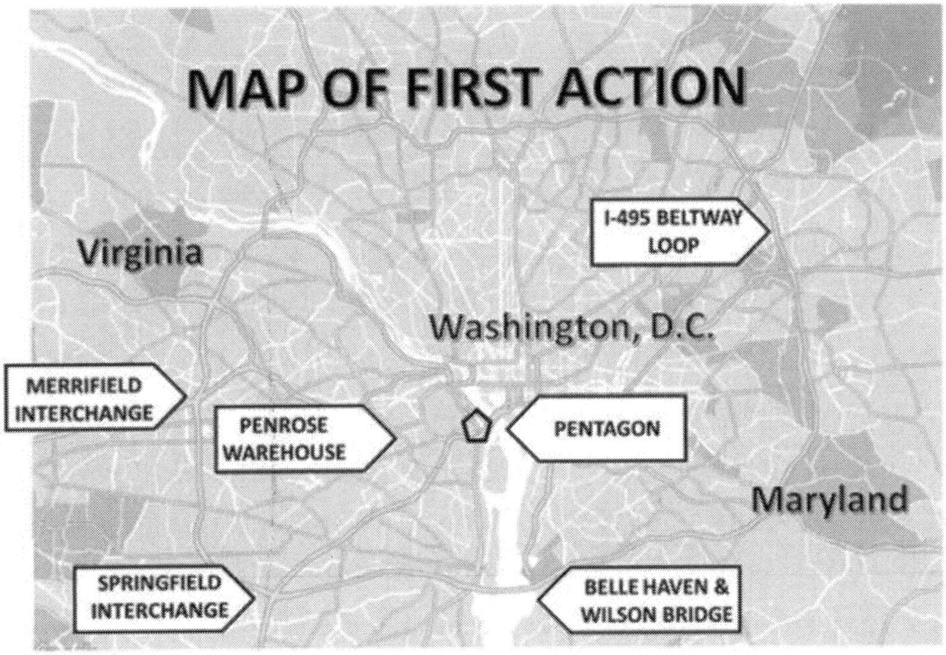

Mike left the Air Force Memorial and drove south on Interstate-395. Both windows were down to supplement the slightly cooled air flowing from the dash vents. The water vapor wafting from the warming asphalt reminded him of Atlantic City and the smell of wet sand along the boardwalk. He needed to make quick progress on the fifth item on his list of problems: the fog Arif wanted to distract attention from his second action. He did not know how to make weather happen, but he did know that mixing a few teaspoons of sugar and potassium nitrate would generate a bit of smoke. Doing that by the ton, he figured, would produce a lot more.

The Dodge zipped along at seventy miles an hour—a rare event usually only achievable late at night or early on weekend mornings. Washington, D.C., is surrounded by three heavily populated Maryland counties to the east and by four even more densely populated Virginia counties to the west. All in all, the district and the seven counties have over five million people. Starting at 5:00 a.m. on any weekday morning, they clog the region's roads with millions of cars shuttling from home to daycare, school, work, breakfast, and other places. The median household income in the region is twice the national average, which means more money to spend on second and third cars, creating even more commuter traffic on the roads. Because of the crowded local traffic, and the truly interstate traffic always passing through the region, average highway speeds during rush hour periods are only about thirty miles an hour.

Since the dawn of the horseless carriage over a hundred years ago, the federal, Virginia, and Maryland governments have struggled to plan, procure, and build an ever-larger network of roadways in the National Capital Region. Overly optimistic growth estimates and aggressive road building by each generation have been continually outpaced by the unfathomable transport needs of the next generation. The result is many billions of dollars spent on road infrastructure that works, but not as well as it should.

Viewing Washington traffic from an airplane, a distinctive feature seen would be the circular Interstate 495 that threads through sixty-four miles of Maryland and Virginia. This is the "capital beltway," twenty-four lanes across at its widest point. If the beltway were a clock face, the downtown tourist area, with all the Smithsonian museums, would be at its center. There is a traffic chokepoint from the south where Interstate 395 intersects the beltway at the seven o'clock position on the clockface. From the west, there is another where Interstate-66 crosses the beltway at the nine o'clock position. There is a third major chokepoint (at six o'clock) in Virginia where the beltway bridges the Potomac River towards Maryland. There are other highways and overburdened intersections in the region, but these are the three Mike chose for his fog action.

While driving, Mike hoped that Sunday morning's lighter traffic volume would also mean fewer Virginia State Troopers patrolling the roads. He would be making some oddball traffic moves and did not need to be pulled over by a road cop asking a lot of questions. With the car's radio tuned to Doctor Dust, he was annoyed by the scratchy 78 RPM foxtrots being played, apparently as a one-off lark. Just ten minutes after leaving the Air Force Memorial, he neared his first destination, the colossal eight-square-mile interchange of I-395, I-495, and I-95 at Springfield, Virginia. About seven miles south of the Pentagon and the Penrose warehouse, the interchange, which locals dubbed the "mixing bowl," was his obvious number one location for launching a fog action.

Slowing to pull into an emergency lane with a relatively promontory view, he studied the civil engineering masterpiece as if for the first time. There must have been a hundred lanes of traffic heading in all directions at dozens of elevations above the ground. There were four or five layers of banked, sharply turning, flyover, and cloverleaf ramps. Massive concrete piers supported even heavier-looking steel-beamed bridges. The whole area was a pedestrian death zone cordoned off by safety fencing, jersey barriers, retaining walls, and endless stretches of brutally ugly fifteen-foot noise walls. To make the traffic flow, and add to the overall confusion, segregated pay-as-you-go express lanes were available on all three highways with their own requisite on and off ramps and overhead monitoring stations.

A half-million cars and trucks driven by locals, through traffic, and mystified tourists passed through the mixing bowl's traffic hades every day. The government had just spent over a decade and nearly $700 million improving the interchange, and Mike had plans to fuck it up, if only for a few hours. The key spot was at the center and bottom of the conflagration. The fog would rise with the sun, and the wind would blow it whichever way—it did not matter. Arif wanted a fog to distract from his action, and this, combined with others Mike was planning, would do just that.

The goal was simply to slow the pace of traffic on the three intersecting highways causing a spreading "ripple effect" slowdown for miles on each roadway. This would happen as visibility dropped for some drivers, while others reduced their speed or stopped to rubberneck and yield to emergency vehicles clawing their way to the scene. Because hundreds of thousands of vehicles would be enroute to the massive intersection from all four compass points, some nearby, and some many miles away, the traffic jam would be monumental, or so Mike hoped. There would be fender benders, and probably a few crashes, but hopefully no one would be injured. If Arif was planning to hurt people with his second action the following morning, that was out of Mike's control, and he knew better than to probe him about it.

It took several frustrating wrong turns, and probably twenty miles of driving, but Mike finally found the correct path to arrive at the center-bottom of the mixing bowl interchange. Parking the Dodge, he stepped onto the gravely concrete to absorb the sights and sounds, imagining stealthily parking a trailer there at three or four in the morning. Overall, he was feeling anxious about Arif's stingy guidance and high expectations. He needed to get busy buying the equipment and supplies for generating multiple large-scale fogs. On Saturday, he would have Arif's thumbs up or down, along with more information he needed. Just the same, thinking about it and then finding this first spot felt good. He climbed onto the car's sweaty vinyl seat to pinpoint the next one.

The Woodrow Wilson Bridge, another recently upgraded and gargantuan roadway project, is seven miles east of the Springfield mixing bowl and less than six miles southeast of the Pentagon. The twelve-lane bridge arcs 70 feet over the Potomac River from Belle Haven, Virginia, to the National Harbor in Maryland. If traffic is flowing, you can drive east on the I-495 beltway from the mixing bowl to the Wilson Bridge in just ten to twenty minutes. Mike planned to slow that down to at least an hour on the morning of his fog action.

Before the interstate highways were built after World War II, U.S. 1 was the main north-south thoroughfare on the east coast. In Virginia, it is still a heavily traveled route between D.C. and south towards Richmond. Just west of the Virginia side of the Wilson Bridge, U.S. 1 crosses over the inner and outer loops of the I-495 capital beltway. Daily traffic across the Wilson Bridge and on U.S. 1 was about half that of the mixing bowl, yet there were still hundreds of thousands of vehicles. That made it a no-brainer second site for Mike's planned second fog.

Parking the Dodge and viewing the site from a distance, Mike could see the same type of ramps, bridges, noise walls, and other accoutrements as the Springfield interchange, but on a much smaller scale. There was only one logical place to park his second trailer for maximum fog effect, so he set off to explore it.

With the first two morning commuter fog locations pinpointed, it was past noon on a ninety-degree day with ninety percent humidity. Giving up on the car's air conditioner, Mike thought about lunch as he drove northwest to the third fog location, where Interstate 66 crossed the beltway nine miles west of the Pentagon. He knew this third spot was flat and wide open, with the same spaghetti pile of high-volume roads as the Virginia Wilson Bridge entrance. He needed to pick the trailer parking spot and learn the ingress and egress routes so he could pitch them to Arif on Saturday.

The three mega highway intersections would host his three biggest fogs, with smoke pouring from horse trailers he would park at each location just a few hours ahead of time. If Arif approved his plan, there would be additional, but smaller, fogs and fires hopscotching the commuter landscape towards and finally, into the Pentagon.

He would use a week of sick leave from work to flesh out the plan's details and prepare his presentation to Arif. On Friday, he would have to go into the office for a few hours to receive his annual performance rating, assuming it would reflect the downward spiral of his so-called career. Croaking along with Hamilton, Joe Frank, and Reynold's *Don't Refuse My Love* on the radio, he decided a roast beef sandwich with an extra-large diet soda would be good for lunch.

***

"C'mon in, Mike," Shaquan Reynolds pleasantly called out to him with a small wave of a toned, yet beefy arm. She was Mike's current supervisor, a retired army warrant officer, and Black Hawk helicopter pilot. She had earned multiple commendations during her tours in the early years of the Afghanistan and Iraq invasions. She was a large woman with a preference for pant suits, and she shared a cramped office in 1D343 with another first-line supervisor. Mike sat across from Shaquan at the small wood conference table designated for the two managers. "Are you feeling better?" she inquired, alluding to the four days of sick leave he had just used.

"On the mend," he offered, adding, "thanks for caring."

She studied him, wondering why he bothered to keep working as an army civilian employee. He was approaching sixty; his stoop was growing more pronounced, and when he did come to work, he glommed around the office in a lethargic shuffle. Mike needed a haircut and to admit defeat in his attempt at a combover. His clothes were old, rumpled, and frayed at the cuffs. There was also a disturbing buildup of tartar on his teeth that ineffectually cried out for a dental hygienist.

They had confirmed his drinking problem one day by serendipitously getting a whiff of his coffee thermos when he was relieving himself. Office scuttlebutt was that he was also addicted to gambling, supposedly confirmed by several providential sightings at the Charlestown, West Virginia, Indian casino. He had no family, drove a crappy car, and lived in a house his late wife left him mortgage-free. For some inexplicable reason, he annoyingly comported himself with an air of noblesse oblige that had no basis in fact. She wondered if he also had mental issues.

At one time, she was told, Mike could be depended on to prep the assistant secretary of the Army for congressional briefings. Now, the office picnic committee has refused him as a volunteer delegate from her division. He had stopped applying for promotion years ago, as she knew. She needed self-motivated workers who could run with projects and complete them ahead of time while exceeding her expectations. Getting rid of him would allow her to hire a younger, more eager go-getter, which would eliminate the workload headaches Mike generated.

Opening the first of two manila folders, she slid it across the tabletop explaining, "Your annual rating is on page two. You need to sign and date the form just below that, then I will forward it to Colonel Back for his review and signature." Mike had been through this ritual too many times. He could just sign the damned form, walk out the door, and leave for the Penrose warehouse. Or, if he chose, he could go into an escalating barrage of confrontational histrionics until Shaquan was flustered, argumentative, and near tears. He had enjoyed doing that to a previous supervisor he had loathed, but Shaquan deserved better. She was dedicated, hardworking, and fair. More importantly, for Mike's purposes, she was pliable, easily manipulated, and insecure. He needed her, but she sure did not need him.

Apparently, when you became a government supervisor, you are issued a booklet of inane "bullet points" to enter on your subordinates' annual performance appraisals. Scrolling down the pamphlet's lists, you would spot one that applied to a particular employee at that particular time and copy it onto that year's rating form. Mike's bullet points used to be things like, "loyal and dedicated employee," and "requires minimal guidance and direction." Glancing at the appraisal Shaquan had just handed him, the bullet points for his past year included, "fails to follow established policy," and "ignores guidance and direction."

The all-important metric on any annual appraisal is your overall rating on page two of the form. Workers that can improve the bureaucracy and will be moving up within it are rated "1". Workers who are just workers are rated "2." People who are air thieves while in the office are rated "3." For twenty-four years, Mike had been a "1" worker, migrating to a "2" when he realized additional promotions were out of his grasp. Glancing at the middle of page two of his new appraisal, Shaquan had accurately rated him a "3." Out of boredom, he thought he would tweak her a little bit, indignantly gasping, "Three?"

"Mike," she began cautiously in a diplomatic tone of voice, "you have not met any of your six performance objectives this year. You don't schedule annual leave ahead of time and you don't turn in notes from your doctor when you use more than three days of sick leave. You have not completed your mandatory training classes and I can't depend on you to complete an assignment—and I don't mean on time, I mean *ever*."

"I've met that last objective," he contended, pointing to the form.

"Promoting POSH (Prevention of Sexual Harassment) and EEO (Equal Employment Opportunity)?"

"Yup, I met that one."

"Give me some examples."

"Well, for POSH, I've never had a harassment complaint filed against me."

"And?"

"For EEO, I mentored Ruby."

"*Ruby*?"

"Yeah, I gave her guidance when she asked for it."

"And Ruby is black, like I'm black, so that counts as meeting your EEO objective?"

"That's it."

"Mike, Ruby transferred out of the office two months ago. When you were on extended, undocumented sick leave, you missed her farewell lunch. Also, you did not complete this year's on-line POSH and EEO training."

Loudly sighing, Mike realized he did not have the heart to harass Shaquan. Grabbing her pen, he signed and dated the appraisal, closed the folder, and slid it towards her. Pushing his chair back to leave, she cautiously slithered the second folder towards him.

"From Colonel Back," she murmured defensively.

The folder held a one-page formal army memorandum, secured by two paper clips. It was addressed to Mike and titled, "Letter of Caution." She was busy studying the tabletop, avoiding his gaze. *What the fuck was a Letter of Caution,* he wondered. Rapidly scanning the three short paragraphs, there was mercifully no mention of Iranians, the over half a million Arif had paid him in the past year, or the Penrose warehouse. It was just bureaucratic gobbledygook about being a shitty worker. "Should I sign this?" he asked.

"No Mike," she said apologetically, "it's yours to keep—a copy will be placed in your Official Personnel File."

Holy shit, Mike realized they were moving to terminate him! Thirty-seven years of faithful service, all but one in this concrete shithole, and this is how they treated him! Closing his eyes, elbows on chair arms, and templed fingertips on his forehead, Mike took a few moments to process the jolt.

Unless you were a clumsy thief or an uncontrolled sexual deviant, it took two or three years to be fired by the federal government. He could join the employee union, file a bunch of baseless grievances, then the process would take even longer. Their objective, he realized, was to force him into retirement, which was not possible. To complete his action for Arif, he needed a valid employee identification badge and DOD Combined Access Card, allowing him unfettered entrance, movement within, and exit from the Pentagon. The bottom line, he realized, was that beyond the slap in the face and hatchet job on his pride, the Letter of Caution was meaningless. He would continue as planned, probably for another year or so, and then he would be living in Tehran, where he would burn the damn letter in the camel dung fire of his mud hut's tortilla oven.

Brusquely pushing back from the table, he startled Shaquan by proffering a firm and brisk handshake with a sincere smile. "Put me on leave," Mike directed as he moved towards the door, flimsy folder in hand. He had too many loose ends to finish before Arif's visit the next day.

Chapter 17

Logistics

August, 2016

$$C_{12}H_{22}O_{11} + KNO_2$$

Arif and Mike stood shoulder-to-shoulder facing the basement's longer cinder block wall, a hip-high table before them. The pole fans droned in the background, their round heads pivoting like spectators at a tennis match, pushing the humid night around the well-lit, but gloomy room. Competing for their aural attention, Doctor Dust mumbled some radio trivia in his calming baritone about the next song on his playlist.

With heads bowed to their task, the two men watched as, with a hiss and whoosh, Mike ignited a blue flame ring on a butane camping stove. He had carefully arranged his utensils and supplies within easy reach on the tabletop, like a TV cooking show. Small paper cups held pre-measured ingredients, awaiting their use in the unwritten recipe Mike was following.

Heating a small saucepan, he began his presentation with the jagged breathing and shaky voice of the truly nervous, made worse by his attempt not to be. He had good reason to be jittery, as his usefulness in the plan was being hotly debated by Arif's superiors. The basement warehouse was needed due to its proximity to the Pentagon, as were the small panel van and forklift that Mike had the foresight to procure. All three would be useful in handling, transferring, and then delivering the weapon. Arif's secret task that night was to evaluate Mike's fog plan and its potential to support the primary action. His guidance was clear—if the American stumbled, as was expected, his presence in the operation was to be terminated.

“I learned to make smoke bombs in high school,” Mike struggled to calmly explain. “Sugar melts at 366 degrees Fahrenheit, so the pan needs to be hot. This is two teaspoons of granulated sugar,” he continued, holding a paper cup with a finger and thumb of one hand. “And this is a teaspoon of water to add to the sugar. Now we mix it to make a paste, and dump it in the frying pan.” Using a small wood spatula, he stirred the white paste until it resembled bubbling egg whites. “Two teaspoons of granulated potassium nitrate,” he called out, selecting a third cup. Sprinkling the chunky white powder onto the bubbling sugar, he continued stirring the mixture ‘til it looked like frothy cream of wheat. “The last bit,” he added, blending in a fine blackish power, “a teaspoon of organic dye.” Without narrative, he slid, poured, and pushed the dark mixture into an upright two-inch-long and one-inch-wide segment of PVC pipe. Into the upright end, he slowly inserted a short green firework fuse, taking care not to let it sink too far into the solidifying mixture.

Arif feigned interest in the pathetic little smoke bomb demonstration. You would not think it to look at him, but Mike had been more dependable—even faithful—than their other American recruits. Pay the others for a simple task, and they will give whiney excuses for doing half-assed jobs. Give Mike a difficult task, and it is done quickly without drawing attention to himself. He was clever, resourceful, discrete, and self-motivated. He also uncannily sensed the need to mostly listen, rarely talk, and never ask questions. They had yet to meet another American with his skill set. Seeing him flail with this last test while so close to the operation’s end was disappointing.

“Last step,” Mike eagerly disclosed, grabbing a heated glue gun and a large metal washer. Arif rolled his eyes in disbelief while Mike focused on his task. “You have to restrict the exhaust to extend the burn time and to get the maximum smoke.” The washer was a little wider than the PVC pipe, with a quarter-inch hole in its middle. Centering the metal disk on one end of the pipe with the fuse protruding from the hole, he squeezed a bead of glue to secure it to the pipe. Blowing to cool the glue, he asked Arif, “Ready?” while sliding him a box of kitchen matches.

“This?” Arif wondered as he pointed to the fuse's end.

“Yup.”

“Do we stay here?” he wondered, imagining the piece of PVC exploding.

“Hasn’t blown up yet. Go ahead; you’ll be surprised,” Mike encouraged the smaller man.

As the fuse sizzled for a few seconds, Mike turned to watch the Iranian's face transform from sour skepticism to stunned surprise. A small flame within the cylinder quickly became a crescendo of sound and flame, reminding Arif of a small jet engine with afterburners activated. A dense plume of purple smoke forced its way out of the washer hole like a volcano, thickly rising, and then spreading among the ceiling rafters. The device entered a twenty-second plateau of steady sound, flame, and smoke generation, then faded to eventual exhaustion after about half a minute. The unique stink of vomit mixed with wet clay and fireplace ashes slowly descended and engulfed the two men.

"Mikel," Arif exclaimed, "یک ابر بنفش (a purple cloud)*!*"

Nervously chuckling, Mike had no clue what Arif had just said, but thought it sounded encouraging. Walking into the dissipating purple haze, he returned with an eleven pound, thirty-gallon fiber drum that looked like a huge "D" cell battery. A metal ring reinforced its closed end, and there was a locking metal lid on the open end with a jagged eight-inch hole in its center. Laughing in delight, Arif immediately understood that the drum would be used to make a very large fog generator. "How many?" he wondered.

"One hundred and twenty—forty each at of three locations, plus a few smaller ones.

Bending to pick up the barrel, Arif judged its heft and durability before setting the cardboard drum down. "You chose well, Mikel. Will you put these in the Pentagon?"

"Two smaller ones—I'll explain."

Picking up a length of the green fuse cord, Arif held it to the roughly hewn hole in the drum top, glancing at Mike with arched eyebrows and expecting an explanation. He was wondering how the fuse would be secured and lit on the big drums.

"Over here," Mike responded, earnestly motioning Arif to his next basement workshop project. "This is an automatic igniter than can be set by the hour or minute." He had removed a cheap round clock face and mounted it to a thin piece of plywood; the battery-operated clock mechanism apparently remained behind the dial as the minute and second hands were visible. Arif bent to inspect a nine-volt battery hot-glued to the board. He followed Mike's finger as he explained and traced the path of thin wires soldered between the battery, the clock face, and a paper tube the size of a tampon. A metal strap and screws secured the tube, with one end extending an inch beyond the edge of the board. "Push this to this," Mike directed, wanting Arif to advance the minute hand half an hour to connect with a pin he had riveted to the clockface, "then cover your ears."

Taking a step back from the worktable, Arif reached out to do as he was directed, fearful of getting an electric shock. Immediately, and before he could cover his ears, something happened at the far end of the paper tube. Like the smoke bomb, it shot flames and roared, but at a higher, screaming pitch. Having forgotten to secure the board, Mike jumped forward to stop its movement across the tabletop, keeping one hand over an ear. Then the damned thing exploded in front of them, startling Arif into a backward hop and making Mike softly chuckle again.

Arif looked at Mike like he'd bought a knife for a gun fight. "جدی هستی (Are you serious)?" he shouted in his Persian code, acerbically enough for Mike to get his gist.

"It's a model rocket engine," Mike explained sheepishly, "that last pop pushes the parachute out."

Pantomiming a toy skydiver drifting to the concrete floor, Arif wondered, "Do you need چتر نجات (parachute), Mikel?

"Beggars can't be choosers," was all he said, failing not to sound defensive. Try to buy anything that goes bang or pop in a big way, and you run straight into the ATF (Bureau of Alcohol, Tobacco, Firearms and Explosives) dragnet. Potassium nitrate was a common agricultural fertilizer that chemical companies produced mountains of every year. Buying it by the ton, as Mike needed to do, would probably require skirting around ATF paperwork because it was also a common bomb-making component. Also, good luck trying to buy an igniter, like his rocket motor science fair set-up—especially not using the internet—without getting on the ATF's radar. The things he built were amateur hour, but they worked, and so far, they had not drawn any unwanted attention. He wondered if Arif understood those restrictions and how likely it was that, once they scaled up their operation, a black-clad SWAT (Special Weapons Assault Team) raid would swarm unannounced into their basement warehouse.

Sensing Mike's frustration, and embarrassed by his own loss of self-control, Arif offered, "متاسفم*'Ana 'asaf*, Mikel," raising a hand to his heart. "That mean's I am sorry in my country. You chose as well as you could. We will help you. Our army has the squibs and timers you need to create a fog. Is that 'okay' to you?"

"Perfect, thanks."

"Now come, let us sit and you tell me your plans," Arif directed, moving to the card table and folding chairs while checking his wristwatch. He had already spent more time visiting that evening than was safe, but his superiors would want more details. With smoke-irritated eyes, they drank bottled water to wash down the lingering taste of the demonstration. "Mikel, in a short time, tell me the plans for your action and how we can help."

"Well, those squibs for a start..."

"Tell me how you will make the smoke barrels, how you will put them and where..."

"Okay..." Mike began, taking about thirty minutes to give a carefully planned and practiced explanation. He started with the modifications he planned for the basement and the machines he would use to produce the finished smoke barrels. Then he explained how he would use horse trailers and a truck to transport and position the smoke drums. Arif intently listened while Mike defended the logic for his selected highway locations with follow-on bus and subway incidents culminating in two actions inside the Pentagon. To make sure their message was blatantly clear to all, a distinctive purple smoke would be released at all locations.

He had anticipated and preemptively addressed most of Arif's questions, which impressed the Iranian. Finally, he explained the overall strategy of the first action, summarizing the timeframes and, most importantly, the expected reaction of the Americans and how his activities would draw attention away from the second action the following morning, which would be the main event.

Without pausing for Arif's interjections, Mike enumerated his supply requisition for the Iranians: ten dozen of the igniter squibs, 3.5 tons of granulated sugar, 5 tons of granulated potassium nitrate, and three helpers the full week before the action date. All the other items, he would obtain using funds from the account while abiding by the $10,000 spending limit for each purchase.

Tremendously impressed with the presentation, Arif was confident he would face little resistance in conveying it to his overlords. They had given Mike bullshit guidance about a "fog" and the پسر عوضی (son-of-a-bitch) figured a way to make it happen using schoolboy devices of his own design. He'd also shown good judgement deferring the nitrate purchases, which Arif's organization could complete without pesky oversight. Mike would be kept busy, monitored closely—and kept far away from any knowledge of the second action. Most likely, the Americans would nab him during his frantic morning, setting off smoke bombs around the city or in the Pentagon. If not then, they expected the Americans would interrogate him sometime in the twenty-four hours between the two actions. Either way, he was to be kept ignorant of the big event, so he could not tip off their enemies.

"Mikel," Arif began, pushing wood shavings and sawdust on the card table into a small pile, "why purple? What is the meaning?"

Relieved that that was Arif's lead-off question, Mike semi-grinned, "It means that color had the lowest price."

"Ever efficient," Arif joked, sweeping the wood bits onto the floor, then adding "you should clean your workshop."

Leaning over, Mike watched the sawdust feather fall to the floor, wondering where it came from. Picking the largest chip, he examined and smelled it. "That's fresh, but it's not mine," he said, slightly puzzled, looking around for the source of the shavings and specks of wood dust.

Arif slowly stood; head tilted back as if viewing stars. Without talking, he motioned to Mike with a forefinger to first be quiet, then to move the card table aside. Taking Mike's wood spatula from the demonstration, he repositioned his chair, carefully stepping onto its rickety seat. Silent as a monk, Mike watched as the short man struggled to reach and poke the ceiling. Instead, the spatula handle magically disappeared into the floorboard above them.

"جاسوسان (Spies)!" Arif declared, jumping down into a blur of purposeful and well-trained movements. With eyes on the ceiling and shifting crabwise between the joists, he signaled for Mike to sit and remain silent. Continuing his search for more peepholes, Arif removed an automatic handgun from under one armpit and a silencer from under the other. Without bothering to look down, he mated the two with rapid twisting motions, then worked the gun's slide.

From time spent with his grandfather's pistol, Mike knew the muted mechanical sounds confirmed a chambered round and cocked hammer. With a death grip on the plastic armrests of his lawn chair, he wondered what Arif would do next. The room began to wobble, so he closed his eyes, waiting for a blast from the gun. *I should have retired*, he silently lamented, wishing he had an intervening deity to call upon. Intensely focused on all sounds, he listened as Arif quickly hustled towards and out of the small door, his rapid shoe movements squeaking on the floor like a basketball player's.

Breathing jaggedly, Mike assumed Arif was inspecting the payday loan business occupying the middle unit of the building and the source of the freshly drilled hole. At this time, on a Saturday, all three of the building's businesses were closed. If the loan shark was working late and opened the door for the small Arabian man, he would probably be getting the last surprise of his life. Mike had only waved and nodded to the heavyset man in passing, never bothering to stop and talk with him. They were about the same age, and he apparently worked with either his daughter, or his much younger wife.

Why would they drill a hole through the floor? For TV or internet cables? To drain a refrigerator or beer cooler? He could ask Suzy Wilson to investigate. Maybe they were bored and nosy, wondering what the oddball basement tenant was up to with his weird hours and endless oldies music. His thoughts meandered to the vodka in his fridge, reluctantly deciding that being caught out of his chair by the gun-wielding Arif was not worth the warmth of a couple quick swigs.

The size of the security breach and how much trouble Mike was in, probably depended on the number of peepholes they found. If there were more than just one, say many more, he would be at the mercy of Arif's group for being a security liability. Scanning the ceiling like he was looking for a slow-dripping pipe, he could not spot more holes. Sweeping the floor with his eyes, he noticed no more wood shavings and dust, although they could have been disturbed by their footsteps or the blowing fans. Checking the bottom of his shoes, he saw that they were wood-free.

After about five minutes outside, Arif returned, moving purposefully toward Mike, still sitting as commanded, both men a little less agitated. With quick wrist and hand movements, much to Mike's relief, he disassembled, unarmed, and returned his weapon to its hidden holster. "Everything for the fog in here," Arif directed, grabbing, and pointing to the opening of the 30-gallon drum. "Leave nothing; be careful to garbage it and not be seen. Now, I need a light."

Mike trashed all evidence of his smoke bomb demonstration and supplies. Arif thoroughly inspected the basement's entire ceiling with a blindingly-bright halogen shop light.

"No more holes," Arif announced, inspecting the completeness of Mike's clean up. "You will not return here," he added, "for one week."

Mike nodded his understanding.

"You will go to your job and have a reason."

Mike waited for clarification, which did not come, "A reason?"

"A reason to be at your job and not here."

"An *alibi*?"

Frustrated and annoyed, Arif shot back, "لعنتى (Damn!) Am I to know everything?"

Remorsefully chastising himself for asking too many dumb questions, Mike reminded himself that *this is a good time to just shut up and do as you're told.* "I understand," were the last words he spoke to Arif that evening.

***

Early Monday afternoon, Mike sat in his 1D343 cubicle, wondering what to do for the rest of the workday. He had spent the morning leisurely reading *The Washington Post* and *The New York Times* in the Pentagon library, followed by a mandatory office town hall meeting in the building's basement auditorium. Then he rode the Metro downtown for a sweltering Caribbean food truck lunch, grudgingly returning to his gray, fabric-lined holding cell to surf internet birding sites. Then the phone rang, which for him was not a common phenomenon. He avoided making calls, and most everyone reciprocated by avoiding calls to him. *Maybe they will go away*, he hoped, waiting for the sixth ring to answer.

"Cappiello," he whispered guardedly, as if responding to a potential threat.

"Pentagon City Mall parking garage," the voice demanded, "level four entrance to Macy's. You be there at two-p.m."

Mike's stomach sank while the cold little cubicle suddenly became too warm for comfort. "Okay," he replied, cautiously replacing the handset.

***

It was about a mile walk from his desk to Macy's, a quarter through the building's corridors, the balance across baking parking lots, then around hundreds of cars seemingly trying to flatten him. Sweat pasted the bookbag to his lower back, accumulating rivulets that worked their way down to his butt crack. As soon as he arrived at Macy's, an unmarked police sedan squealed to a stop and Detective Rodriguez overvigorously signaled for him to get in. Weaving through and out of the crowded parking structure, the two remained silent as the car entered the rhythmic flow of Crystal City afternoon traffic.

Arif did something, Mike thought. He was paying Rodriguez two grand a month for "business protection" insurance and now it was about to pay off—or not. Either way, *keep your yapper shut*, he counseled himself. Let the cop talk. Push comes to shove; his insurance policy would be null and void if Rodriguez needed to arrest him to cover his own ass.

"Anthony Turner," the detective began, careful to watch Mike's facial reactions and drive at the same time. "You know him?"

Mike could have responded negatively, which would have been truthful, or he could have just shook his head side-to-side. Instead, he stared out the windshield, as if he were alone and bored.

Leaning into the passenger footwell, Rodriguez wondered, "What size shoe you wear'n, Mike? I'd guess you're between an eleven and a thirteen, that 'bout right?"

Mike stared mutely ahead, imagining plaster casts the police had made of some unknown criminal's errant footsteps.

"Fine, be an asshole. I'm here try'n to protect you, and you disrespect me. Listen, butt wipe, Tony Turner's dead. He's also the payday loan guy above your little basement hideout in Penrose."

Feeling like he'd been gut punched, Mike hung his head, not in disbelief, but more in defeat and dread.

"Ahh, got your attention now, motherfucker. Yeah, he's dead and you know why, don't you?" Rodriguez demanded while rolling past a stop sign.

"H-how?" Mike inquired meekly, seeking to understand Arif more than the crime.

"Well, first someone drilled him in the gut with a gun, we figure a .38 or .45. Then they made a sticky mess drilling a half-inch spade bit into his noggin, leaving the hardware behind along with a partial size-nine shoe print." As Mike began heaving and grasping the seat belt release, Rodriguez swung the car curbside, lowering the passenger window. Twisting out the opening, Mike hurled his mango jerk chicken and nearly conch fritters lunch down the side of the car onto the street in several waves of warm puke.

Moving the car forward a few spaces, Rodriguez kept it in park with the air conditioning blowing hard. He studied Mike while lighting a smoke. He had the little bastard where he wanted him, and now it was time for some bonus pay. "Here's the deal, Mike. You are in deep shit my friend. You know the who and why of today's little homicide in Penrose. I don't know what you're doing in your bat cave, but I know it's not the defense work bullshit you told me last year. I also know you got Suzy Wilson on your monthly payroll."

Mike shot him a sideways glance.

"Oh yeah, I know that—I'm a detective. I could find out a lot more, but I won't because you and me have a business arrangement. I'll protect you because that's what I said I'd do and you've been paying your monthly premiums. Thing is though, something like today, that is a mighty big claim on your policy."

"How much?" Mike muttered, eager to escape the car and go home.

"Well," Rodriguez began, wondering how much would be too much, "the way I see it, an accident like the one today requires a big deductible..."

"How fuck'n much?" Mike screamed.

"Twenty-five grand—cash...in hundreds would be good. Plus, the monthly premiums continue."

"Check the mailbox Wednesday night," Mike snarled, grabbing his backpack and exiting the police cruiser with a slam of the door.

Chapter 18
Production

May, 2017

Suzy Wilson parked her new, but leased, Mercedes in front of the Asian nail salon, which replaced the payday/car title loan business she had loathed. Tony Turner, the dead renter, had grabbed at her too many times for his passing to be mourned. *Good riddance, you pervert,* she thought, lighting a long, thin coffin nail. Satisfied to gaze upon a trash-free lot, she made a mental note to call the window washer now that tree pollen season had ended.

Slowly working her way around to the rear of the building, hip bursitis made each step less of a sure thing on the sloping pavement. She had seen the permit and inspection papers for the gas line Mike had ordered; she wanted to see what other changes he had made. Leaning on the retaining wall of the cement ramp leading up to the basement's large roll-up door, she smoked and scanned. A large restaurant-grade exhaust fan had been vertically mounted on a cinder block wall and was noisily doing its job. Mike had overflowed his five allotted parking spaces. There were three rusty and smelly-looking farm trailers, the type for moving animals around. They were neatly aligned with their towing things, all sticking out in the same direction. He had apparently bought a beater pickup truck to haul the trailers, and he also replaced the garbage dumpster with a larger version. His white van was also parked out there. Looking as if she smelled something rancid, Suzy decided her once orderly back lot looked like that of a mini stockyard that did plumbing work on the side.

The other tenants should have been complaining, she thought. Then she recalled Rodriguez's intimidating presence after Tony Turner had been corked last August. His "investigations" left the butcher and beauty supply tenants feeling violated. They were probably still too shaken by the murder and its rumored link to the weirdo in the basement to register a grievance with her.

With double jets of mentholated gas satisfyingly streaming from her nose, Suzy flicked the butt and turned to warily make her way up the ramp, one hand brushing the rough concrete wall for support. The roll-up door was only one-third open, and she was uninvited, but curious—and greedy. Rodriguez, while flashing a clunky and supposedly expensive watch, had clued her in: If she played it right and her timing was good, she could easily soak Mike for a pile of cash.

Adjusting to the dim interior after ducking under the door, she saw that the spacious, but gloomy basement had been transformed. Two metal summer camp bunkbeds were stationed as if to guard the door. Clothing and personal items spilled from the mattresses, gym bags, and small suitcases. Recoiling from the scent of a skanky towel hanging nearby, she stealthily moved on. Wood pallets were stacked waist high with carefully positioned paper bags, the same type used for BBQ charcoal, only bigger. The pallets were double-stacked and shrink-wrapped, blocking her view. On the balls of her feet, with sandal leather quietly gliding across the floor, she edged sideways through the pallet maze, guessing there were fifty or so of the square columns. The smell of something vaguely familiar caught her attention; it was a burnt, yet sweet baking smell. Raising a hand to her nose, she noticed a purple stain on a finger and wondered where it came from.

She could discern a TV credit card commercial among multiple fans, blowers, and other odd sounds in the room. While she could not see them, she smelled the musky odor of multiple men doing physical labor. Something, she told herself, was different; Mike had tacked a layer of white plastic-lined insulation, like a bulbous cloud, across the entire ceiling. He was trying either to keep something in, or something out; she had no idea which or what.

Stacks of large cardboard drums began where the pallets ended. There seemed to be hundreds of them, like a forest of mature, light brown tree trunks, reaching to the cloud-covered ceiling. She sneaked forward, careful to remain in defilade, and saw the four terrorists busily at work. The sudden bark of an amplified saw made her jump, jouncing a stack of three empty drums. Looking up from his work, his goggles fogged by purple dust, Mike failed to see Suzy spying on him just three car lengths away. Bent over an empty drum, his attention returned to cutting a semi-round hole in the drum's metal lid with an annoyingly loud jig saw.

Apparently, the men had been at their task for some time, probably days. Each robotically shuffled through their required movements, alerting one another with grunts, hand signals, and an occasional barked universal word or two. Their limited, yet effective shared vocabulary included "fuck, okay, huh, pussy, coffee, stop, shit, television, pizza and asshole," among other erudite gems. Suzy also sensed something else odd about Mike's helpers—their clothes, hair styles, and general way of moving about just seemed—foreign. There was a short but husky oriental, as well as a tall, muscular dirty-blond with a prominent forehead. The third man was also short, but slim and had darker features, including a closely cropped black beard. One unifying denominator among them, including Mike, was a light patina of purple dust from head to toe.

Empty paper bags and wood pallets were accumulating in one area; the remnants of a McDonald's breakfast littered a large central workbench the men were positioned around. An open liter of vodka stood among the refuse, along with a scattering of water bottles. *Mike should have listened and started with AA* she thought, *he would be sober and happier by now*. Judging from the trash accumulated in several of the tan barrels, the men were working their way through all five major food groups—pizza, burgers, chicken, tacos, and booze. She noticed that whenever one of the three workers had a slack moment, they would pivot to the wall-mounted TV, which seemed to be tuned to a celebrity gossip channel.

Whatever they were doing, she decided, looked about as legitimate as counterfeiting money. The oriental man's task was to fill five-gallon buckets. She recognized the familiar blue, white, and yellow colors of Domino sugar on one of the bags, which he poured to the brim of blue buckets. Sacks of another white powder, which she did not recognize, were used to fill orange buckets. He moved quickly, using a razor to slice open a sack, pour its contents without spillage, and then toss the empty bag onto the pile behind him.

The tall blond manned a four or five-foot-tall stainless-steel mixer that a bakery or commercial candy maker might use. She watched as he dumped a blue bucket into its large kettle, along with what she assumed was water. Thumbing a control panel, the mixer's agitator lowered itself while blue and yellow/white flames flared beneath kettle's charred bottom. *That explained the new gas line*, she thought. A second mixer, which looked brand new, stood nearby covered with plastic sheeting; she guessed it was a spare.

A fresh burst from Mike's saw jolted her again as he began to work on a new drum top. She wondered how many of the hundreds around her he would be cutting. The tall man motioned to the short, dark one, who was preoccupied with the TV, then began pouring from an orange bucket into the kettle's boiling sugar and water slurry. The third man added a dark powder from a large plastic bag, raising a purple-tinted cloud that wafted towards, and then into Mike's new exhaust fan. *What the hell were they cooking?* Suzy wondered. *It sure ain't something to eat.*

With the mixer churning, its operator left his station, reaching for a ready-made shot of vodka, greedily wincing as the warmth flowed over his tongue and downward. The final steps seemed to begin as the tall and the shorter, dark man pulled on paisley and plaid oven mitts, not bothering to wear matched sets. With the mixer beater raised, the smaller one grunted as they lifted the heavy steaming kettle by its handles. A portion of the dark foamy contents topped-off a nearly-full drum; the rest was poured and scrapped into another drum prepositioned next to the first.

Moving with purpose, the bearded man capped the drum with one of Mike's lids, rapidly working a tool like a car jack to secure it. At the same time, the blond reached a gloved hand into the jagged lid hole, inserting long-ways what appeared to be a foam brick. Those steps were done; the men wedged the lip of a four-wheeled hand truck under the edge of the completed drum. She could only guess what it might weigh, but they made it look heavy as they manhandled it to a corner crowded with thirty or so other drums, none of them double or triple stacked.

Suzy's legs were tiring; she needed to burn another one, and she thought coffee would also be good. *I'll yack with Mike when he's alone,* she decided, turning to wiggle her way back through the maze of drums and pallets. Then Mike spotted her. Shoving the goggles off his face to confirm who it was, his face registered deep consternation and disappointment. Like a lawn sprinkler, his head snapped 180 degrees to see if the other three had noticed. Mercifully, they had not.

Bolting after Suzy, Mike's primary concern was for her safety—and by extension, his own. Only nine days away from the first action, there was no margin of error available for potential security lapses. Just from being where she was, and seeing what she undoubtedly saw, Suzy was in way too deep for Arif's razor-thin comfort zone. Another rearward glance revealed that the other three men were preoccupied with something other than his movements. *They'll think I'm taking a dump*, he reasoned, *so he had about that much time to take care of their visitor.*

"Suzy," he called out after ducking under the roll-up door into the glare of the early summer morning.

Stunned, she tried with middling success not to show it, "Mike! Well, I just thought I'd drop by..."

"Where's your car?"

"Up top," she said with a sideways jerk of her head.

"Let's go," he directed, quickly leading the way down the ramp, around the side of the building to Mercedes shimmering in the front lot."

Short on breath, she caught up with him, declaring "I gotta smoke."

"Suzy," he pleaded, "I'll talk and you smoke, but we need to get in the car."

"You're filthy!" she said indignantly, "you'll get that purple shit all over my leather seats."

Looking down at the tinted arms and legs protruding from his t-shirt and shorts, he couldn't disagree. He had to make this lightning fast anyway. "Fine, just-get-in-the-fucking-car—now!" he screamed, immediately regretting his loss of control. Warily, she fumbled through the rote steps of producing and lighting a cigarette with what Mike could see were lightly trembling hands. Sucking in a near-bursting breath, he held it for a few heartbeats, then let his chest slowly deflate. With newfound, if still exasperated calmness, he softly pleaded, as if in open-palmed prayer, "Suzy, please, just do it...it's important."

She acquiesced, taking time to make the engine purr and the AC blow while sucking on her death stick. Mike segued straight to the only resolution he could see—other than Arif's quick and final solution. Bending down to the open window, he whispered, "Twenty grand in cash and you keep your mouth shut. Do not come back 'til I'm gone and don't let anybody stick their nose in the basement while I'm still here."

Drawing in another drag, she grinned the self-satisfied smile of rewarded nefariousness. "When and where?" she wondered coyly.

"I'll be gone weekend after next..."

"No, I mean when and where will you pay me?"

"Your office, Monday next week. There is no way I can get to the bank this week. That work for you?"

She smiled up at him, savoring another long drag of the cigarette. "Next Sunday is Memorial Day, Mike, so next Monday the banks ain't open. Besides, I wanna go shopping next weekend for all the sales," she whined. Anxious to send her away, he quickly agreed to a noon, Friday delivery. As the car backed up, she called out when he turned to leave, "Make that twenty-five, Mike—you promised me a bonus. Plus, I never saw a thang!"

Like a Halloween witch, she cackled as the car glided away. He did not care; he'd just saved her from a terminal visit with Arif. But even that minor accomplishment did not assuage the guilt he felt welling up inside him. Suzy could not see it, but as he descended to the depths of Lake Despair, he was pulling her down with him. He realized that shoveling hush-up money at her and Rodriguez was like offering a band-aid to someone he had already made terminally ill. There was a clock ticking in his head, counting down the time until the Iranians' second action. He still had no clue what it was, but he sensed that anyone near the Pentagon early on the last day of May would probably be in jeopardy. The money would keep Suzy and Rodriguez safe and happy up to that point. Beyond that, they would be on their own to face the consequences of their lousy life decisions and unsatiable greed—just like him.

***

Mike returned to the basement, hearing a ruckus from the work area on the far side of the long room. Edging toward it, just as Suzy had, he crouched within the drum stacks, observing his mini–United Nations workforce goofing off. The Iranian was busy jabbing three bent McDonald's straws into one of the foam blocks on the workbench. They flared up, out, and away from each other, like half-eaten candy canes. For some reason, they all found it hilarious, clinking their grimy glasses together in a three-way vodka shot salute.

"嘿！(Hey!)," offered Mr. China.

"اینجا! (Here!)," saluted Mr. Iran.

"отъебись! (Fuck off!)," ordered Mr. Russia, doubling over in laughter at his deception.

Grasping another foam block, China made engine sounds, like a child at play, as he piloted the second block towards the one with the protruding straws.

"رونق! (Boom!)," Iran bellowed, as the two blocks came into contact.

“轰隆隆！ (Kaboom!),” China piled on while sloshing more drink into the glasses.

“четыре утра (Four-a.m.!),” the Russian screamed, holding aloft that many fingers then thrusting two fists into the insulated ceiling. As his arms blossomed out like a ballerina’s, he delicately sprinkled imaginary pixy dust onto the floor. That performance led to more howling laughter and another potato juice salute between them.

Idiots, Mike thought, watching purple whiffs rise from the mixer’s kettle. They had left it stirring and the gas flame burning, allowing the smoke mix, which had dried out, to apparently self-ignite. Soon it would be a roaring hybrid inferno and smokestack, but he would wait a few more seconds to pop from his hiding place and grab a fire extinguisher. Like a child and the proverbial hot stove, the men needed to learn the hazards of what they were doing and the consequences of fucking off. Then it began.

“دود! (Smoke!),” Iran announced, pointing at the kettle.

“火！(Fire!),” China astutely added.

With flames scorching the overhead portion of the mixer and threatening to melt the ceiling insulation, Mike could barely make out Russia’s form in the billowing, dense purple cloud. The fool was trying to douse the growing inferno with booze bottle remnants. Ignoring him, Mike emptied the sub-zero contents of a carbon dioxide extinguisher into the kettle’s inferno. With his eyes clamped shut and his breathing suspended, he could feel his forearm and facial hair being singed. After what seemed like forever, the extinguisher was empty, and the last crisis, at least for that day, had been abated.

***

That evening, the four men lounged in front of the TV, surfing for something they could agree to watch. Because he had ventured out to buy supper and other essentials, Mike looked clean, but exhausted. The other three, not having bothered to shower, remained purple-tinted except on their hands and in circular patches scrubbed clean around their eyes and mouths.

Mike stopped surfing when the TV hit a news channel featuring a speech President Donald Trump had made that day.

“شیطان بزرگ! (The Great Satan!),” Iran hissed at the screen.

“我们的敌人！(Our enemy!),” China proclaimed.

Russia took his time growling up a surprisingly large loogie, and dramatically standing to launch it at the president, missing the TV screen by over a foot. Cringing as the fresh oyster gathered a purple hue sagging down the basement wall, Mike turned up the volume, confident it would annoy his three guests:

> ...But no discussion of stamping out this threat
> would be complete without mentioning the
> government that gives terrorists all three—
> safe harbor, financial backing, and the
> social standing needed for recruitment.
> It is a regime that is responsible for so much
> instability in the region. I am speaking of
> course of Iran...Until the Iranian regime is
> willing to be a partner for peace, all nations
> of conscience must work together to isolate
> Iran, deny it funding for terrorism, and pray
> For the day when the Iranian people have
> The just and righteous government they
> deserve...Thank-you...and God Bless the United
> States of America.

Chapter 19
First Action

4:00 a.m., Monday, 30 May 2017

Straining to carry a block of concrete, Mike dropped it from waist height onto the gritty grass, bending to drag it beneath the trailer's jack stand. As if pulling a cannon's lanyard, he yanked the trailer's power cord from the truck, then disconnected the safety chain and safety brake connections. Pausing to daub eye-stinging sweat with a t-shirt sleeve, he noted the time: 4:10 a.m. Even at that early hour, highway traffic swished all around him, with the sound of bridge overpasses rhythmically clicking and clacking under the strain of their loads.

Like an automaton, he had efficiently performed the tasks expected of him, ignoring an inner human voice screaming for him to stop. With a prisoner's sigh of resignation, he popped more antacid tablets, trying to quell an angry stomach ulcer. He had started at midnight, emplacing the Springfield Mixing Bowl and Belle Haven Woodrow Wilson Bridge trailers without incident. The detonators on all three trailers would activate at rolling intervals between 6:00 and 6:20 a.m.—in less than two hours. *Stop thinking, and just do*, he hissed at himself, bending to rapidly crank the trailer tongue up and free of the truck's hitch.

Three steps remained, and then Mike needed to drive thirty-two road miles south just to work his way another twenty-nine miles north to the Pentagon. Every minute he delayed meant more cars on the roads and a greater likelihood of falling behind his tight schedule. Feeling for deflater valves in a pocket, he bent to screw them onto the trailer's two roadside tires. As the air hissed out in close harmony, he positioned two orange and white safety cones behind the trailer. From another cargo shorts pocket came a hunter orange-colored sticker, the size of an index card. Peeling the backside, he slapped it at eye level onto the rear gate of the trailer.

After he drove away, the goal was to make each trailer look like an unlucky farmer had blown two tires, abandoning it to reclaim later. The traffic cones added an aura of safety consciousness and a law-abiding nature to the absentee farmer. The orange placard was a facsimile of those used by the Virginia State Police to signify a completed inspection and the need to tow an abandoned vehicle from the highway emergency lane. Without the benefit of a computer, Mike had managed to forge a plausible-looking sticker for each trailer—when viewed from twenty feet while passing at highway speeds. If the ruse worked, the three trailers would remain forlorn and unmolested for a few early morning hours until the first action began.

Climbing into the pickup, Mike's thoughts were on the VDOT (Virginia Department of Transportation) commuter lot in Triangle, Virginia, his next stop. He would take a short hop on I-66 East to I-495 South, then onto I-95 South. Trial runs showed that, if driven at the speed limit, the trip would take about half an hour. Grasping the truck's ignition key, he hesitated, his eyes drawn to the left outside mirror. Neon blue pulsed behind him in the giant intersection's half-light. Bending to look closer, he made out the edge of a car, mostly hidden by the livestock trailer. *Fuck!* As if punched in the chest, his heart suddenly pounded, and his breathing became jagged. Struggling for composure, he watched the Virginia State Trooper exit his vehicle.

Donning a feed store hat, Mike was ready with a bullshit story and, if need be, cash to wiggle his way free of the cop. *Make it quick*, he thought, preparing his driver's license, insurance, and registration papers for review. In the mirror, he could see a powerful light beam dancing around and through the trailer's ventilation slats. The trooper was tall, rail thin, and a bit stooped. Mike watched as he bent to inspect the flat tires, the brass deflator valves still attached. *Shit!* Finally, he sauntered to the truck's cab, his appearance starched, polished, and intimidating. From beneath a forward-tilted campaign hat, the trooper silently examined the stranded motorist and his truck's odd interior with a long black flashlight held shoulder height.

"Good morning, sir," was the salutation Mike expected, or possibly, "license and registration, please." A third probable greeting would have been, "So, what seems to be the problem?" This trooper was wired differently, offering no banter as the men examined each other in a silent Mexican standoff. Mike noted that his free hand rested lightly on the grip of his side arm.

"Where'd you get that sticker?" the trooper finally asked, the light and gun hands steadily remaining as they were.

With no time for games, Mike's succinct response was the truth, "I made it."

"Forgery, in Virginia," the cop began, as if reciting a bible verse, "is a Class 5 felony punishable by up to ten years in prison and a $2,500 fine. Plus, processing fees."

Good to know, Mike thought. *I have been pulled over by a talking law book with a nasal tidewater accent.* He knew when it was best to shut up and listen; this was definitely it.

"What happened to those tires?" the officer wondered, nodding over his right shoulder to the side of the trailer.

"I let the air out—to make them look like flats."

"The Virginia penalty for a highway emergency lane violation," the lawbook with legs continued, "is a jail sentence of up to one year and a fine not to exceed $2,500 with driver's license suspension of up to one year."

Tempted to ask about processing fees, Mike remained silent. Checking his watch again, he noted the pre-dawn lightening of the sky.

Beside and behind Mike, the trooper illuminated another thirty-gallon fiber drum where the tuck's missing passenger seat should have been. "What's in the trailer?" he demanded.

"Fertilizer."

"What for?"

"The farm..."

"Bullshit!" The trooper barked, taking a half-step back and pivoting to squirt a fine stream of dark brown spittle to the ground. "What I see here is a handoff of whatever contraband you're transporting. I see you fixing to leave here, then somebody else arrives, hooks up the trailer, fills the tires, and drives on down the road. The flat tires, that fake sticker, and those traffic cones make it all look legitimate. That about it?"

"Close, but no prize," Mike replied, unable not to zing one on the surprisingly perceptive trooper.

Reaching behind his hips, the trooper produced a set of chromed handcuffs, jingling them while menacingly asking, "You ready to be arrested?"

"I've got plans for today."

"Aaand?"

"I'd like to pay those fines—and fees?"

"Aaand?"

With both hands held above the steering wheel, Mike announced he was getting something from the glove box, slowly producing a tan envelope that he passed to the trooper. "That's ten grand if you let me drive off right now."

"Aaand?"

Mike withdrew and passed another envelope, wondering how many it would take to get back on the road. He had a total of ten, but was hoping to bring as many as possible with him when he and Arif left America later that day.

Stowing the handcuffs and holding the flashlight in the crook of an arm, the trooper rifled through the envelopes. "What about the trailer?" he murmured, still examining the cash.

"It's yours; I'm gone," Mike called out as he started the truck and pulled away, watching in the mirror as the cop watched him drive off. *Twenty-five minutes behind schedule*, he thought, *he needed to get to Triangle ASAP.*

***

The VDOT manages dozens of regional commuter parking lots to reduce congestion on Washington, D.C., area roadways. Drivers can park for free at their local lot, then catch a bus, vanpool, or carpool ride for a cheaper and less stressful trip to work and back. Mike picked the Triangle, Virginia, lot for its large size—over 800 parking spaces—and for its strategic location. Wedged between I-95 and Route 1, the primary north-south corridors to and from Washington; a cloud action there would quickly draw attention.

Driving aggressively from the Merrifield interchange, at about 5:15 a.m., he arrived at the Triangle lot. It was a quarter-hour past the weather service's official sunrise time, but it was still semi-dark on the gloomy, overcast, and windless morning. The plan was to clean himself with a wet towel and change into his Pentagon work clothes. *That will have to wait*, he thought, swinging the truck into a space at the center of the blacktop acreage. Exiting, he removed the fill caps from two five-gallon jugs of gasoline stowed behind the driver's seat, rolling one over to spill. Activating the twenty-minute delay on a detonator, Mike carefully passed it through the drum top's cut hole, placing it in the recess made in the solidified smoke mixture by the already removed foam brick. With windows down, work backpack, and travel suitcase in hand, he stopped to make sure he had the remaining cash and his lanyard with Pentagon ID and DOD CAC identification. Smelling rank and looking ragged from his overnight endeavors, he hustled to get in line for the 5:30 a.m. bus to the Pentagon.

Completing a turn across multiple traffic lanes, the bus arrived as scheduled, rumbling up a curving incline towards its half-awake queue of passengers. A cross between a Greyhound and a municipal bus, it had double rows of seating for sixty or so passengers. Boarding with his baggage, as if heading to the airport via a Pentagon Metro connection, Mike made his way down the narrow center isle to the five-across bench seat in the rear, relieved to find he had the entire seat to himself.

While other passengers dozed, stared at nothing, or examined their glowing smartphones, Mike wolfed down a double stack of Pop Tarts with water and more antacid. Other than the state trooper, the emplacement of the three trailers was hectic, but non-eventful. He was exhausted, but he still had a busy morning ahead of him. He would be done by 9:00 a.m., provided he avoided any more delays. Then he would meet Arif an hour later to begin his new life as an international fugitive. As the bus merged onto the I-95 North express lanes, he imagined the commuter havoc about to begin.

At 5:40 a.m., his pickup would begin belching a purple cloud visible for a quarter mile, then it would burn somewhat dramatically. People planning to park and ride from the Triangle lot would instead decide to either drive themselves to work, go home, or find another commuter lot. Police and fire vehicles, with lights blazing and sirens blaring, would push their way through the crowded roads towards the burning truck. Passing rubberneckers would slow the flow of traffic to vicariously absorb the excitement. Radio traffic reporters would feature the unusual events taking place, encouraging north-bound travelers south of Triangle to steer clear of the area and take alternate routes.

Mike wondered how much of that chaos would truly happen. The key was volume—tens of thousands of vehicles in a small area in a short timeframe. Traffic flow would undoubtedly be impacted, but probably not dramatically. How long the smoke drum and truck would burn, and how long until the purple cloud dissipated were unknowns—they had never been tested. Besides, he reasoned, that was more a factor of how quickly the local fire department arrived to douse it all with water.

For this southernmost outpost of the various cloud actions, the most important factor was visibility. The radio traffic reports would highlight the unusual events that occurred in Triangle. Then they would really get spun up over the Merrifield, Springfield, and Belle Haven interchange brouhahas. After someone connected the dots, the story would leap to the newsroom as one of local interest. When Mike finished in two hours, the story would then jump to the national level because—well, because he was mucking with Washington, D.C., and the Pentagon.

At 5:55 a.m., the bus threaded through the labyrinth of the Springfield Mixing Bowl. Pulling himself up to see over the seat back in front of him, Mike momentarily glimpsed the first trailer, far below and to the left, wishing he could see it begin to cook off in five minutes. As the bus droned on with the engine vibrating beneath his seat, he rested with his eyes closed and a self-satisfied grin on his face. He recalled how last July Arif had cryptically ordered, "You will build a fog, a fog to hide the second action." *The last ten months had been crazy*, he thought, *and where he was headed would probably be crazier*.

About 6:20 a.m., the bus approached the Pentagon reservation, and he stood to lift the sixty-pound suitcase onto the rear bench seat. It was the type with small wheels and an extendable handle, sized to fit within a plane's overhead bins. They had filled its two halves with as much smoke mix as they could, cutting a postcard-sized hole in one side for the device's exhaust. Slowly and quietly peeling back the duct tape covering the hole, Mike delicately lifted the loose end of a green fuse cord. After lighting it, he would have ten seconds to exit the bus before the purple smoke began belching from the suitcase, possibly starting a fire, or possibly not. The performance of the suitcase device was unknown. It had not been tested because of the possibility of attracting unwanted attention. Mike would not see his handiwork on the bus either, but he knew it would initiate more than a little pandemonium as he continued his nine-hour-long morning commute.

With the bus parked curbside behind four others, the passengers slowly, silently, and methodically exited for their short walk to the building. Some riders remained onboard, planning to continue their commute across the Potomac River and into downtown Washington. Grabbing his backpack, Mike lit the green fuse. Counting off one-one thousand, two-one-thousand...he purposely reached the exit steps at twelve-one-thousand. "Hey," he warned the driver, nodding towards the back of the bus where whiffs of purple smoke were rising, "I think I smelled something burning back there."

In less than five minutes, he passed under the bus terminal's long, white tent-like canopy, up a flight of concrete steps, along a string of gray metal barricades, past a half dozen unsmiling and heavily armed PFPA guards, then down a long escalator into the dank and dreary Metro Pentagon Station. A blue line train took him one stop south to the Pentagon City Station. Trying to stay within the schedule's allotted fifteen minutes, he quickly meandered towards his Dodge sedan parked at the Fashion Centre Mall parking garage.

The masonry parking structure had five levels, all large enough to fit a short, three-ring circus. Mike had pre-positioned the Dodge in the northwest corner of the fourth deck. Pausing at the outside retaining wall, he gazed north for evidence of his bus action, but detected none. The Pentagon and its commuter center were a half-mile away, and shrouded behind the earthen berm supporting I-395 and its traffic load.

Standing between the Dodge's two open left-side doors, he stripped, cleaned, and changed. The towel bath felt refreshing in the still-cool morning air. With a comb and water, he tried to tame hair that had not been trimmed in over three months. Clothed in his well-worn work shirt, slacks, and shoes, he vowed never to wear them again after arriving in Iran.

Like the truck, the Dodge had been reconfigured to cram a thirty-gallon smoke drum into it. Mike opened the windows and toppled an awaiting gas container. Gently grasping one of Arif's detonators, he set it to blow at 7:55 a.m. The device was the size of a very small box of breakfast cereal with a plastic, army-green shell. One hinged end opened to reveal a readout and buttons, like a home thermostat. The current time had to be pre-set, and then an activation time—within twenty-four hours—could be quickly entered. After finishing that task, Mike reconfirmed the presence of his Pentagon credentials and $80,000 in traveling cash. Removing another rolling suitcase from the trunk, he made his way back to the Pentagon City Station.

Waiting at the far end of the underground platform, he boarded the first car of the northbound blue line train for the five-minute hop back to the Pentagon. He and the driver, ensconced in a stainless steel and one-way black glass enclosure, were the only passengers. Laying the suitcase flat on the subway car's soiled carpet, Mike ripped off the duct tape and lit the fuse. By the time the train pulled into the Pentagon Station, the car was filling with acrid purple smoke. Yanking the emergency stop cord, Mike felt his way to the driver's compartment as the two exit doors automatically opened. Urgently pounding on the driver's door, he yelled, "Fire! Stop the train. Fire!" He figured there was a good chance that an inattentive or inept driver would continue to the next stop; that could not happen.

On the agonizingly slow ride up the station's long escalator, Mike prepared to enter the building for his final day of government work. Gazing up, he saw two PFPA cops checking building IDs and directing exiting subway riders to proceed in a direction away from the bus lanes. He thought looking bored would be the best way to blend in with the other workers. To do that, he pretended he was doing dishes at the kitchen sink, something he loathed. On the adjacent down escalator, a half-dozen PFPA officers suddenly appeared, high-stepping as fast as they could down the metal steps. Sufficiently bored-looking, Mike crested the escalator, presented his credentials to the guards, and then appeared to mindlessly follow the backside of whoever was in front of him.

The pedestrian traffic barriers had been rearranged, and he heard the constant back and forth of urgent chatter on the PFPA radios. Taking a quick, but still bored, glimpse, he saw the entrance to the bus lanes was barricaded and guarded. Workers arriving on other buses were being routed to the far end of the commuter station and given the option of walking to the smaller south building entrance, or towards an alternative path to the main entrance. He could also partially see and hear multiple emergency response vehicles hovering around what he assumed was his 6:30 commuter bus.

Outside the main building entrance, the PFPA had partitioned the decreased inflow of workers into six lines for hastily arranged bag checks and body wanding. It was 8:15 a.m.; Mike was a half-hour behind his original schedule. He would have to move quickly and improvise once inside the building to still catch the 9:00 a.m. free DOD shuttle to Reagan National Airport.

The other Pentagon workers were unusually animated, talking nervously with each other, and pointing to this and that outside the building, some with eyes glued to their smartphone screens. Both uniformed and civilian security officials dashed out of the building towards the Metro station. "Wonder what's going on?" he murmured with a shrug to the lady in front of him.

A large and overly muscular PFPA officer, testing the limits of his uniform shirt, searched the inside of his backpack. "Open this," he directed, pointing to Mike's toiletry bag. Satisfied with the backpack's contents, including the unseen cash in tan envelopes, he motioned for the next person in line. Standing spread eagle in front of another PFPA officer, Mike submitted to, and passed screening by a hand-held metal detector. Finally arriving at the waist-high entrance turnstiles, he scanned his DOD CAC card and was admitted to the building.

Mike was concerned about somebody pointing at him and shouting, "Him, that's him! I saw him do it!" To avoid that, he would take the rat's path to his desk. The concourse, escalators, elevators, and main corridors were all heavily trodden. Less well traveled was a network of hidden stone staircases, narrow interior hallways, dank service tunnels, and rear exits that led him most of the way to room 1D343.

Passing through the big room's grimy double doors for the second-to-last time, Mike saw co-workers clustered in small, excited groups. Passing quickly, he saw they were watching something on the internet and heard conversational snippets including "Springfield," "purple," and "bus." *The bastards*, he thought. *They had treated him like dog shit on the sidewalk for years—something to be noted only if necessary, and otherwise avoided. When he eventually was identified as the day's purple smoke terrorist, they'd gush to anyone who'd listen about their close work relationship with him. Well, fuck 'em all and fuck 'em hard.*

He arrived at his desk damp from his fast walk through the building. He removed two backpacks from his locked wardrobe cabinet, both containing Amazon boxes filled with twenty pounds of smoke mix. Unzipping each, he stacked the boxes and quickly carried them out of the room. Nobody seemed to notice or care.

His plan for the last two devices was to make a shoutout to the long-forgotten anti-Vietnam and counter-culture spirit of his youth. In 1972, the Weathermen group bombed a Pentagon fourth-floor woman's restroom after midnight. No one was hurt, some damage was done, and their point was made. Lugging his heavy boxes in front of him, he knew just where to set them off on his way to meet the airport shuttle.

A barren and lonely interior hallway connected the third and fourth corridors, across from 1D353. Traversing it without passing anyone, he arrived at a small and empty two-seat and two-pisser men's room. Many of the Pentagon's restrooms are sized to accommodate dozens of visitors at a time. The unmentioned history of the smaller restrooms is that they were designated as "colored only" back in the less enlightened era of World War II and the 1950s.

Setting one box atop a toilet seat, Mike lit the fuse and fast-walked the second box to the outside courtyard. Traveling counter-clockwise, he passed dozens of workers taking an early morning smoke break under the overcast sky. Using a little-used exit door beneath a corridor apex, he entered another empty and underutilized men's room. Positioning the second box like the first, he lit its fuse. Dodging maintenance workers on their electric carts, his passage led to the rear entry of the main lobby.

He had five minutes to exit the building and catch the airport shuttle bus. Then the building's fire alarm loudly reverberated, and white strobe lights flashed around the three-story main entrance vestibule. Trying again to look bored, Mike approached the bank of fifteen entry/exit turnstiles. Like directing traffic, the PFPA officer held up a palm to stop him.

"Main entrance is closed," he mouthed expressively to compensate for the shrill of the fire alarm.

Trying to appear puzzled or flustered, Mike asked, "Why?"

"Police activity. The announcement went out to use the south building entrance."

Mike looked beyond the officer and out the main doors, which were swinging open and closed. "Well, I need to catch the airport shuttle that leaves in less than five minutes!"

Like a stuck phonograph, the guard crossed his arms and repeated, "Main entrance is closed."

Curious about the impact of his Metro station action, he followed up with, "Well, if I go out the south entrance, can I take the subway to the Airport?"

"Metro's closed."

"Police action?"

"Sir, you need to move on."

Mike turned and began his rat's path to the building's south entrance. Missing the shuttle was a non-event—he would hail a taxi in Crystal City, a half mile from the south entrance. All-in-all, he was surprised at how smoothly last night and the morning had transpired. Arif would be pleased. Whatever the Iranian's second action would be following morning, Mike had provided the requested distraction.

His thoughts shifted to the restaurants in the Reagan airport and what he would have for breakfast to celebrate his job well done and the start of his new life, first in Quebec, then Iran.

Chapter 20
Flight

10:00 a.m., Monday, 30 May, 2017

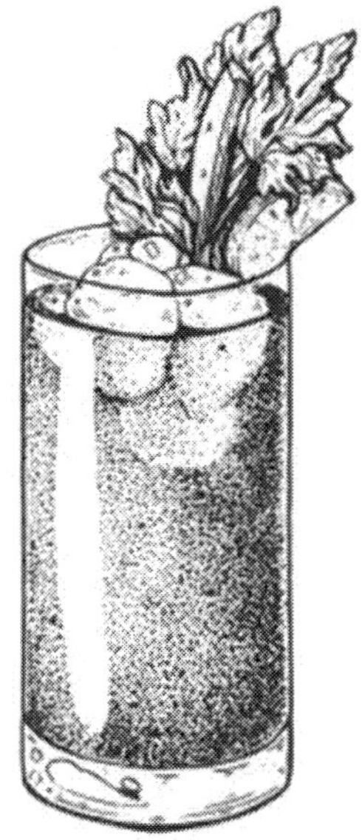

The setup at Ronald Reagan International Airport was typical, with taxis and bags on the bottom, check-in on top, and everything else accessible from a vast concourse in the middle floor. Even before exiting the taxi, Mike noted several two-person patrols of navy-blue-clad TSA (Transportation Security Agency) officers toting automatic rifles; one of them also had a dog that sniffed whatever it passed. *Stand down,* he thought with a smirk, *I'm done making purple fogs.* Up and to his left, a Metro train smoothly rolled to its airport stop. The yellow line train, he noticed, came straight from downtown and back; the blue line train from the Pentagon would probably be out of commission for a few more hours while the subway fire was investigated.

The unwritten plan was for Mike to rendezvous with Arif around 10:00 a.m. on the concourse level beneath the American Airlines check-in area. The exact time was agreed to be flexible, but no later than 1:00 p.m. to make the 2:00 p.m. Air Canada flight to Montreal. Arif would provide Mike's tickets and new identity documents, including, he assumed, an Iranian passport. "Do not be late and do not get caught," Arif had admonished him, "there will be no other planes for you."

The newish terminal was a gothic tribute to commercial aviation, with a runway-long nave trimmed with mustard-gold piers supporting high vaulted ceilings. As a patriotic flourish, an excessively large American flag hung high above, barely ruffled by a soft, air-conditioned breeze. Unlike its predecessors, this cathedral was brightly lit by acres of clerestory sheet glass and was lined with multiple stores, restaurants, and bars, one of which Mike gravitated towards.

"Double bloody vodka," he muttered to the barkeep, "no Tabasco." Sliding his aching body onto the barstool, he had a line-of-site view of the American ticket kiosks on the terminal's balcony. He would have no trouble spotting Arif when he arrived on the concourse. From a hanging slate and chalk menu, Mike ordered the British breakfast, ravenous for the eggs, toast, beans, fried tomatoes, and whatever else the kitchen needed to move out of the cooler that morning.

"You hear about the Pentagon?" the barkeep asked, leaning back on the counter to surf news channels on the TV mounted above them.

"Not yet," Mike mumbled into his drink.

"Terrorists maybe—multiple fires, purple smoke and who knows what else."

"Put on NPR!" The only other patron called out. "It's on the radio...WAMU...88.5!"

As the bartender bent to work hidden controls, Mike wanted to pump his fist in the air and shout out loud in victory. Instead, he used his cold and wet drinking hand to rub out a triumphal grin. Emerging from somewhere, the cook joined the others in keenly listening as a lady reporter gave her brief update. "Another!" Mike called out for a refill, which the barkeep acknowledged with a gentle 'in a minute' hand signal.

Watching over a shoulder for Arif's arrival, Mike thought the NPR reporter did a fair job explaining the mess he had made that morning. She covered the truck and car incinerations; she got the three beltway interchanges correct. She also mentioned "purple smoke" multiple times, so that was good. He especially wanted to hear how bad traffic was screwed up, but she just said that "it was a mess." The reporter took the big leap of wondering if "some type of message or protest" was being made. *A gold star next to her name*, he thought. Finally, she yammered about a 1:00 p.m. Pentagon press conference. *Maybe he and Arif could catch it before their 2:00 p.m. flight.*

Mike was extra full from breakfast, and with a slight buzz, he was ready for a short nap somewhere that Arif would be sure to spot him.

***

He had been asleep for a while when something woke him. The wide expanse beyond the glass wall and a distant taxiing airliner instantly oriented him as he groggily peered up at Arif. Except it was not Arif, and there was no celebratory exchange of Middle Eastern greetings.

"Sir," began the smaller of the two TSA officers, both of whom cradled serious looking weapons in black-gloved hands, "can we see your ticket, please?"

*Fuck...*Mike's brain instantly processed several response scenarios, the most tempting being to haul ass and try to outrun the airport Gestapo. Instead, with heart slamming away, he looked up and semi-defensively announced, "I'm waiting for someone."

With this brief exchange, both officers satisfied their curiosity about the graying, heavy-set man they had observed sleeping for several hours. Bottom line: he could be a vagrant, but he was not a threat. "Sir," the smaller one continued, "you need to move on. The concourse is for arriving and departing ticketed passengers." Looking down at Mike, they both wondered what his next move would be. This was the point where some people became indignant, lathering themselves up to hurling professional insults and, on rare occasions, challenging their mothers' honor. Those assholes, they knew, could be cuffed and detained until they apologized after finding a better attitude.

Mike was more concerned about the time, 12:40 p.m., than he was about the two cops. "Okay, no problem" he sighed distractedly, scooting off towards the Air Canada gates in the older section of the airport. Leaving the updated and airy concourse, he felt the walls closing in on him with the look and feel of the depressing Pentagon corridors he was eager to forget. The original 1930's-era terminal had the ambiance of a very large basement, or fallout shelter, with its masonry walls, minimal windows, and low ceilings.

Mike, constantly scanning for Arif, randomly strolled a circuitous route in front of a TSA security checkpoint that blocked his access to the airport gates. *Did Arif miss me while I was sleeping? Is he late? Did something happen? Should I even be hanging out here if he does not show up? Maybe he got grabbed, and now they will be waiting for me.* Mike cursed the man's aversion to electronic and paper trails—no banks, no people, no paper, no phones, and no internet—wishing he could just call the bastard for an update.

He needed to dodge the two TSA guards, and any others that crossed his path. Under a hanging TV screen stood a mute gaggle of travelers, transfixed on what Mike recognized as the blue background of the Pentagon Briefing Room. The press conference they had mentioned on the radio in the bar that morning was about to begin. Blending into the gathering, he continued his visual hunt for Arif with ears attuned to the TV.

***

Nervous chatter in the brightly lit media room suddenly subsided as Army Lieutenant Colonel Steve Bennett appeared from the rear side door of the speaker's dais. His camouflage battle dress uniform sleeves were tightly folded around firm biceps; his trousers were bloused into desert tan boots. With a briefing book in hand, he nervously claimed his position at the podium. An American flag stood proudly behind him, accompanied by the familiar white-trimmed oval with a graphic image of the building suspended before deep blue floor-to-ceiling drapes. For the benefit of the less imaginative and situationally challenged, the words "The Pentagon, Washington, D.C." were spelled out in smallish font at the base of the oval, and the podium prominently displayed the seal of the Department of Defense.

LTC Bennett, middling in height and bespectacled with a fresh high-and-tight haircut, gazed down at the neatly arrayed bevy of reporters, happy to note a vague, if wavering, sense of confidence. *I can do this*, he assured himself. He was nearing the end of an uneventful professional development assignment in the Pentagon's Public Affairs Office. Without warning, or much time for preparation, he'd been thrust front and center into the national media spotlight.

No briefings were planned for what was expected to be an uneventful post-Memorial Day Tuesday. The press secretary was overseas with her deputy; the next three officials in the offices' pecking order were on vacation, sick leave, and emergency leave. As a bauble for his annual evaluation and over-a-beer bragging rights, LTC Bennett had been officially designated the acting DOD press secretary for that one day. When the Secretary of Defense abruptly ordered a presser on the morning's purple smoke fires, all eyes turned to the army lieutenant colonel sitting quietly at his desk surfing the web for news on the morning's weird events.

In a dizzying whirlwind, the public affairs professionals prepped LTC Bennett for the first, and most likely, last press conference of his army career. *Thirty minutes, max*, they ordered; *a ten-minute brief with one graphic...use the pointer on the lectern...then a twenty-minute Q&A. Don't rock, swivel, or sway in your boots, and keep your hands to yourself. Remember, short and quick answers, but never say "I* don't know," *or worse,* "no comment." *Also, watch out for reporters turning questions into speeches—cut them off with a smile. Keep your eyes on the back of the room and watch for hand signals from the director,* they said, *like a third-base coach. Speak clearly, but not too fast, and don't breathe heavily into the microphone. Also, watch your annunciation, avoid acronyms, and do not use technical jargon—especially that army tanker lingo you like—stay away from that. Another thing: no interjections like,* "uh-huh, and okay." *Metaphors, analogies, and colloquialisms? —avoid them like the plague. Be sure to maintain eye contact with the audience, appearing confident, sincere, and honest. Stand up straight, be energetic, do not cross your arms...and never point at somebody with a finger—just use your knuckles. Above all, and this is important, try to look comfortable and relaxed!*

"Good afternoon," Bennett began with the shaky gravitas of a mortician about to announce a tornado warning, "this will be a short news brief on the series of fires this morning inside and around the Pentagon with questions allowed afterwards." A quick glance to the back-of-the-room director got him an "OK" hand signal. Not wanting to misspeak, he carefully read directly from the briefing book.

"At approximately zero-six-thirty hours this morning, a fire was detected inside the passenger area of a bus parked at the Pentagon Commuter Station. About ninety minutes later, a second fire occurred on board a Washington Metropolitan Area Transit Authority subway train. During a scheduled stop at the underground Metro Pentagon Station, a subway fire was detected. There were also smaller fires inside two separate Pentagon restrooms, occurring at approximately oh-eight-thirty and oh-eight-forty hours."

"That makes a total of four fires this morning on the Pentagon Reservation: the bus, the subway car and two interior bathrooms. A common thread among all four fires is that witnesses report a large volume of purple smoke being generated."

LTC Bennett could hear the culmination of muted smartphone keystrokes, like rain on a pond, as he looked at the reporters. "All four fires," he continued, "were quickly reported and extinguished. There were no injuries other than minor smoke inhalation, which was treated on-site. Physical damage inside the Pentagon was minimal; there was minor damage to the Metro subway car; the commuter bus sustained significant damage."

Pausing to check on the back-of-the-room coach, a female reporter startled him as she bounced onto her feet from the third-row to ask a question. "Please," he intoned with a preemptory raised palm, like a dispassionate debate monitor, "Ma'am, we'll answer questions in a few minutes." Without a trace of self-awareness or impinged dignity, she sat back down, and he continued.

Extending his pointer, Bennett stepped to a large easel-mounted graphic of the Washington area road network with five yellow blocks highlighted. Without the benefit of notes, he segued into a situational assessment of the battlefield. "In additional to the incidents within the Pentagon perimeter, there are reports of five similar incidents in the area of interest." Pointing to the lowest yellow block, he continued, "The first event was a single vehicle fire here, at Triangle, Virginia at about oh-six-hundred hours." Pushing the pointer along with his narrative, he continued, "The second event was eighteen miles north, here at the Springfield interchange of I-95 and I-495. Flanking eight miles to the right, the third event was here, just west of the Wilson Bridge. Finally, flanking nine miles to the left of Springfield, there was a fourth event here, just north of Merrifield, VA."

The briefing coach looked like she was trying to saw her own head off with a rocking horizontal hand and forearm motion. *Better speed it up*, Bennett thought. "The fifth incident was here," he said, pointing to the last yellow block. "Another single vehicle fire in a parking garage half a mile from the building and around the same time as the bus and subway incidents. In total there were nine events, all generating either an intense column of purple smoke or a purple obscuration haze."

Returning to the lectern, he completed the scripted comments in the briefing book. "I've been authorized to announce the creation of an inter-agency task force led by the FBI (Federal Bureau of Investigation) that will analyze all of this morning's fires. The Army Criminal Investigation Division has been designated the lead DOD task force element. Other task force components include the Metro Transit Police, the Arlington Virginia Police, the Virginia State Police, and the Washington Metropolitan Police."

"Due to the unknowns and out of concern for their well-being, the Pentagon workforce was dismissed at noon today. Whether they return tomorrow, as scheduled, will be determined after additional investigation and analysis. Also, out of an abundance of caution, the Force Protection level for the Pentagon Reservation has been raised from Normal to Alpha. This higher rating indicates a possible threat of terrorist activity."

"I'll take questions now," Bennett offered, receiving another "OK" hand signal from his coach. Gazing down, the twenty or so reporters reminded Bennett of a trout farm pond at feeding time. With a slight thrust of his knuckles at the nearest reporter, he murmured. "Right here."

"Robert Jaeger, *Fox News*," the reporter began. "Sir, in your experience as an army officer, can you suggest what type of device or process was used to start the fires and produce the purple smoke? Also, do you think military grade devices were used?"

"Most likely, Robert, they were IEDs—improvised explosive devices. IEDs can be incendiary, pyrotechnic, and noxious, which these obviously were. They do not necessarily have to be explosive or lethal, which these were not. As for military ordnance—that's always possible, but in my experience unlikely due to the high level of ammunition surety used by the DOD." Bennett vaguely aimed his fist towards the rear rows, letting the reporters sort out who would speak next.

An unusually young and tall man slowly stood, threatening the low ceiling with his head. "Keith Muckerman, *Defense News*: Could this be the work of one deranged or disgruntled person, or do you think it's the work of an organized group?"

"It could be either, Keith. It's too early to determine who is responsible, and no person or group has yet to claim responsibility. That said, in my mind, nine incidents over such a wide area in only a few hours would indicate the work of more than just one person. The planning, logistics and expense of these actions would also indicate an organized group versus a lone-wolf operator." Satisfied with his answer, Bennett shifted his fist to the right, where a pert, dark-haired woman arose.

"Thank-you, Myrna Molina, *El Tiempo Latino*: Is it possible that a Pentagon employee is responsible for these fires?"

Bennett's heart skipped a beat as he was consumed with that very thought. *It could be a crazy ass officer, or more likely, an unhappy enlisted man, but there were not that many enlisted personnel in the building. It could be a disgruntled civilian or contract employee—maybe someone who had been stewing for decades in the oppressive atmosphere of the Pentagon. Whoever it was, they had the wherewithal to get the devices into the building and then escape undetected. Also, he doubted that one person could have initiated all nine of the incidents. Yeah,* he thought, *I would bet my next paycheck that whoever or whatever was responsible had inside help.* With those thoughts, his terse reply was, "Myrna, we will have to wait and see what the task force uncovers on that issue. Another question?" he asked, rubbing his fist across the front edge of the podium.

A gray-haired, heavy-set lady struggled to stand up. "Cookie Shindo, *The Community News*: Is it possible that this could all be an overblown cisgender birthday reveal? Also, since the color of purple represents strength, transformation, and power, do you think today's events could be a message of increasing societal awareness and acceptance of transgender rights?"

I didn't see that one coming, Bennett told himself, *and what the hell is cisgender*? "Ugh, Cookie, those are both good questions, but there is no indication currently that either of those events have transpired. Next question?"

An attractive and professionally dressed woman, who reminded him of his sister, stood and locked eyes with him. "P. Susan Inglese, *The Washington Post*: Lieutenant Colonel Bennett, could today's events possibly be some type of political protest against the current administration's collusion with Russia in last November's presidential election?"

Holy shit, Bennett thought, *I'm not even touching that thing*. "Susan, that's an interesting perspective, but we have no knowledge, at this time, indicating any type of political protest." Anxious, to move on, he scratched his nose, eager for someone else to pop up from the audience.

Sylvia Pigati, the NPR reporter covering that morning's events on the radio, stood and announced herself. "Sir, there were nine fires this morning, four of them on the Pentagon Reservation and a fifth only half a mile from here. Whoever is responsible for this, and whatever message they are trying to convey—do you feel they are deliberately targeting the Department of Defense and its headquarters?"

Yes, I do, Bennett told himself, noting the briefing coach swinging her nose from left to right. *But I won't go there*, he decided. "Sylvia, we don't have the level of detail at this time to make that determination." The coach was again trying to saw her head off, so Bennett waggled his fist to the left adding, "We have time for one more question."

"Thank-you, sir" the last reporter began, "William Landers, *The Washington Times*. Lieutenant Colonel Bennett, following up on the NPR comment, and considering the terrorists attacks on September 11, 2001, is it possible that these fires and purple smoke are signaling, or even obscuring, the hostile intent of another attack on the Pentagon?"

"Bill, let's all pray that that's not what's happening today, tomorrow or forever. Thank-you all for attending, we will provide additional information as it becomes available."

With that, LTC Bennett strode out the stage door, stress sloughing off his shoulders and ready for a celebratory beer; yet he knew he would be working non-stop with the rest of the public affairs staffers until the crisis was resolved.

***

With darkening reality, Mike lost interest in the televised press conference, returning to the curving, narrow hallway connecting the old and new terminals. Stopping at a bank of chest-high cast metal windows, he watched as the 2:00 p.m. Air Canada flight taxied towards the distant runways. *Maybe Arif's just late*, he considered, *or maybe I'm just an idiot that's been used and fucked.* Either way, he was screwed.

Loitering much longer at a high-security venue, Mike reasoned, was probably not the best of his diminishing options. That state trooper he had paid off at the Merrifield interchange could report him, but not without putting himself in jeopardy. Suzy Wilson knew everything, and she probably compared notes with Detective Rodriguez. Either of them could catch a fever of civic responsibility and eventually report him, but again, not without incriminating themselves. Whatever happens, the FBI and ATF will soon be dissecting the Penrose basement for evidence and clues. Mike knew that the hundreds of surveillance cameras he had walked beneath that morning at the Pentagon were the real immediate threat. The investigators would be studying his grainy images by now, with a confirmed identification of Mike not far behind. Then the government would hunt non-stop until they treed him.

Chapter 21
Class Reunion

2:00 p.m., Monday, 30 May, 2017

Leaving the airport, Mike took a cab to a grungy Alexandria tavern he liked to visit during his Sutton Towers apartment days. Settling into a sticky booth farthest from the door, he was relieved to not recognize the man and woman working the bar. *Probably the new owners*, he guessed. "Cheesesteak and Grey Goose," he ordered, "double and neat—and keep 'em coming." He gave the woman two hundred dollars to keep her distantly attentive. The bartender and his few patrons were ignoring a replay of the Pentagon press conference he had seen at the airport. Soon enough, he figured, they would be looking at him on that TV, and if they remembered, they would yack forever about the Pentagon terrorist being *right there...in that booth in the back*.

The fucking Iranians had hosed him, he decided. "Do not betray your friends," Arif had warned him. That was clearly a one-way threat. At least Kazim had given him a dog—he had been a true friend. "You will plan your action for early morning," Arif had declared, "the number two action will take place early the second morning." Mike figured that meant about twelve hours. Then Arif had thrown out his truly ominous tidbit, "You will not be safe here after the actions." *Well, too late now,* Mike thought.

Last night, when he had hitched the first trailer for the Springfield Mixing Bowl, Arif had told him to never set foot in the Penrose warehouse again. He had noticed that the Chinese and Russian workers were still in there. They had cleared an area inside the chaotically messy room large enough for the white van. Signaling to the bar for a refill, Mike thought about that and his two erstwhile helpers.

They had stuck three McDonald's straws into that foam block, losing it in laughter when the Chinese man vroom vroomed another foam block towards it. They both went, "boom, boom, boom" then the Russian did his stupid ballerina act with the falling pixie dust—after that, he held up four fingers. *That's it, that's all he had,* Mike realized, and he was too exhausted to make any sense of it. His eyelids were sagging; the booze was kicking in. Limply waving for his refill, he was asleep and dreaming before it arrived.

Mike The Vulture, took flight. A meandering silver ribbon stretched from one wingtip to the other on the moonlit landscape. The unnatural outline of the Gateway Arch rose to greet him as he flew home to Kansas. The geometric shapes of the land below yielded a few, then a sea of starlike lights. He saw the three straws, realizing he had flown the wrong way; his van was below, in between the Air Force Memorial and the Pentagon. A fireball sent Mike spinning out of control towards the fresh lunar crater below, with the entire Pentagon building wobbling on its rim. "Wake up Mike, we have to clean the dishes." Unconscious recognition of the voice from the past, and the firm shaking of his forearm, slowly rocked him awake.

Mike studied the man currently sitting across from him in the booth. His thinning hair was now gray, he wore thick glasses, and he had probably gained over a hundred pounds, but Mike still recognized his friend from college. "Ahmed," he groggily murmured, adding, "درود بر شما (peace be upon you)."

"And unto you, peace, my friend," Ahmed returned warmly, impressed by Mike's breezy use of Persian. "We have much to talk about, but not here—there is little time and we must move." Sliding a foam cup of coffee across the table top he added, "You might need this."

"To Quebec?"

"No, those plans have changed. You were being watched at the airport, so we will use a fallback plan."

Ahmed, Mike thought with woozy wonderment, *of all people.* They had not seen or heard from each other since the end of college, in the spring of 1979. *He was somehow involved in all of this.* "There is little time," he had said—*well, no shit! Their fricking bomb was going off in what, about ten hours?* "What time is it?" Mike struggled to murmur with his dry mouth.

"Almost six," Ahmed replied, confirming with a glance at an expensive-looking watch.

"Ten hours," Mike added ominously.

"Almost," Ahmed reluctantly confirmed. "How did you know?"

"I had a dream," Mike casually replied with a shrug.

The men studied each other under the gloomy, low wattage of the hanging overhead light. Mike instinctively knew to shut-up and listen at this point. Ahmed would give him whatever information and guidance the Iranians cared to divulge, and then he would do exactly as he was told—that was the only way to stay safe with them and out of the grasp of whoever was trailing him. In a way, finally understanding that Ahmed was apparently someone important in this crazy venture brought back the sense of security, trust, and belonging that Kazim had offered, but Arif had lacked. "I trust you, Ahmed," was Mike's only reply.

They had tried to keep Mike in the dark about the details of the second action, Ahmed thought. His divination of what was about to happen was not surprising—he had proven over the years to be reliable, resourceful, and self-sufficient. Given his loyalty—along with the remote likelihood of him negatively impacting the second action at that late-hour—Ahmed felt compelled to give his college friend a quick explanation.

"After university, as I had hoped," he began, "I became involved in the revolution. They needed someone who sounded like an American to manage logistics with overseas suppliers. I quickly made important contacts and learned how to broker and move international shipments. By the end of the war with Iraq in 1988, I bought my first jet. Then I went solo and built a good business—in Paris—that is where my wife and children are."

"So, you're wealthy now?"

"Wealth", he self-consciously replied, "is relative, but first, back to Iran, where, in the mid-eighties, I saw your name on a list of Americans under recruitment by the Ministry of Intelligence.

"Kazim?"

"Exactly. Leaping forward to 2015, I recommended you for the operation we are executing tonight."

"Arif?"

"Yes, but here is the bit you should know—this is *not* an Iranian government action."

That bit is surprising, Mike thought, sipping coffee—he needed to burn off his alcoholic fuzziness and focus on what Ahmed was saying. "What about the Chinese and the Russians?"

"The men you met were hired mercenaries, carefully picked for their cultural heritage."

"*Were*?"

"They are still alive, but the Americans will soon find them in need of medical attention—and without documentation."

"But with their DNA intact."

"Exactly! Why were you not this smart back in Lawrence? Which reminds me—how did things turn out for your mother?"

Mike understood that he was politely asking when Joy had died. "She married one of her lonely-hearts customers. She claims to have stopped drinking and lies about living happily in Arizona."

"سبحان الله! (Glory be to Allah!)"

"Don't overdo it, Ahmed" Mike responded dryly.

"Where were we?"

"DNA from Russia and China."

"Right...tonight, before the second action, the Americans will rescue the injured Russian and Chinese men, most likely, we figure, taking them far enough away to survive the blast. From their DNA, they will eventually figure out where they are from

"And the second action will be blamed on the Chinese and the Russians, and not on the Iranians—or whoever."

"'Whoever,' as you called us, are a small group of my friends."

"Other billionaires?"

"Yes, but we do not have a formal organization or name."

"No banks, no help, no paper, no phones, no internet."

"Those guidelines are harder to adhere to at our level, but you have seen how effective they are."

Half-way through the coffee Ahmed had thoughtfully provided, Mike realized he was talking too much when he should have been listening, but the conversation was going well, so he continued the two-way banter. "Who was watching me at the airport?"

A man-and-woman team, the same one that has been watching the Penrose warehouse for a few weeks. They are Americans, but we do not know what agency they are from."

"I'm guess'n they're clueless about the second action?"

"They were so focused on your preparations for the first action that it diverted their attention—as planned. My congratulations! The planning and execution of the first action were brilliant! We were amazed at how much you were able to do on your own.

"I tried," Mike responded humbly.

"The weapon was only briefly in the warehouse last night. It has been circling Washington on the I-495 Beltway all day."

"In my van?"

"Yes."

"Should I probe about who's doing the second action and why, or just let it be?"

Checking his watch, Ahmed fidgeted in the booth's seat. "We need to get on the road, but I will give you the quick and unclean: My friends and I want to save America from itself. More specifically, we do not want communist or religious autocrats centrally controlling global markets and finance.

"And mucking up your ability to earn more money."

"Let me explain it with some history: *Look back over the past, with its changing empires that rose and fell, and you can foresee the future, too.* Marcus Aurelius said that almost two thousand years ago."

"Who?"

"Aurelius was a Roman emperor, but you are missing the point. Empires, caliphates, sultanates, and dynasties—call them what you want, but they all come and then eventually go. Ming, Mongol, British, Dutch, Aztec, Egyptian...not in that order, but you get my point. The Germans, Japanese, and Russian Soviets had a go at it just a few years ago. Hundreds of empires over a span of four thousand years driven by spirituality, nationality, tribal brutality, fear, greed, and other noble causes."

"I get your point, Ahmed. You and your big bank account buddies are worried about the Americans fucking up their current position on top of the global heap."

"Yes," Ahmed sighed heavily. "It is obvious to us that the Americans are shattering into ethnic, racial, religious, gender and political factions."

"No more assimilating in the melting pot?"

"Correct, and that lost cohesiveness and unified focus is a problem for us because it leads to geopolitical gridlock and poor strategic planning. While Americans obsess over cultural, climate, and rights issues, their global influence is diminishing. For them to retain great power status, they need to at least maintain, or better yet, keep expanding their supersized economic, political, and military strength."

"Which, you and your friends believe, is opening the door for global power competitors in places like Russia, China and Iran."

"Yes, and China is our biggest near-term concern. Here is another historical quote for you, '*Clearly, a civilization that feels guilty for everything it is and does will lack the energy and conviction to defend itself.*'"

"That from Assilius, too?"

"Aw·**ree**·lee·uhs, Mike," Ahmed gently corrected like a school teacher. "The second quote is from a Frenchman named Revel, and he was right on the money. The American political class is not only becoming even more corrupt; it is also unusually polarized. One side wants day, the other night. Both want unlimited spending and borrowing."

"I've been reading *The Washington Post* every day since 1980, and you're right about the political situation in Washington, but the second action seems a little extreme. If anything, it will screw up your business deals for a few years. Isn't that like spiting your nose to cut your face?"

Ahmed returned a quizzical look, "I have never understood that one."

Mike shrugged again, "Me neither, but what I mean is how do you figure you'll be 'saving America from itself?' Won't you just be creating a huge opening for those 'communist and religious autocrats you're worried about?" The coffee seemed to be helping him think clearly, so Mike added, "Also, what about American counter-strikes and all those second and third order effects? You may be igniting a global war—but that would be good business for an arms dealer and his buddies."

Insulted, Ahmed pressed against the seat back, struggling not to return an insult. Deeply exhaling while heavily leaning forward onto his elbows, he carefully responded, "First off, Mike, I am here because of our friendship. Others wanted you gone by now, but I intervened. I am a small part of something much bigger. You said you trusted me, and you can. Yes, I broker war materiel, but my partners' businesses are not defense-related and are all over the map—literally. The dangers here are extremely high, and we have spent years arguing and strategizing. The bottom line is that we think the risk is warranted given what is at stake—and we do not believe the Americans will launch a nuclear counterstrike if we muddle who made the second attack and why.

"You're not going to issue a manifesto, or take credit?"

"No, and that is part of the plan. Listen, I have one more quote, then we need to move." Ahmed waved towards the bar, and two husky, dark-clad men slowly arose to exit the tavern.

"Your men?" Mike wondered.

"I cannot move without security; it is too risky. Now, do you remember me reading Sun Tzu in college?"

"No, not really."

He was a Chinese military strategist before the Christian era. He said, "'*Let your plans be dark and impenetrable as night, and when you move, fall like a thunderbolt.*' That is what we are doing with the second action tonight. We think it will shock some sense into the Americans and move them to get their shit in order.

"Shock therapy."

"A thunderbolt."

"Slap upside the head," Mike added, making both men snork, recalling the easy friendship that had bonded them back in the late 70's.

***

It was approaching 7:00 p.m., the coffee was gone, and so were Ahmed and his bodyguards. Mike needed to pee, and he also needed to escape the growing after-work crowd in the smoky tavern. Ahmed had left a car for him with specific instructions that Mike knew would be a mistake to ignore.

There were nine hours before the second action would rip through downtown Washington and send the entire world into a tizzy. It was kind of exciting to think about the effect it would have, yet he wondered how many millions would be impacted. He still had time to be a hero and try to stop the whole thing, but he needed mental space to think and possibly plan a rescue operation with a chance of working.

Threading Ahmed's Ford Explorer through early evening traffic, he wove his way onto I-395 North towards downtown D.C. He exited toward Potomac Park, passing the gleaming white dome of the Jefferson Memorial on his left. Leaving the Ford, he strolled the islet's perimeter walkway towards the day's lowering sun.

Nine people knew he was responsible for the first action. Ahmed and Arif, obviously, but he was probably safe with them if he continued to be useful and loyal. The state trooper, Detective Rodriguez, and Suzy Wilson, also knew. After the second action erupted, any of them—if they lived—could grow a conscience and report him. More ominously, the unknown man and woman at the airport that Ahmed had mentioned knew about him and were filing reports to their superiors. With that thought, Mike slowly spun in a circle, scanning his surroundings for anyone who may have been trailing him.

His Russian and Chinese helpers could also identify him. Even from a hospital bed, they would be able to grunt at headshot pictures and finger him as the crazy purple smoke guy they worked with in the Penrose basement. Mike realized that if nine people knew what he had done, then hundreds of other people already knew or could easily find out. He was now a known domestic terrorist, and that would never change.

The park closed at sundown, so only a few pedestrians were there that Tuesday night. Arriving at Hain's Point, Mike had a beautiful view towards Reagan Airport as the setting sun managed to shimmer through the cloud cover and reflect off the boundary channel waterway. The picnic tables had been moved and replaced, so he picked one he thought would be closest to where he had last met with Kazim in September of 2003.

Sitting backwards on the bench, leaning on both elbows with legs stretched to the water, he recalled the significance of that day. It was when his promotions at work had ended and his sour attitude towards life had begun to blossom. He smiled, recalling his decimate, Lenny, the guy with the thick Boston brogue. That day, he treated Mike to lunch at the Indian Museum. It was also the day that Kazim gave him Potawatomi, which turned out to be a going-away gift. *Everything was downhill from there*, he thought.

The big jets overhead were landing instead of taking off that evening, so it was a good spot to reminisce and think. He had been careful, but he was also greedy and stupid. Now millions of people would be impacted, and some would die. Who knew what would happen tomorrow morning after the second action ignited? He doubted the atomic bombing of Washington, especially the Pentagon building, would happen without retaliatory strikes being launched from bombers, submarines, ships, and in-ground missile silos. What was the purpose of all that hardware if not to defend a nation's capital city?

Ahmed's guidance, not surprisingly, was odd yet logical. Mike was to rendezvous with him six hours south on I-95 at the North and South Carolina border, where a large RV awaited them. This would avoid the interstate traffic pileups that were expected in the morning. Ahmed mentioned climbing a tourist tower shaped like a large sombrero hat to see the glow of the 4:00 a.m. blast, but Mike hoped they would be too far away to see anything. While the country reeled from the shocking news of the second action—and whatever craziness happened afterwards—they would hide in the RV among many others in the Smoky Mountains. When the time was right, they would continue to Savannah, Georgia, and Ahmed's awaiting yacht.

For years, he realized that anger, resentment, and envy had controlled him. Maybe if his mother had not been such a scumbag; maybe if his wife had not died so suddenly; maybe if he had never befriended the weird Iranian dishwasher in college. His life had been a slow-motion mistake. Now lots of people would be hurt, and he would be hunted like Osama bin Laden after *he* attacked the Pentagon. Living with Ahmed would be interesting and probably fun for a while, but eventually he would be eating a baguette in Paris, and then notice the laser sight dot shimmering across his chest. Then he would either be imprisoned or just dead.

He had fucked up, as usual, but what could he do now? He could call the Pentagon Police or Detective Rodriguez. They could probably intercept the white van at the Air Force Memorial and shoot it out with whoever was inside, but could they defuse the bomb before it exploded? *Empires rise and fall*, Ahmed explained. Who was he to stop the course of history? Was America *a civilization that feels guilty for everything it is and does?* He had no doubt about that. Finally, *falling like a thunderbolt*, seemed to be inevitable.

Mike stepped onto the concrete ribbon between water and land, the dusky surface of the darkening waterway reflecting his mood. He could jump into the cold water. The current would slowly push him past the Pentagon, the airport, and even the Wilson Bridge if nothing snagged him along the way. Eventually, the Potomac would painlessly put an end to the lonely vacuum that had been his life.

Suddenly, he sensed, but could not see, a pair of kingfishers skimming along the river's surface, their wings nosily ratcheting in rhythm. The birds' surprising passage jarred Mike from his dismal reverie. *Yes,* he decided, stepping away from the barrier's edge, *but not now, and not like that.*

Chapter 22
Enigma

9:00 p.m., 30 May, 2017

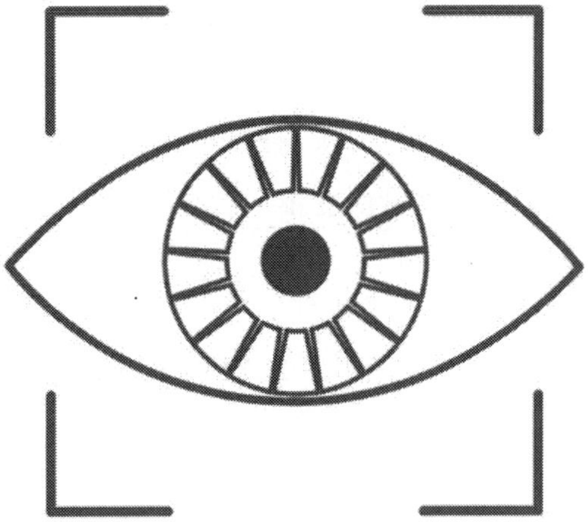

Mike parked as close to the main Pentagon entrance as he could. The entire sea of empty parking spaces was reserved by number for others deemed more essential than he would ever be. At 9:00 p.m., though, he could park wherever he wanted. He followed the edge of the sidewalk toward the building entrance, focusing on appearing normal. A pair of PFPA guards observed his slow approach. One of them silently moved to stop Mike so that the other could inspect his building pass. Satisfied, they allowed him to proceed.

Multiple other officers studied his passage through the main entrance's big wood doors. An ALPHA force protection level, still in effect after that morning's first action, had the guards on alert for the unusual or unexpected. Standing spread-eagle for a weapons check, Mike studied another arrival as she swiped her CAC card at a turnstile; he did the same.

The large bullpen in room 1D343 was always a dreary and soul-sucking place. Swiping to enter the double entry doors, he found the room eerily unpopulated. *It feels like a mausoleum*, he thought, threading through murky shadows cast by random computer monitors, plant lights, and emergency exit signage. Finding the right cubicle, he shoved the desk chair aside and built a firm pillow from two reams of copier paper. Curled in a fetal position half-way under the desk, he wept, recalling things from the past and mostly regretting them. Eventually, he fell asleep on the soiled carpet next to a small mound of used tissues.

The two agents looked down on him, half expecting his savage snoring to expectorate something from deep within him. Both held their snub-nosed .38 specials were ready for duty as the male agent nudged Mike awake with his foot. "Rise and shine, Cappiello," he cooed with a soft kick to Mike's ribs. Sluggish from sleep, Mike studied the four dark trouser legs and shoes that were assaulting him. The shoes were black leather with soft-soles—a *good choice for the Pentagon*, he thought. Bending and rolling, he squinted up at the silhouette of a tall, thin, black man wearing a business suit with hands clasped on a handgun extended his way. "Roll over face-down," the man growled, to which Mike willingly complied. "Now put your hands behind your back."

With Mike restrained, the trio left the big room, marching through the building's long corridor, encountering no others on their journey. *Where were they going?* He wondered. *Would a black SUV with dark windows whisk him away to some off-site location?* Pivoting left, the male agent paused at a door no different from the thousands of others in the building.

With a swipe of a card hanging from a lanyard, and a few pecks on a keypad, the door clicked open. Inside was a small vestibule leading to a gleaming elevator entrance. One after the other, the agents bent to face an eye-scanning biometrics reader, patiently waiting for a glowing red circle to turn green with a muted "Bing." Entering the elevator, the trio dropped for less than five seconds when the doors swished open. Mike guessed they were now somewhere in the building's basement.

Ceiling lights flickered on as the three entered a snug office suite sparsely furnished with a conference table and several generic work cubicles. The room was as institutional and styleless as anywhere else in the Pentagon. Mike sighed, murmuring "I didn't know where we were going, but I gotta say, I thought it'd be more interesting than this."

"Of all the generals and admirals in the Pentagon," the male agent retorted, "only a handful has ever been in here, Mike." Uncuffing him, the agent swept an arm towards the table adding, "Consider yourself special, and have a seat." Mike claimed a straight-back metal chair, observing as his captors draped their navy-blue jackets on chairbacks opposite him. Both sported tactical belts with cuffs, tasers, revolvers, and spare ammo. The woman, a petite Asian, also carried a telescoping baton. Clunky hand-held terminals were tapped to life and placed on the tabletop before them, followed by glances at clunkier watches on their left wrists.

"In sync," intoned the female agent.

"Same here," the male agent mutely replied. "Pass that ash tray over here, Mike," he directed while shaking a loose cigarette from his pack. "I'd offer you one, but we know you don't smoke."

"Gimme one," Mike mumbled, watching as the surprised agent noisily struck a stick match against its small cardboard coffin. "I'm going to start right now."

"Here," he said, tossing the pack and matches while leaning back to blow smoke sideways. "Smoking's a poor choice," he chided. "Okay, Mike, my partner will explain the lay of the land, such as it is, then basically we're just going to talk to you for a couple of hours."

"Talk? That's it?"

"Actually, a bit more than that," the female began to disclose, pushing forward onto her elbows. Both agents became busily focused on their terminal screens, which glowed in varying hues. A wall-mounted monitor behind them was illuminated with a black-and-white headshot from years ago. Mike would not be told, but the interview was being recorded and transmitted to others remotely monitoring the two agents' progress.

"First off, Mike, you're being detained, but not formally arrested."

"When will that happen—being arrested and all?"

Ignoring him, she continued, "We will conduct what we call a 'soft interrogation' which basically means we ask questions and you answer them. You need to remain seated," then motioning towards a shrink-wrapped bundle on the table she added, "there's drinking water if you want it."

"What about Miranda rights and a lawyer and all that?"

The agents shared the knowing look of close and experienced confidants. They had done this many times. Mike was following the usual script, which was disappointing considering all that he had done the past ten months and the surprising effectiveness of his stunts the day before. They hoped he would say or do something out of the ordinary to enliven an otherwise humdrum assignment. To perk up the day's work, they had wagered a tenth of an ounce of gold. She would win if Mike was politically motivated; he would win if he was just another disgruntled worker grasping for payback. The gray area in the middle of religious or other oddball motivations would be considered a draw.

"We're not the police," the female replied, "and you will not be entering the criminal justice system. You do not need to be mirandized and you don't need an attorney—we're beyond all that."

"Beyond all that..." Mike contemplated. "Just who are you, the FBI?"

"That was an insult," the male agent deadpanned. "Look, Mike, we're not on anyone's organizational chart, just call us what we are, an enigma. So, to keep things simple, and to keep us on schedule this morning, we work for an outfit called Enigma and our job is to quietly make problems go away."

"Make problems go away..." Mike slowly repeated while exhaling a choppy fog of tobacco smoke. "Okay," he decided, wrestling a water bottle from its shrink wrap. "I'll answer your questions, just help me get oriented first."

"Oriented?" she asked.

"Yeah, first off, what do I call each of you, Agent X and Agent Y?"

The male agent glanced at his watch, retorting with, "Just to keep things moving here, you can call me...Conway."

Picking up on her partner's theme, the lady offered, "And I'll be Tammi...no, no wait, I want to be *Loretta*."

"Good," Mike replied, "second to last question: what's this room and how come you can smoke in it?"

"Technically," Loretta replied, "it's called a Sensitive Compartmented Information Facility...a SCIF.

"A spic?" Mike wondered, pulling her leg.

"S-C-I-F, Mike. There are others in the building; this one is ours. It was built after the nine-eleven attacks, when the Patriot Act created our organization—Enigma. The SCIF gives us secure privacy and linkage to the intelligence internet."

Mike ground his cigarette into a stub on the ash tray. "And smoking?"

"Who gives a shit, Numnuts?" Conway growled while balanced on the back two legs of his chair. "You done with your fuck'n questions?"

"Just one more thing...and I do appreciate you two humoring me here...what's the schedule for tonight?"

Loretta checked her terminal, curtly replying, "One hundred eighteen minutes."

"Then what?" Mike asked.

"Goddamnit!" Conway exploded, standing, and leaning in towards Mike. "One hundred eighteen minutes and then you are done! With the proper introductions and make'n up shit, we've lost time and have to get back on track. Here is your schedule, Mike: you tell us why you did the crap you did, then we are going up on the roof to continue your little séance with a hard stop at zero-four-hundred hours."

Mike looked confused. "On the roof—of the Pentagon?"

"Yes," Loretta replied calmly.

Still puzzled, Mike wondered, "What's 'zero-four-hundred?'"

"It's four-a.m., Mike," Loretta explained.

Conway thumbed a short message on his terminal: SMOKING, MILITARY TIME. The previous investigators had missed that Cappiello was obviously a smoker. Also, how could anyone working over three decades with the army not know the military twenty-four-hour clock lingo? Maybe Cappiello was a dimmer bulb than they thought.

"Okay, I'm good," Mike retorted, "no more questions from me. You ask, I'll answer and we'll stay on schedule."

Sharing a glimpse of relief, the agents slightly repositioned their chairs to study their captive from opposing angles. "Show and tell time, Mike," Conway explained. "We'll show you what we already know, then you tell us what we don't." The captors would audit his posture, hand movements, facial tics, respiration, voice, heart rate, and eye movements to detect Mike's lies and evaluate his emotional responses. This analysis would influence their follow-on questions, hopefully increasing the effectiveness of the interrogation.

"Do you recognize this first image?" Conway asked.

Sighing, Mike decided to be quick, concise, and emotionless—not hard to do at almost 3:00 a.m. with little sleep. "If it's me, I needed a haircut."

"It's from your intern class pic at Red River Army Depot in 1979; you were an honor graduate—belated congratulations on that. Then you were assigned to the Pentagon in March, 1980."

"Yup," Mike mumbled while downing a slug of water, watching the image change to an outside shot of a large brick building.

"You lived in an apartment in this complex from March, 1980 to October, 2012."

"Looks pretty nice," he demurred as the monitor changed to an image of a foreign-looking man. A fuzzier shot, maybe from a telephoto lens, replaced the headshot of the foreigner.

"This is you and Kazim having a picnic on Hains Point in September, 2003. Do you remember that?"

"Kazaam!" Mike joked, like a thought cloud from a Batman fight scene.

"*Kazim*, Mike, was actually Lieutenant Colonel Naghi Panahi of the Republic of Iran's Army."

"Do you know where he is now?" Mike wondered.

"Well," Conway retorted, watching for Mike's reaction with a smirk, "We don't know where his body is, but his head was found in a roadside culvert."

Visibly revolted, Mike wondered, "Where?" as the image changed to an outside shot of a crappy-looking townhouse.

Ignoring Mike's inquiry, Conway continued, "From October, 2012 to the present, you have lived in this dump in Woodbridge, Virginia. You're not much on landscaping and maintenance, are you?"

"I guess not" was Mike's cryptic response, as an image of another, younger, foreign man came up.

"Colonel Meysam Hedayati," Loretta explained, "from their Air Force. For twelve years, Mike, you were a 'sleeper asset,' someone the Iranians had compromised and could reactivate if needed."

"Hedayati," Conway grumbled, "you're lucky he didn't deactivate your ass. He has knocked off more sleepers than he has bothered to wake up." The monitor changed to an outside shot of what looked like a walk-up bank, or dentist's office.

"So, Mike," Conway sarcastically continued, "here is where your little 'secret' bank account was. Tell us about the money."

Mike wondered how much the government did not know about him and the men in the pictures. So far, they seemed to know just about everything and had spent a lot of time and effort monitoring them. He noted they had not mentioned the man from Paris he had met. "The first guy gave me money, like you said," Mike improvised. "I spent it all on hoes and blow. The second guy, he gave me a lot more—there's almost eighty grand in my backpack."

"Guilty as charged," Mike exhaled with a wave of his hand at the next image of the Penrose building. He wondered what depressing real estate wonder would appear next, and he was not disappointed. It was a fuzzy image of two guys, also foreign-looking, next to a wide-open roll-up door.

"Who are these men?" Loretta wondered.

"Eager to end the inquisition, Mike slowly opened the water, crafting another lie for the agents. "I don't know, we weren't properly introduced, and they didn't have a handle on English."

***

Like many of Washington's majestic monuments, the Air Force Memorial is somewhat isolated, with limited ingress and egress options. Sited on a barren hilltop surrounded by highways, a cemetery, and a fingertip of urban sprawl, the memorial has only one lightly traveled access road and entrance gate.

With heavy bolt cutters in hand, the Russian swung open the memorial's wide metal gate arms. Slowly rolling past him, Mike's white panel van crept closer to the three spot-lit silver arches soaring towards the early morning clouds. "Ждать! (Wait!)," he shouted while placing a new lock on the gate. Climbing back into the passenger seat, the three men continued onward.

"那里(There)," the oriental man pointed from his cramped spot behind the van's front seats.

"Иди сюда (Go here)," the Russian piled on.

Ignoring both, Arif edged the van onto a maintenance road, then around the backside of the memorial's small visitor's center. He wanted the weapon on the grassy hilltop, sloping gently down to the hulking Pentagon in the distance." این است (This is it)," he halfheartedly announced, applying the parking brake before killing the engine.

"Здесь (Here)," the Russian offered, passing a pack of Marlboros and a lighter. He also pulled a fresh vodka bottle from beneath the passenger. Enjoying a cool cross breeze, the three men retreated to private thoughts. In less than two hours, they would all be martyrs, and their families would be justly rewarded. Yet they felt depressed. For the two helpers, the past few weeks had been a blur of new experiences and glimpses of the mythical America they had heard about all their lives. Now, with nothing to do but wait, emotions and memories cascaded over them as they waited to die. Softly, the Russian began humming a slow, seemingly melancholy tune known only to himself.

The Asian man took a cigarette, but knew better than to drink anything other than water as he monitored the status of the weapon. He held a solid-looking, olive-drab terminal the size of a chocolate box that glowed with rows of red digital numbers. A braided silver cord connected the terminal to what looked like a white kitchen freezer—type of horror movies kept in basements stocked with dismembered body parts needing defrosting. The bulky weapon filled the back of the small van, wedging its operator up against the two seatbacks. He could not do maintenance on the bomb, but the readouts would indicate if it became unstable enough to abort the mission. So far, whatever he was tracking apparently met his parameters for a 4:00 a.m. detonation.

The adjacent Arlington National Cemetery operated two roving one-officer patrols twenty-four hours a day. Like clockwork, one of them would inspect the memorial's entrance gate hourly after closing time. After that, it would rejoin the other in its lonely vigil of the nation's eternally resting warriors, heroes, and statesmen. Had the gate inspection happened as scheduled, the white van parked atop the hill would have been clearly visible. If the officer had chosen to investigate, he or she would have surprised the three mopey foreigners waiting for the second action to happen. Mike's purple clouds the previous morning prevented the gate inspection from happening. Raising the force protection level from Normal to Alpha meant that more patrols were needed closer to the Pentagon. Therefore, the two cars that could have detected and deterred the terrorists were instead slowly driving in large circles around the building, and not the cemetery.

The Russian's soft, gloomy humming had morphed into a mid-range, off-key rendition of his chosen native folk ballad. Annoyed, Arif swiveled in his seat to spew a short burst of offensive-sounding Persian in protest. Brandishing his handgun, he took two seconds to shoot the unsuspecting Russian in the knee and the opposite shoulder. More deliberately, he leaned in to hold his victim steady, placing the warmed muzzle of the gun against the Russian's left cheek, and firing carefully across his oral cavity. The wild-eyed Asian man was next, but it was more of a challenge due to his resistance and the cramped space he was occupying.

Covered with the bloody mist of his victims, and with ears ringing, Arif exited the van. Sprinting towards the memorial's gate, he entered a car Ahmed had prepositioned for him. Smiling and laughing a self-congratulatory howl, he sped towards a highway entrance. He had about ninety minutes to put as much distance as possible between himself and the monument. Keying a preset number, he waited for his burner phone call to be answered.

In a soft blurry rush, a young female answered, "Pentagon Force Protection Agency, how may I help you, sir or ma'am?"

In a solid, mid-west American accent, Arif urgently replied, "There has been a shooting with two victims."

"What location, sir?"

"The United States Air Force Memorial. Look for the white van—and hurry!"

With the cell phone bouncing and skittering on the roadway behind him, Arif headed west towards Columbus, Ohio.

***

"So," Conway continued as the monitor in the SCIF switched to an aerial photo, "here's your handiwork at the Wilson Bridge yesterday." Leaning in towards the image, Mike could see brightness where a trailer had become an inferno, releasing wisps of purple-looking smoke.

"To much breeze from the river," Loretta commented, noting his concentration. "It blew away the haze, but there was enough of a distraction to back up traffic for an hour or so."

"This one was better," Conway interjected as an aerial shot of the Springfield trailer was displayed. "Looks like all the cars mixed your smoke bomb into a hurricane type cloud. Impressive and effective, A-minus on that one."

Ignoring him, Mike peered at a third overhead shot, which he assumed was taken from a helicopter. The purple smoke rose straight up in a dark column for a bit, then a breeze gave it an anvil-shaped head like a thunderstorm cloud.

"Better call your insurance company on your truck and car, Mike," Conway snidely added as close-ups of the torched, tireless, crumpled, and roofless vehicles where shown.

"The bus may have been your best work," Loretta commended Mike as that image appeared. "The entire back roof collapsed, and you burned a chunk out of the white canopy at the Commuter Station."

"Damaging federal property," Conway tut-tutted, "you could do time for that one."

Calmly gazing at the agents as they impassively studied him, Mike declared, "I'm bored. Spare me any more pictures. I planned it, I did it and overall, it looks like I did an effective job."

"Seventy-nine minutes," Conway intoned, as if reading an oven timer.

"Mike, we have two questions for you." Lorretta explained, "First, we want to understand why you decided to work with the Iranians, that is, we want to understand your motivation."

Tired, weak, and feeling nauseous, Mike decided to let the agents work for their pay. *He had just told them he wanted money for drugs and sex. That was, and would remain, his primary motivation. Their next question would probably be about the motivation of whoever paid him—the foreigners in the slide show. He didn't feel like dictating a novel during his last hour, so he would just play spin-the-bottle with them, giving quick and evasive answers.* "You wouldn't have any bourbon down here, would you?" he wondered. "Another nail would be great too," he added.

"Bars' closed, Numnuts," Conway growled. "Answer the question!"

"Ask a question, and it'll be answered," Mike calmly replied in a neutral tone, "as promised."

Visibly annoyed, Conway began verbally hammering out a list, like a poem he had been forced to memorize. "You grew up poor in the rural Midwest; your single mother was grifter. A Pentagon job was your big break. The ladies rejected you, and your only true friend was a dog. Enter Naghi Panahi—Kazim. He became a friend, making you feel important. You finally figured out that the defense department is a fraternity with uniforms and guns. You didn't belong and you'd never move up, but there was always a bed pan needing to be scrubbed. That point, my friend, is when smart people retire and move on, but not you. Your mid-life bride tragically died. You spiraled deeper into depression and gambling issues, grasping a bottle on your way down. Enter Meysan Hedayati—Arif, toting serious cash. He was not the new friend you needed, but he made you feel like somebody with important things to do."

Appearing to be chagrinned and embarrassed, Mike pivoted his flushed face towards a blank wall, using a hand to massage the back of his head. *Damn...his life would make a good TV movie.*

"Eventually, you knew you had problems," Loretta tagged in. "Was Arif's offer worth walking away from your federal retirement benefits? Was it even possible to walk away, or would you have to escape? Maybe they would hunt you down in—I'm guessing here—Las Vegas? Tell us, were they meeting you at the airport yesterday; did they promise to take you to Iran?"

Spinning to face his tormentors with a look of expectancy, Mike waited for what would come next.

"Looking for this?" Conway taunted him, pulling Mike's credit card-sized cardboard list entitled, 'Problems' from his dress shirt pocket. "We found it in the trash."

Clapping while pretending to sigh in defeat, Mike sarcastically added, "Bravo."

"Sixty-three minutes," Loretta called out, "we need to leave for the roof at thirty minutes."

Seemingly deflated and humbled, Mike was actually thinking about a restroom. "Let's just skip me, since there's not much mystery there. Your next question is about the Iranian's motivation, no?"

"That's correct," Loretta confirmed with a slight nod, like a game show host.

"We never talked about politics—theirs or ours; it was kind of a taboo area for them. The second guy yakked about making that purple smoke; the first guy talked about family, and that's about it. I would say you already know more about them than I could ever guess."

"We're leaving in half an hour, Numnuts," Conway said while stifling a yawn, "why don't you give it a try?"

"Okay, but first tell me why you didn't stop me."

"As in stop you from doing dumb shit like yesterday morning?" Conway asked.

"Yeah, you could have saved me from myself if you wanted to."

"We're not a social services agency, Mike," Loretta apologetically explained. "We monitor and take copious notes. Our adversaries do the same. It's like a glacial game of checkers, and about as exciting."

"Until someone really fucks up—like you did," Conway smirked.

"Then," Mike recalled, "you make the problem go away."

"Answer the question, Mike" Loretta lightly pleaded, "as promised."

"I will, on the roof."

"You want to go there now?"

"Yup."

Chapter 23
Jumper

2:45 a.m., Tuesday, 31 May, 2017

U.S. Air Force Memorial

"Base, unit twelve," the PFPA patrol unit called in.

"Go ahead, unit twelve," the communications center responded.

"I've got eyes on the 11-54 (suspicious vehicle), top of Air Force Hill." With the access gate locked, the officer continued alone on foot, cautiously approaching the white van. With one hand needed to toggle her microphone, she had to choose between a flashlight and sidearm for her second hand. She chose the gun. "Stand by, base."

"Base, standing by."

Crab walking counterclockwise at a safe distance, she could see a body slumped and bloody through the open passenger door window. "Police!" she screamed, while crouching into a shooting stance. "Show me your hands!" Instead, the door clicked open, and a big body rolled out, falling hard to the ground headfirst. One foot and calf of the body remained attached to the vehicle at an awkward angle

"Base, 10-53 (person down) with possible gunshot wounds. Request EMT and backup ASAP."

"Roger, unit twelve, backup and medics. How many suspects?"

"Stand by, base" she replied. Examining the Russian, she judged him to be unarmed, unconscious, and alive. It looked like he had sustained multiple gunshots. Slowly continuing around the front of the van, she probed the open driver's window with her weapon held firmly in two outstretched hands. Illuminated by the red glow of the bomb's control panel, she could see a brownish sheen on the inside of the windshield. Slowly opening the door and peering between the seats, she observed the digital figures as they continued to automatically update. The moans of a second man, who lay behind the seats, startled her. Shining her flashlight into the grim scene, she noted the large metal box wedged into the van's cargo space. Hearing the sirens of her approaching backup, she radioed, "Base, unit twelve."

"Go ahead."

"There's a second 10-53 with gunshots. Also, a possible Code 10 (bomb threat)."

***

Mike leaned against the hip-high safety railing that branched its way around the top of the giant building. Crossing one leg over the other, he sought as comfortable a stance as possible while handcuffed behind his back. With a smirk and a sense of schadenfreude, he observed the activity half a mile away on the Air Force Memorial hilltop.

Blue, red, and yellow beacons pulsated from a dozen emergency vehicles. Centered among them and bathed in spotlights, was a white panel van. The scene stood out like a lit-up carnival in the cool, overcast night. Conway and Loretta failed to make the connection between it and their interrogation. The Americans would have to quickly neutralize whatever was in the van. With about half an hour to go, there probably was not enough time for them to stop what had already begun.

Loretta checked her buzzing terminal, her face dimly highlighted in the glowing screen. After a minute of quick texting, she gave a curt nod and thumbs-up to Conway. "Oh-four-hundred, no deviations," she reported, "and they want his thoughts on the Iranians."

Leaning next to Mike on the railing, Conway asked Loretta to call out five-minute intervals. "Friends of yours up there?" he asked, nodding towards the memorial, "We'll know soon enough. Come on and lift your veil for us, Mike, give us a peek at their motivation."

"Twenty-five minutes," Loretta quietly intoned.

Pushing off the rail, Mike wearily shuffled a few steps towards the edge of the rooftop. He felt drained, thirsty, and needed his pain pills. "Unbind me and I'll give you some thoughts," he said, stopping short of the five-story drop-off. "I'd like to feel my hands again."

Without hesitation, Conway removed the shackles, adding "You're ready, we're ready...now talk."

"Why Iran and the United States can't be friends?" Mike inquired, as if being asked to run another mile after completing a marathon.

"That's it," Conway directed, bored and ready to finish the night's work.

"Well, he began," beginning to feel woozy, "there's the whole religious, oil and Israeli thing."

Loretta softly called out, "twenty minutes."

"Old news, Mike," Conway critiqued.

Scratching some rooftop grit with his right shoe, Mike mumbled in return, "I remember Jimmy Carter and the embassy hostages, that was some bad blood there. Then there was the Saddam Hussein thing where he invaded some other country over there."

Conway softly groaned, "That second one wasn't even the right country, Mike."

"9-11 and Osama bin Laden?"

"Nope."

"Ah-ha, I've got one, the Iraqi nuclear program! They want to build a bomb and the U.S. and Israel won't let 'em."

"Pathetic, Mike," Conway frowned, examining a dead cigarette butt with disgust, then flicking it away. "For some reason we thought you would be telling us something new. How you get from snarling traffic and smoking the Metro yesterday to old news geopolitics is not making much sense."

Loretta restrained herself from blurting out questions, instead reporting "thirteen minutes," with more urgency than she indented to.

Still facing the spotlight-lit spires in the distance, Mike mumbled. "Turn the tables and it'll make more sense."

"Tell tale."

"Imagine that every decade or so, your part of the world is invaded by the same foreigners. They use slick weapons to kill members of your family, your church, and your town. The invaders defile your religious beliefs and destroy most everything they touch. After they leave, your daily life is harder than it should be because of economic and political sanctions controlled by the same foreigners."

Conway paced towards Mike with crunching roof grit, announcing each step. "Something's missing, isn't it, Mike?"

"Big time," Mike replied.

"Your juvenile stunts don't make any sense...unless they're part of something bigger—a whole lot bigger."

Conway glanced at Loretta, who held up nine fingers, signaling the remaining time while unclipping her taser. "Finish your testament, Mike, you've got about five minutes, then we need to move on."

"That's it," Mike sighed, "that's all I got. Let me burn one more before I go."

Hearing their familiar honks, Mike broadly grinned at a flyby of ducks, easily seen in the urban light reflecting off the overcast night sky. "Gadwalls, Pintails or Wigeons," he announced, "flying north for the summer."

***

The plan was simple and had proven reliable after years of discerning use around the country. The target would tragically suicide via some eye-wincing process. The media, already spun-up by whatever brouhaha needed suppressing, would report it. That morning, as the sun illuminated the country from east to west, Americans would be plied with a news update. A lone—and now deceased—Pentagon employee was the source of yesterday's purple smoke fires and traffic snafus around Washington. It would not be a screaming headline, just another press release among many others. A second Pentagon news conference that day would imbue the story with official gravitas. News networks, platforms, and old school papers could choose to announce, post, and print it—or not. Most people, especially those outside the national capital region, would ignore it, and the situation would quiet to a whimper, then soon be forgotten.

Mike's leap from atop the Pentagon was planned, but not with onerous detail. The possible outcomes were understood. Contingency plans were in place should the unexpected happen. His 240-pound body would take about two seconds to hit the concrete pavement below at forty-five miles an hour. Anyone falling seventy-one feet has a fifteen percent chance of survival. Given Mike's age, the hard landing, and the lack of obstructions to slow him on the way down, he was not expected to live. Just the same, Loretta had been provided with a toxic lancet to prick Mike the moment they pushed him off the roof. His death, while tragic, was guaranteed. As a precaution, Pentagon security camera records would be reviewed and digitally edited as required.

At 3:59 a.m., an untraceable call was brusquely answered by a monotone male voice, "Pentagon Force Protection Agency, how may I help you sir or ma'am?"

A hysterical female replied, "There is a man...on the ground...and he's not moving!"

"Where are you located, ma'am?"

"He's...I'm outside—I was going to work."

"Where outside, Ma'am?"

She hesitated, audibly breathing fast and hard enough to sound hyperventilated. "Outside the Bay 400 entrance to corridor four," she replied, hastily adding, "send help, quick!" A Pentagon employee reporting to work at 4:00 a.m. is not unusual. One supposedly using a restricted and little-used entrance is uncommon. Being able to technically describe that entrance, like the building's architect, is very unusual. She could have been there and accidentally encountered Mike's body, but that would be impossible. Her actual location was in a Roslyn, Virginia, office building two miles away.

"We'll send a unit to investigate," the PFPA voice droned before hanging up.

The Enigma group knew that, left on their own, the PFPA would take several days to officially report Mike's demise. An investigation would be required. Other law enforcement and military jurisdictions would be consulted. The next of kin had to be notified. The longest pole in the tent would be getting through the internal Pentagon review and approval bureaucracy. The two-day timeframe was for a run-of-the-mill jumper.

It would take two minutes to identify Mike's remains and alert the news media. After Loretta transmitted a confirmation picture of Mike from above, press releases would be sent linking him to the purple smoke events the day before. Citing "sources within the Pentagon," enough information would be provided to hopefully quell further introspection. The obligatory request to respect the privacy of the recently deceased's family would also be included.

An inquisitive reporter or inspector might be motivated to investigate the odd timing of the 3:59 a.m. phone call followed by the 4:01 a.m. press releases. If necessary, this would be addressed, but the plan assumed that no one would be diligent enough to bother with, or fund, an in-depth review. Celebrities, politicians, athletes, and criminals were newsworthy. Deranged nobodies doing odd shit in the vast federal workforce were not.

***

The press releases were prepared, but never sent. At 4:00 a.m., a detonator triggered uranium fission, which induced atomic fusion within the weapon hidden in the white van. At the same moment, Mike began his ungraceful plunge from the Pentagon's rooftop, his arms, and legs pinwheeling in the air like a cartoon character. Conway and Loretta would have shared a good laugh over the sight, but there was not enough time for their brains and facial muscles to react. A tenth of a second later, an over 5,000-degree Fahrenheit fireball incinerated them along with Mike, his being reduced to a momentary shadow on the crumbling façade of the Pentagon.

Chapter 24
Bunker

8:00 a.m., Tuesday, 31 May, 2017

"Talon to BUNKER" Major Elliott announced into the microphone of her full-cover CBRN mask. Her breath's condensation was fogging the SCUBA-like lenses from the inside. Soon, she would have to remove it and risk inhaling radioactive particles carried into the helicopter by her nine passengers from the White House. The alternative was to continue wearing the mask and possibly jeopardize the upcoming landing at the P-COOP site, code named BUNKER.

"This is BUNKER, state your flight status, Talon," the reply came as expected on the new frequency listed in the OPLAN.

"Andy," Elliott ordered her co-pilot on the helicopter's intercom, "you take control, I'll work the coms; I'm fogging up."

"I have the aircraft," the second pilot rotely announced while stretching his legs to reach the foot pedals and gently grasping the cyclic and collective controls with gloved hands.

"BUNKER," Maj Elliott continued, "we are a flight of two. Talon One has crew of five and nine pax, one visually confirmed as the POTUS. Talon Two has crew of five and one pax."

"Stand-by, Talon," the clipped voice from BUNKER replied.

The helicopters slowed as they descended through the dissipating cloud cover towards the green hardwoods carpeting the rolling Appalachian Mountain landscape. If there were borderlines drawn on the treetops below, Elliott thought, they would be able to see which areas were in Maryland, West Virginia, or Pennsylvania. They were nearing Gettysburg and had flown just seventy or so miles from the early morning atomic blast. From their current vantage point, she realized, you would never know it was anything other than another morning in early summer.

They had departed Quantico around 0640 hours, evacuating the POTUS from the White House about forty minutes later. Now they were on final approach to the BUNKER complex. *Nothing to write home about*, she thought, *just two quick hops through the fresh, post-nuclear wasteland of Washington, D.C.* Her breathing grew shallow and a little jagged as she wondered what would happen next. Were her family and friends at Quantico and in Minneapolis safe? Would this presidential hideout be blown to bits by another bomb? Maybe this was the beginning of the end...*don't think about that shit,* she caught herself, *just fly the bird, do your job, and don't fuck it up.*

"Talon, BUNKER," the voice on the radio crackled.

"Talon One," Maj Elliott responded.

"Cleared to hover and land, terminus runway three-two, look for flares."

"Hover and land, terminus three-two, flares, Talon One."

"One other thing, Talon, state the pax in Talon Two."

Elliott paused before responding, trying to recall the unexpected passenger's particulars. "Marine Colonel Richard Pawlowski, assigned to the Pentagon NMCC—believe he's an assistant director."

"Roger, Talon. Remain in the aircraft for decontamination instructions."

"Remain aboard pending instructions, Talon One," she repeated as Capt. Stone descended towards a hill capped by a red and white arial and an operating radar.

A single, unimpressive red flare marked the landing zone—not that it was needed in the wide-open space carved out of the hillsides for the exclusive airport. A few small jets and other helicopters gleamed in the emerging morning sun at the opposite end of the lone runway. From their colorful livery, Maj. Elliott could tell they were assigned to the military's top brass and, most likely, to other government bigwigs. They had probably not flown directly into the shitstorm, like the Talon flight had, and therefore would not require decontamination.

The radio crackled again, this time with the staticky background sound of a handheld terminal. Elliott scanned the runway, unable to identify whoever was directing their arrival. "Talon One," the familiar voice began, "power down, do not disembark. Talon two, disembark one pax, and prepare to return to Quantico. Copy?"

Elliott shot a glance at her co-pilot, wanting to gauge his reaction to the odd events greeting their arrival. Andy just shrugged his shoulders, encapsulated in the bulky, hot, and increasingly uncomfortable CBRN protective garment. He felt sorry for the Talon Two crew that would have to endure another hour or more in the suits on their return flight.

"Talon One, power down, remain onboard," Maj. Elliott replied to BUNKER, followed by the Talon Two pilot repeating his guidance.

From about the midpoint of the runway, a half dozen green four-passenger golf-cart-type vehicles approached them. "UTVs," Andy commented on the intercom."

"Huh?" Elliott replied, not really wanting a discussion, but eager for something mundane to settle her thoughts.

"Utility Terrain Vehicles, that's what they're riding—electric too. Twenty grand apiece, easy."

"Talon One," the radio voice continued, "disembark nine pax, POTUS first," then adding sternly, "DO NOT remove CBRN garments or respirators."

Elliott observed as the train of odd little vehicles approached, like a giant caterpillar wending its way down the tarmac, each driven by one driver shrouded in white protective garments and a black rubber mask. "Crew, you got that guidance?" she asked on the intercom, receiving an affirmative reply as the door ajar warning flashed on the helicopter's instrument panel. Craning to see over her left shoulder, Elliott watched as the passengers shuffled down the steep steps, then bumbled around each other in their restrictive and unfamiliar protective garments. Eventually, each was gently guided and pushed into a UTV seat. "Andy, what's the radiation meter reading?" she asked.

"Forty-nine rads," he replied, holding the meter up to his mask. "We're still glowing."

"Why's that?" she demurely wondered, her focus on the apoplectic freakshow outside.

"Fallout sticking to the airframe? Plus, whatever the passengers tracked inside."

"Shit," was her quiet and preoccupied reply, as they heard the changing pitch of the Talon Two rotors as the turbines revved up for their return to Quantico. "Something's weird here," she softly mumbled, watching the line of UTVs depart, "something's off, I can feel it."

"Talon Two, cleared for immediate departure," the BUNKER voice continued.

"Talon Two, returning to Quantico," the pilot reported as the soot-dusted green and white machine lifted off into the mid-morning sky."

"I do not know what could be more 'off' than this morning," Andy began semi-sarcastically. "We're at the P-COOP wearing nuke suits at eight in the morning; we landed on the south lawn in a blizzard of fresh fallout and a forest fire of office buildings; we flew by the Pentagon half-falling into a nuclear bomb crater; the roads were clogged by not-moving cars with people shooting at each other, and we woke up to an orange sky way before sunrise. Yeah, I would say there is definitely something 'off' about today."

"Yes, to all that," Elliott gently responded in a muted and neutral tone while watching the UTVs recede from the high perch of her pilot's seat. "I've just got a hinky feeling about this."

"Hinky?"

"That's what detectives say in true crime books—when they think someone's not being forthcoming, or hiding something."

The radio crackled, "Talon One, stand-by for decontamination after the POTUS delegation. All weapons, ammunition, and incendiaries are to remain onboard the aircraft. Confirm."

"Roger," Elliott replied, repeating the order verbatim. "I'm ready to take this damn thing off," she complained to Andy, pulling on the round air filter to find a more comfortable fit of the mask that seemed to be suffocating her.

***

They had been waiting for almost ninety minutes, Maj. Elliott realized after a quick glance at the cockpit's mission clock. The morning cloud cover had dissipated, allowing the sun to begin roasting the Talon One crew stuck inside the Marine One helicopter. Through the multiple layers of their protective garments, she could hear Andy lightly snoring, his head resting against the frame of an opened cockpit window. Behind them, the three-man crew was quietly lounging on the presidential reclining leather seats. They had left the aircraft's passenger door open for the minimal cooling effect it offered.

The sweat's pooling under my butt, Elliott realized, relieved to see two of the green UTVs finally zipping down the runway towards them. "Talon to BUNKER, request guidance" she called on the radio, hoping to speed things up.

"Disembark for decontamination," came the terse reply.

Leaving the airstrip, the UTVs followed a gravel path through the surrounding forest to an encampment that looked freshly erected. There was a structure set up in an "H" pattern formed by two large windowless tents and a wheel-mounted trailer. Everything was in desert tan, with a concrete pad surrounded by about a half-acre of gravel. The trailer formed the center of the "H" and connected on either end to the tents which formed two goalposts of the configuration. Elliott realized she had seen the same set-up on a combat tour in Iraq. *They would strip naked in one of the big tents; get blasted by a shower inside the trailer; then be issued replacement clothes in the second tent.*

The decontamination site was operated by white-suited individuals wearing elbow-length green gloves and fireman-type breathing masks. Following their muffled guidance and hand signals, the Talon One crew crunched their way from the UTVs to the first tent. *How many men are going to see me naked?* she wondered. Everything—wedding bands included—but not dog tags, went into plastic-lined drums. The shower, gentle as a car wash, came after a dousing of foam soap that stung like astringent on a fresh cut. All five of them were as clean as they would ever be, and, they were told, less radioactive than they had been.

A new set of UTVs and drivers drove them zig-zagging through an array of jersey barriers past an aggressively armed security checkpoint. They entered a large, brightly lit tunnel bored into the mountainside following a paved, two-lane road for, Elliott guessed, the length of two football fields. Along the way, the UTVs passed an indoor pool the size of half a gridiron "Drinking water?" Andy murmured from his accustomed seat to Elliott's right. Jerking to a stop, the drivers directed their passengers to folding tables and chairs, where a clerk began familiar military in-processing steps by handing each of them a clipboard of forms to complete.

A safety briefing was followed by a quick tour of the facility areas that were not off-limits to helicopter crews. At the first stop, they were provided a paper sack with toiletries, changes of underwear, and a second bright orange, one-piece jumpsuit like the ones they were wearing. Their guide assigned Elliott to a forlorn-looking women's cinderblock dorm with double bunks. The others placed their belongings on bunks stacked four-high in a much bigger men's dormitory. Communal, but not co-ed, baths completed the basic training meets high school gym class vibe of the P-COOP. "Not exactly James Bond," Andy derisively quipped.

Everything seemed to be either stone, metal, glass, or concrete. Harsh fluorescent lighting accentuated the basement-like atmosphere. The bunker occupants wore yellow, orange, red, and other-colored jumpsuits by function, which visually popped in the bleak surroundings. Caves are naturally cooler than the outside air, and Elliott wondered if a second tee-shirt would help warm her. An audible hissing of air was ever-present, as was a barely perceptible hum of generators and the scent of spent diesel fuel. It also smelled like hotdogs, which, Capt. Stone figured, were for lunch that day. For snacks, vending machines were provided in the stone-bored tunnels. On their way to the cafeteria, the Talon One crew passed multiple "executive suites," with twin-sized beds and the low-rent look of 1960's tourist cabins. These were reserved for high-level politicians, administrators, and military leaders.

***

Maj Elliott loitered at the end of the cafeteria line, pretending to add sugar and cream to her coffee cup. Finally, as Colonel Pawlowski approached the drink station, she asked with a smile, "Sir, can I join you for lunch today?"

Startled by the unknown woman's bold familiarity, Pawlowski reflexively scanned her orange jumpsuit for its missing rank, name, and branch of service insignia. During that second, or two, he also wondered what his wife was doing at that moment back at their quarters on Quantico.

Proffering a hand to the tall colonel she offered, "Major Gwynn Elliott, sir. I was the lead pilot for the Talon extraction this morning."

"Oh!" he responded. "That was quite the adventure—as is this hidey-hole," he added while nodding his head to the rows of folding tables, "Pick a seat."

Moving to an empty table away from the other eaters, she sat down on the hard bench while the colonel placed his tray opposite her. Listening closely, she heard the muffled sound of something hard hitting the bench as he sat down and squirmed slightly with a focused look of concentration. "Comfortable, sir?" she asked knowingly before biting into a hot dog.

Busted, he thought. *This woman, this major, was playing him. He should have stashed it in his clothing bag on his bunk—but then, what good was it if he couldn't immediately use it?* Suddenly not hungry, he waited for her next move.

Elliott smirked over the rim of her plastic cup, enjoying the look of unwanted wonderment the colonel was trying to suppress. "That could be a knife or brass knuckles in your back pocket, sir, but I'm gonna guess it's a gun—and not one issued with our underwear and shoes."

"That obvious?" Pawlowski groaned in defeat.

"Kind of..."

"You turning me in?" he sighed, defeatedly.

"Never," she murmured, conspiratorially, "but I am curious what you're planning to do with that thing."

Sitting straighter, he wiggled his hips to reposition the gun and ate a bite of hotdog. "It's a derringer," he explained, "five-shot, twenty-two long-rifle. Plus, I have hollow points in it."

"That might sting somebody."

"You get close enough to leave a powder burn, and it's all you'll need."

"I'm just a pilot. I prefer my marksmanship from a distance."

"I carried it in Kabul, in Bagram, and in Al-Fallujah—more for surprise than defense."

"It would be a good noise maker, I suppose, but how'd you get it through decontamination?"

"Sleight of hand—I palmed it here, put it in an armpit there, then stepped on in it the showers. Nobody bothered to notice.

"Anywhere else?" She wondered with a dropped chin and arched eyebrows.

"Uh-uh, it didn't go *up there*, if that's what you mean."

Her crooked smile faded as she leaned towards him, and with a lowered voiced inquired, "Do you get the feeling there is something 'off' about this whole thing?"

Discretely scanning their surroundings for anyone eavesdropping, he leaned in, adding "I've wondered about a few things."

"I think there's more going on here than what we've been told," Elliott whispered.

"Women's intuition?" he asked with a smirk, which she brooded over and ignored. "It is odd—very odd—that a ground burst nuke could go off in Washington without *somebody* on our side knowing about it...I mean, that's just impossible to believe."

"You think it was an inside job then?"

"Probably not—I hope not, but I have the same feeling about all this that you do."

"Something 'hinky?'"

"Exactly," he added. They sat silently while Pawlowski finished his lunch and the cafeteria emptied."

"If there's a brig in this hellhole," Elliott thought, "you'll be in it before dinner time walking around with that lump on your butt."

"I could put it in my socks or underwear, but it'll probably fall out."

"And stink," she added dismissively.

"There is a five-p.m. meeting with the president, "he whispered, "I assume to plan a nuclear counterstrike. I plan to drop in on it—that's my area of expertise."

"With that gun?" she asked incredulously and loudly.

"Shhh! It doesn't do any good," he softly muttered, "if you don't have it on your person."

"You're nuts, sir."

"Maybe, but I get the sense you may be a kindred spirit. Are you ready for a challenge?"

"What? Crash a meeting with the president—with a gun? I'm not even invited!"

"Neither am I," Pawlowski demurely added, draining his can of Diet Pepsi.

"You are crazy!"

"You say you have a hinky feeling, but you're not bold enough to act on it. This is a *once-in-a-career* opportunity, major. I've slipped into a few four-star meetings without being challenged. Usually, and this is the case today, there's too much confusion and anxiety for anyone to notice an extra attendee or two. If we do get noticed, we just walk out. If we stay, we get to witness history."

"We?"

"You and me."

"And your five-shooter?"

"Which I need you to carry."

Maj. Elliott was regretting her lunch date. Yet, the chance to attend a historical meeting with the president, and who-knows-who-else would never come again? She reached up to feel the wire support at the base of the bra she was issued that morning. *There would be room for Pawlowski's derringer in there*, she thought.

He watched her lose herself in thought while probing the outside of her jumpsuit. He knew what she was considering. He leaned to one side while quickly scanning the room, then removed the derringer, silently handing it to her under the table. "Meet me here at sixteen-fifty," he directed intensely, "then we'll go to the meeting."

She felt the warmth of the metal and wood. The entire pistol fit within the palm and fingers of one hand; it weighted about half a pound. Her conscience screamed for her to pass it back to the kooky colonel and walk away. "Okay," she mumbled, rising to find her bunk and contemplate the idiocy of what they planned to do.

Chapter 25
Crisis Management

5:00 p.m., Tuesday, 31 May ,2017

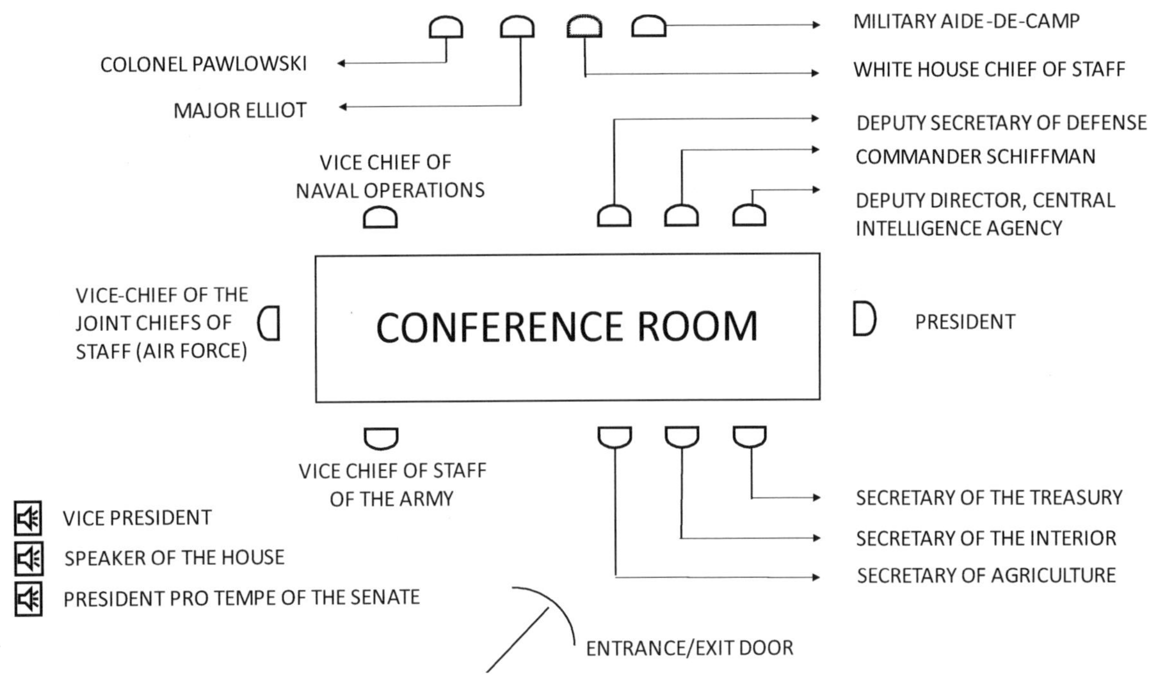

President Donald Trump entered the sparsely furnished conference room, followed by his military aide-de-camp. His two-man Secret Service detail remained posted outside the room's only door. The presidential seal was smartly embroidered below the left shoulder of the one-piece navy-blue jumpsuit issued to him after the humiliating decontamination process. The garment was too snug around the midsection for his comfort and vanity. It was also deeply creased from years of storage awaiting a crisis, and a size 3X president that necessitated its use. His aide lugged a cheap-looking black vinyl briefcase that held the prerequisite secrets required to initiate the annihilation of a significant portion of the world's population.

The president briefly scanned the musky brown-paneled room, and its dozen or so occupants rose from their seats in deference to him. Plodding across the office-grade carpet in his newly issued boat shoes, he scowled his way towards the executive chair awaiting him at the head of the conference table. Plopping heavily into the seat, he let out a long sigh, attesting to the emotionally jarring events of the day, and the weight of decisions yet to be made. He carried an unopened can of Diet Coke, his staple accompaniment for long meetings, placing it gently before him.

At the opposite end of the table, three somber, yet determined-looking faces stared back at him. They represented the Joint Chiefs of Staff, he knew, but he did not recognize them. *Probably second-or third-string alternates for the no-notice meeting,* he surmised. The president assumed the acting chairman would be the one directly across from him, and that the other two on either side of him were also four-star generals or admirals. All were in uniform—not the fancy ones with all the bells and whistles on display, but subtly different camouflage patterns. Also, as he noted upon entering the room, they were armed with pistols holstered at their sides.

The others seated at the table, as well as two more seated along the right wall, next to his aide, were mostly wearing jumpsuits. Not blue and embroidered like his, but bright orange with white tee shirts visible at the neckline—like inmates in a city jail. He recognized the three men in orange seated to his left, but not the uniformed naval officer and the jump-suited man and woman on his sides. *Those in jumpsuits got the pressure washer treatment,* he thought, his eyebrows kneading at the fresh memory. He wondered why those in uniform did not.

As usual, there were large monitors hung around the room for videoconferencing, but none of them seemed to be turned on. Background noise and someone faintly talking annoyingly came from a speaker phone positioned at the center of the table. The president knew the others would be reciting from detailed reports, mind-numbing charts, and obtuse government records. He would rely, as always, on common sense and the business acumen that had made him rich, famous, and powerful.

The funerial silence of the room was broken by the youngish naval officer nervously cleared his throat. Swiveling to face him with raised eyebrows, the president noticed he was earnestly focused on an opened notebook. The president wordlessly motioned for him to speak. "Mr. President," the officer began, desperately wanting, but failing to control a nervous quiver in his voice, "I'm Commander Peter Schiffman, a BUNKER Operations Chief." The president nodded his understanding. "The objective of this meeting is to assist you in determining a course of action in response to this morning's attack in Washington, D.C." Schiffman paused, watching as the president again silently browbeat the room and its occupants, then indicated for him to continue with another nod. "The proceedings are being recorded and I recommend we start with a record of participants."

"Okay," the president quietly responded in a soft tone, leaning forward onto his elbows and folded hands.

"The meeting attendees are based on the order of presidential succession and the need to provide you with advice and guidance."

"Got it," the president responded flatly.

"Sir, we have a voice connection to the vice president, who is aloft. The house speaker and the senate president pro tempore are also on the phone from the G-COOP site in Virginia.

"That the place they call the CLUBHOUSE?" The president gruffly interrupted.

Dislodged from the measured and practiced delivery of the familiar notes before him, Schiffman squirmed as he realized improvisation would be required. "Yes, sir," he began, "the code name for the G-GOOP is CLUBHOUSE.

"And that's were Congress is hiding?"

"Sir, the congressional leadership is there, along with the heads of major federal agencies."

Trump snorted in response; his raised eyebrows signaled Schiffman to continue.

"The secretary of state and the attorney general are both enroute to secure locations and are unavailable." Schiffman paused, and the president waved for him to continue. "At the table, as you know," Schiffman began, while pointing with an upturned hand and reading from his binder, "we have the secretary of the treasury," to whom the president nodded. "Also present are the secretary of the interior and the secretary of agriculture."

"Steve—Ryan—Sonny," Trump offered in somber salutation. The three secretaries nodded with seriously grim looks, mumbling inaudible return pleasantries.

Inhaling deeply, Schiffman continued with a mortician's gravitas, "Mr. President, The secretary of defense and the chairman of the joint chiefs of staff (JCS) are both confirmed deceased." Trump reacted to that news by settling back into his chair, and cupping his lower face with his hands. "The deputy secretary of defense and the vice chairman of the JCS are present in their stead."

"Understood," the president softly offered, leaning forward once again, "please continue."

"The director of the Central Intelligence Agency and the secretary of the Army are both reported to be incapacitated."

"How bad?"

"Sir, injured enough to be unable to travel, but we don't know more."

"Okay."

Again, pointing with his hand, CDR Schiffman added, "The deputy CIA director and the vice chief of staff of the army are here." The president nodded to the woman in an orange jumpsuit to his right, then towards the gaggle of military brass at the end of the table. "Finally, sir," Schiffman continued with a more confident voice, "the chief of naval operations is in-transit from foreign travel and is represented by the vice chief of naval operations."

"So...," the president began slowly, studying his can of Diet Coke, "we've got the VP, the house and senate, treasury, agriculture and interior," he paused looking for stragglers he may have missed, "plus the spooks and the Army, Air Force and Navy...no Marines?"

"Sir, the commandant was delayed."

"Who're they?" the president asked Schiffman, waving a thumb towards a man and woman seated along the wall with his military aide and chief of staff. Both immediately rose to stand at attention.

"Marine Colonel Richard Pawlowski, sir!" The man seemingly shouted in the hushed atmosphere of the room.

"Marine Major Gwynn Elliott, sir!" the woman immediately, but more sedately, snapped following him. Both stood ramrod straight with eyes forward, like first summer academy plebes.

What the fuck? Schiffman thought, glancing behind him, amazed that these two had the balls to weasel their way unauthorized into *The Meeting That Could End the World.* "Mr. President," Schiffman began warily, "Major Elliott was your pilot this morning; Colonel Pawlowski ordered your evacuation from the White House.

"Good," the president responded in a disinterested murmur. "The Marines are here; sit down" he boorishly directed Pawlowski and Elliott with a curt pass of his hand. Retuning his gaze to Schiffman, he sighed, adding "Let's move on."

"Mr. President, Schiffman continued from his position at the center of conference table, the Joint Chiefs will update you on this morning's bombing in Washington." The president's gaze shifted to the uniformed generals at the opposite end of the table, where the tall, slim one on the right rose to speak.

"Sir," he began hesitantly, unaccustomed to giving ad-hoc presentations without the benefit of the review, analysis and professional briefing materials provided by a staff of hundreds.

"Just tell us what we know at this point," the president suggested, sensing the general's unease.

"The weapon was a low-yield ground burst."

"Which means?"

"Which means several important things, sir. First, the weapon was not delivered by a missile or aircraft. Second, we estimate its yield at just ten kilotons."

"Which means?"

"Sir, that is smaller than the bombs dropped on Hiroshima and Nagasaki that ended World War II. Today's weapons are at least a thousand kilotons—with multiple warheads on each missile. Also, Mr. President, the bomb was a ground burst as opposed to an airburst."

The president thought of the black-and-white pictures he had seen of the Japanese cities. The bombs had scraped the landscape clear, and everything looked like an ashen fireplace hearth. He wondered if Washington, D.C., would look the same. The general had confused him, but not wanting to look unknowledgeable, he asked, "Tell me more about the on-the-ground thing."

"Sir, depending on the desired damage, a weapon can be detonated anywhere from miles to a few hundred feet above the target. High-altitude bursts target utilities and electronics. Low altitude burst maximize physical damage."

"And on-the-ground?" the president wondered.

"Well, several things, Mr. President. First, there's less immediate physical damage due to the shielding provided by nearby buildings. Second, there is more fallout because half of the bomb's energy is directed into the ground, as opposed to into the air. That's what got the Pentagon, sir—the large crater. Finally, the ground burst indicates that our enemy may not be capable of delivery by an aircraft, submarine, or intercontinental missile."

Enough of him, the president thought, motioning dismissively for the Vice Chief of Naval Operations to sit down. *No use getting bogged down in technical details. It was a small atom bomb on the ground—amateur hour. But who the fuck did it and why? Terrorists? Some whack job? How do you retaliate against that?*

"Mister President!" the vice chairman bellowed from his end of the table, slamming a fist for emphasis. "The world is watching and awaiting our response! Our forces are at DEFCON One awaiting your orders!"

Startled, the president calmly studied the general, who seemed to be ready to shake a decision out of him. Glancing at his aide and the black bag at his side, he wondered if he could order the launch of hundreds of nuclear bombs—and what would happen after that. *DEFCON One,* Trump remembered that term from movies, *military people around the planet would have their fingers on big red buttons, just waiting for his nod to attack.* "General," the president began in purposefully calm tone, "who do we attack?"

"Well," he began.

"Mr. President," the only female at the table softly began, "I have information you need."

It was the lady deputy from the CIA, sitting just a few feet away on his right. The president nodded, softly adding, "Go ahead."

"Sir, we've been monitoring Iranian operatives and a civilian defense department employee that we believe are involved in the attack." The room, which had been as subdued as a wake, erupted into a crescendo of astonished murmurs and whispers.

With the hand of a tabletop elbow slowly massaging his brow, the president, as surprised as everyone else, simply responded with, "Let's hear it."

"The low-level employee had been selling unactionable data for several decades."

With eyes closed, face flushed, and massaging his temples, the president thought of the multiple questions raised by her revelation. *I need to move fast here, and this goddamned lady is going to make me work for it.* The others in the room were glad they would not be the recipients of his impending outburst. The president rose to stand behind his large chair, grasping its tall back with clenched hands. "I'll ask quick questions," he tersely told her in a controlled tone, "and you give me really short, direct—and honest answers."

"I will, Mr. President."

"Who the fuck is responsible for this bomb?"

"We don't know with one-hundred-percent certainty."

Game over, the president thought. *He would not nuke anyone unless they could definitively prove their guilt. Just the same, they needed to protect themselves from more potential bombs.* "Who is the 'low level' employee?"

"His name was Michael Cappiello, he was a GS-13 working in army logistics."

The president heard a muffled curse come from one of the generals, probably the one from the army. "'Was'—is he dead?"

"Sir," she hesitated, "he was on the Pentagon rooftop being interrogated by two of our agents when the bomb detonated."

He counseled himself to stay focused. *The details can wait for later.* "How were the Iranians involved?"

"They'd been grooming Cappiello, and others, for years, paying for low-level intelligence of little value."

"Then they wanted more."

"Exactly, Mr. President. In the past two years, they had Cappiello set up a small warehouse near the Pentagon."

"What for?"

"We believe as a staging point for the weapon."

"But again, we're not sure?"

"Correct, but we can confirm the purple smoke devices were assembled in the warehouse."

"Purple smoke?" He vaguely recalled that news update from...*hell, just yesterday*.

"At nine locations, including inside the Pentagon. That was Cappiello with the Iranian's help. We believe it was a distraction from what happened at the Air Force Memorial.

"Air Force Memorial?" the president wondered, holding two index fingers up like the monument's curved arches. In all the excitement and movement since the explosion, no one had told him exactly where the bomb had detonated.

"Yes, sir, that is where the bomb exploded. We suspect the Russians and Chinese may be involved as well."

Scratching his scalp through his famous, but now disheveled, hairdo, the president returned heavily to his chair. "Suspect, but again, not sure?"

"We believe they helped assemble the purple smoke devices. We know two men were shot inside the van used to transport the weapon to the Air Force Memorial. Both men are being treated, under police guard, at the Fort Belvior Army hospital."

Jesus Christmas, I couldn't make this shit up if I tried, the president thought. *Stay focused...*" Okay, the army civilian was spying for the Iranians—that we can prove?"

"Yes, sir."

"We think the Iranians provided the nuke, and we suspect the Russians and Chinese helped—but we don't have proof?"

"That's correct, Mr. President."

"Okay," the president exhaled with an exhausted sigh, falling back into his leather chair. He opened the Diet Coke and drank a third-to-a-half of its room temp contents. "We have considerable means for a nuclear response, and the joint chiefs are eager to use 'em. Who gets it, where, and how much are up to me."

"Affirmative, Mr. President," she responded while checking the JCS end of the table for affirmation.

Trump glowered at Shiffman, doubting that he, or anyone else in the room, could provide him with additional details of the morning's attack. *I'll follow my gut, but I won't make a stupid knee-jerk reaction. First, I need more info, and then I need time to think about a common-sense decision.* "How long will all that take?" he queried softly to the tabletop. Unsure who should reply, the attendees remained mute. "If I order a nuclear attack, how long will it take to happen?"

"Sir," Schiffman began, "because we're at Defense Readiness Condition One worldwide, and because your orders are expected, it should take about ten minutes?"

"Just ten minutes to bomb Tehran?"

"Ten minutes to launch continental United States and submarine-based missiles—which will take another fifteen to thirty minutes to reach their targets. If your chosen plan includes aircraft delivery of bombs or cruise missiles, those actions will take considerably longer."

The president leaned back in his chair again, his head cocked sideways on the high, padded back. *Jesus,* he thought, *this is a fucking mess.* He glanced askew at the deputy CIA lady parked next to Schiffman. *She knew about the crazy civilian bastard and didn't stop him. That deputy SECDEF on the other side of Schiffman, a professional bureaucrat, no doubt, he was not much help either.* Looking down at the table's end, he saw the three hawks in uniform staring holes into him. *They want to make this train wreck a million times worse.* "Steve," he said, turning to face the secretary of commerce, "I'd like your thoughts."

"Well, Mr. President," he began, shifting forward onto his elbows, "it's a mess."

"No doubt," the president replied, happy to have found a confederate among the assembled experts.

"Global markets stopped trading as news of the attack spread."

"Stocks, bonds, commodities...gold?"

"All of them, Mr. President, worldwide. I don'tt think they will reopen until this crisis is resolved. People fear much worse will happen. The markets will crash if they reopen before that fear resides."

"What about the banks?"

"They're closed too, the Federal Reserve as well. For one thing, the data management infrastructure has been terribly damaged—nationwide—by this morning's event. The investment banks won't trade because they can't price things. The retail banks that tried to open today were mobbed and had to close. I heard some news about shootings and fatalities. People are panicking, as I guess, they should be."

The president thought about that, imagining mayhem on the streets of New York City with unfettered looting, assaults, and power outages. "Steve, what should I do?"

"Consider this, Mr. President, we are already carrying historic levels of debt. At some point—and nobody knows when—the market for U.S. government bond sales will begin to taper off. We will be forced to pay more interest for the money needed to cover on-going budget deficits. That was probably going to happen without this morning's attack, but now it's here. Also, the cost of rebuilding the federal government will be huge."

The president felt better and drank the rest of the Diet Coke. He understood exactly what the Treasury Secretary was telling him. *Why make this shitstorm worse if we are already approaching a financial black hole?* His gaze shifted to the secretary of agriculture; he needed to hear some more good advice. "Sonny, help me out here."

"Mr. President," he began in his deep Georgia drawl, "I'll make it short and sweet for you."

"Do that."

"If we don't clean up this clusterfuck real soon, many millions of people are going to be hungry, cold, ill-clothed and short of medicines. Plus, there will be no power, no clean water, and no gas for the car. It's that simple. Also, I'm not just talking about this country. This shit's already beginning to ripple out to the rest of the world. It's already a real bad deal, why make it worse?"

The president watched as the three military hawks opposite him held a mini-conference in hushed tones, with their arms and hands urgently churning the air in front of them. "Okay, Ryan," he told the secretary of the interior, "I need to hear from you."

"Mr. President," he began, "we don't need to talk about national parks, forests, wildlife, logging and mineral rights—those things will all be fine in the long-run."

The president sensed the secretary was bullshitting his way out of a tight spot, but tried not to show it. *I'll fire his ass later*, he thought. "Good, is that it then?" was all he said.

"No sir, I'd like to offer you my opinion, if you want it."

That, is what he needed...assuming it was good advice. "I do. Go ahead."

"The bomb was puny by today's standards—about ten kilotons. It was also delivered by truck—not by missile. Both of those things indicate non-state actors—terrorists. The bomb went off in a park at four in the morning. If it had exploded on the National Mall at four in the afternoon, damage and fatalities would have been much higher. That indicates whoever is responsible wanted to send a message more than maximize damage and death."

"And what do you think that message was?" came a sneering challenge from vice chairman of JCS at the far end of the table.

The secretary did not miss a beat. "I don't know, and apparently, neither do you*, general*!" he barked back.

"Gentlemen!" the president interceded with a raised palm. "Let's all keep our cool; Ryan, wrap it up."

"The immediate damage was to the Pentagon, so if there's a message, that's our big clue," he said, glancing down at the vice chairman. "We know about the army civilian's involvement. We are aware of the incidents involving purple smoke and the warehouse. We know there are two foreigners in the army hospital—who may or may not be from China or Russia. The CIA tells us, they believe the Iranians are involved, but they don't have concrete proof. Finally, no one has stepped up to claim responsibility for the bomb."

"Good summation, Ryan. Very helpful. Thank-you," the president replied. He remembered the three phone participants, but decided to ignore them. The VP was just a rubber stamp. The Senate and House would just ask for trillions more of emergency deficit spending to "rebuild" from the bombing. He pushed back from the table and rose to his feet, both knees audibly popping. "Here's what we're going to do right now," he announced—"nothing."

The vice chairman shot to his feet, bellowing, "Mister President!"

With arched eyebrows and a sullen look, the president studied the four-star general across the room and wondered if his agitation would segue into something worse. As a businessman, few people dared to openly confront him at such a high level. His enemies typically hired a phalanx of cutthroat attorneys to slowly do their dirty work for them. The Washington politicians, he soon learned, were worse. They would leak information to the press, then use their committees, hearings, subpoenas, and other dirty tricks—even the courts, to resist him. Rarely had anyone dared to challenge him face-to-face.

"Sit down, general," the president calmy seethed, "and I'll explain." Visibly breathing in huffing gulps and with tension knotted in his reddened face and throat, the vice chairman reluctantly returned to his seat. Turning to face Commander Schiffman, the President directed, "We'll reconvene at eight-a.m. with the same participants."

"Yes, sir," Schiffman replied.

"Keep track of the time for this schedule I'm about to give—I don't want go over an hour."

"Yes, sir."

Pivoting towards the deputy CIA direction with a scowl, the President demanded, "I want to know more about this Pentagon employee and why he was not stopped. I want more details on the Iranians, and I want to know more about the Russian and Chinese men in the hospital—along with any new developments. You will have ten minutes, and Commander Schiffman will enforce time limits for each speaker. Also, and this is for everyone, no slides, and no back-and-forth except between me and the speaker.

To the three generals seated at the other end of the long table, he directed, "I want conventional and nuclear response options from the Air Force, Navy, and Army. Five minutes each, including overnight updates. Also, no foreign invasions and no boots on the ground." Swiveling left to face his cabinet secretaries he said, "Steve, Sonny and Ryan, you get five minutes each for updates and second thoughts, if you don't need the time, then don't use it." His attention turned to the right-side wall, where Pawlowski and Elliott were silently gasping at the sudden presidential attention. "Colonel...?" the president began, "and major...?" he continued.

"Pawlowski, sir," the Colonel replied calmly.

"Elliott, sir," the major replied, following the Colonel's lead, and wondering what was coming next.

"I'd like your thoughts in the morning—five minutes each. Pretend you're not in the military, just at home with family—what would your thoughts be and what would you want the government's response to be for this mess? You will be our representatives for American citizens. Can you do that?" Both officers responded affirmatively, their attention drifting to their presidential homework assignments.

Commander Schiffman was ready when the president looked at him. "Fifty minutes for all speakers, sir."

"Mr. President..." came the grating voice of the speaker of the house over the audio line. "I believe the house and senate should be given the opportunity to speak."

Grimacing and kneading his forehead, the president committed another political faux pas while making half-hearted amends for his Freudian slip. "Commander," he began, "let's give the house speaker and the senate president three minutes each on the phone tomorrow morning." He doubted that an atom bomb could break the enmity of his political oppressors, but for decorum's sake, he would pretend to listen to them.

"Thank-you, Mr. President," came the insincere reply on the phone, almost imperceptibly incensed by being limited to just three minutes.

"Good," the president continued, sitting upright with arms on the table and rubbing his hands together. "Here are my thoughts: We need to address the public's panic and fear—lets meet again at six-a.m., and do another emergency broadcast message no later than eight-a.m. We need to take care of the dead, the wounded, and the sick. We need to stabilize things in Washington and provide food and shelter to those who need it. Most of that, I expect, is already beginning to happen. We also need to know for certain who is responsible for the bomb *before* we decide on an appropriate response. Maybe more information on that will come in during the next twelve hours. Then we need to focus on rebuilding." The president paused with a self-satisfied scowl and slightly nodded his head. *Good plan*, he told himself. He also realized he needed to pee and was thus eager to end the meeting. Rising to his feet, he nodded to this chief of staff, adding, "Let's huddle."

Chapter 26

Decision

31 May and 1 June, 2017

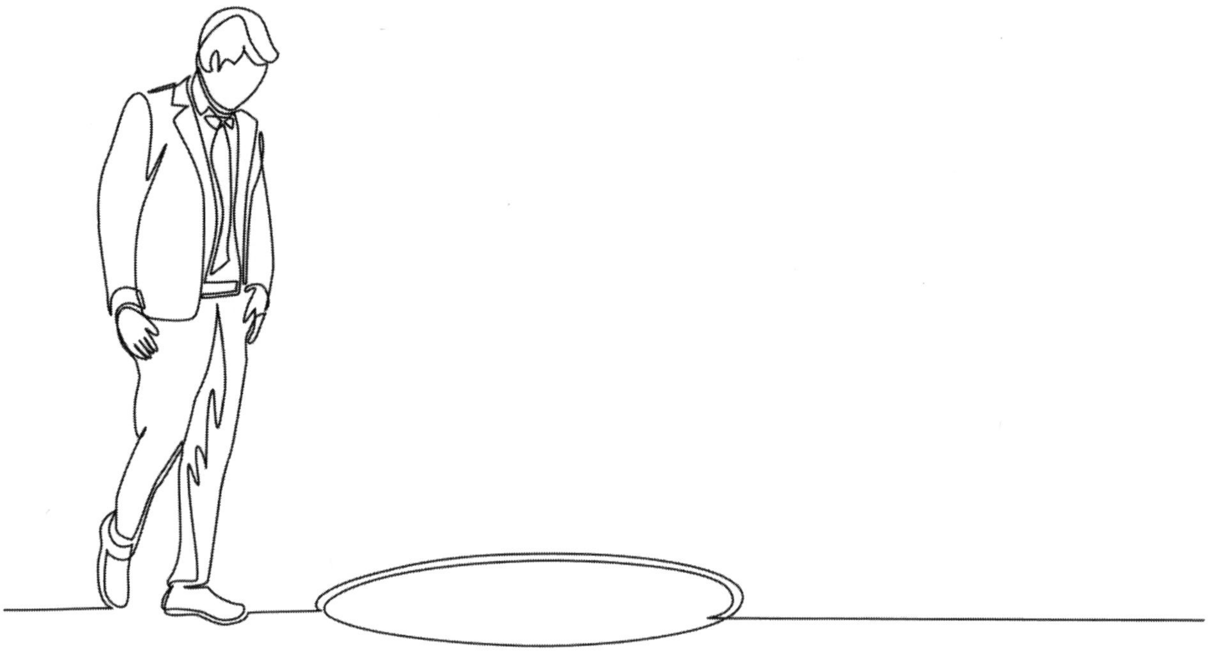

Propped against the headboard of his queen-sized bed, the president glanced at the wall clock in his bunker quarters. “I’ve got an hour max before the pill kicks in,” he told his chief of staff occupying a rattan chair in a corner of the small room. After a long swig of Diet Coke, he added, “I want to be clear-headed and refreshed before I make a decision tomorrow morning.”

The man in the chair nodded in silent agreement, holding a pen and notepad, awaiting the overnight to-do list he knew would be forthcoming. That morning, he had grabbed three random White House staffers by surprise for the trip to the P-COOP. The timing of Ahmed’s bomb had limited his selection to those working through the night. The ideal team of staffers would have included legal, national security, foreign policy, economic, military, and communications advisors. The three-person support team that boarded Maj. Elliott’s rescue helicopter included a deputy associate counsel, a video editor, and a speechwriter. Whatever overnight tasks the President was preparing to dictate, these were the White House aids the chief of staff would use to complete them.

"Review the message traffic coming in from other countries," the President began. "Look for powerful clues on who bombed us."

"Got it," the chief of staff mumbled.

"Find out how bad the out-of-control situation is out there. They will be worst in the big cities with weak law and order...looting, arson, and gunfire. Then we need to move in a strong army presence where it's needed the most."

"Got it."

"I need to know what my legal options are, and are not."

"You mean who do you have to confer with, the War Powers Act, and what not?"

"The whole thing. Can I make a very, very though decision on my own, or do I have to work with the unfair morons in Congress?"

"We'll find out."

"Get started on the emergency message for tomorrow...no bullshit, just facts they can use. We'll do a quick update after the six-a.m. meeting.

"We've got a good speech writer with us."

"Did he do this morning's message?"

"*She* did, Mr. President."

"Good—tell her not to be too fancy, like that boring speech this morning. We need to be honest, but not too scary. We need to calm and reassure people. Also, call the vice president on his plane and see what he's thinking. Ask him if he has any really good ideas for the meeting in the morning."

"Do you want us to contact the House and Senate leadership at the CLUBHOUSE bunker?"

The president winced, looking expectantly at his chief of staff for a punch line that did not come. "Do they need help planning investigations and hearings to blame me for all of this? I wish I *did* have the Russian contacts they accuse me of; then I could call the Kremlin and get some amazing intel. Which reminds me, if any of the really big leaders, like the ones from the G-8, call tonight, I want you to talk to them. Don't wake me up unless something huge happens." The president opened a second Diet Coke and seemed to drink most of it before shifting to lay on his back, still clothed in his jumpsuit and boat shoes.

"Do you want something to eat tonight?" the chief of staff wondered.

"Millions and millions are probably not eating tonight," the president mused, staring at the ceiling. "They had these Nathan's hotdogs at Coney Island; they were amazing. They boiled 'em in beer—which I don't drink, but they were still very good. I would always eat two—with yellow mustard, not the spicy kind. I'm not hungry tonight."

"I understand, Mr. President."

"Tell me, Chris, what do you make of all this?"

The chief of staff knew this opportunity would be coming and was prepared with a short and concise response he hoped would guide the president in making his momentous decision. "We're in a deep dark hole of our own making," he began.

"I'm falling into one with this sleeping pill," the president jibed, rolling onto his side.

"We've spent the last sixty years creating or responding to one mistake after another, and now we're where we are, and someone figures it's a good time to attack us."

"I'll rattle off some really awful mistakes, then you tell me who that someone might be."

"Deal."

"Sixty years of mistakes...Vietnam for starters."

"Yup."

"The savings and loan, dot-com and home mortgage implosions."

"Good so far."

"Drugs, immigration and the disgusting 9-11 slash Afghanistan slash Iraq fiascos."

"All of the above, Mr. President. We've been bouncing around like a pinball, responding to one crisis after another. This one, just this morning, is probably the biggest one yet."

"All more the reason not to totally fuck up our response. Now, before I nod off and forget, tell the guards to wake me at four-thirty and tell the first lady I'm asleep. But, before you go, tell me who you think attacked us."

"If it was the Russians or the Chinese, there's not much we can do about it. If we attack them, it will quickly escalate, and the hole we're in will become the world's largest crater. The rest of the planet will be dragged down with us. Mr. President, it just doesn't make any sense to do that."

"Believe me, I really, really agree with that. Just the same, what's the good of all these goddamned nukes if you can't use 'em?

"Watch out for the generals at the end of the table in the morning, they've got itchy trigger fingers."

"I've noticed," the president mumbled softly. "What about the radical Muslims?" he wondered, his speech slurring.

"The CIA knows more than they have told us so far. The answer may lie with that Pentagon employee they mentioned—what the fuck were they doing on the roof of the building..." Hearing the president's light snoring, the chief of staff stopped talking, quietly exited the executive quarters, and began his long night of completing his boss' taskers.

***

Twilight was falling in the National Capital Region, ending a stress-filled and incredibly worrisome day for its surviving residents. The immediate victims were not alone, as most of mankind monitored the sketchy and repetitive news reports of the blast that day in Washington. According to conventional wisdom, a massive nuclear counterstrike by the Americans was imminent. The apprehension over the unknowns and follow-on consequences of the expected American vengeance would interfere with billions of people's sleep that night. Many sensed that global hysteria, unrest—and violence were percolating and about to boil over.

The time of day had little impact on the survivors burrowed deep within the wreckage of the Pentagon. Without interior electric lighting, their shelter-in-place spot was as dark as a cave. They had stumbled upon each other while exploring the building's smoky, jagged, and crumbled remains. Eventually, it was agreed that a five-hundred-seat auditorium, deep within the building's basement, and well shielded from the bomb's radiation, would make a good group shelter.

The highest-ranking officer present, a naval captain, assumed command, and the others respected the authority of his rank. Water was slowly rising in the lowest levels of the big, open room, but not fast enough to pose a problem. The elevated stage became a rustic field hospital, and the room's four corners were each designated for food and water, quartermaster supplies, an armory, and headquarters staff. They designated latrines in the outer hallway, and personal sleeping quarters were to be claimed in whatever theater chair was not already taken.

The uninjured were assigned to the scavenger parties responsible for securing supplies. One team made multiple trips to the building's food court, another to the medical clinic. An operations officer knew of stockpiled emergency rations and civil disobedience equipment, the latter a bountiful supply of flashlights, batteries, and, surprisingly, flare guns. Because the radios were not working, the commander assigned a two-man team to continuously fire signal flares into the leaden sky that hung above Washington that day.

Over three hundred personnel, about half military and half civilian, eventually found their way to the auditorium. About a quarter of them were injured enough to visit the stage-based medical facility. Some remained there, requiring care beyond the rudimentary services available at that moment. It was agreed that the dead encountered throughout the day would be left where they lay, more as a practical solution than out of a lack of compassion for their fallen comrades and co-workers.

Twenty miles south of the Pentagon, the Fort Belvior Army Airfield was abuzz with activity. The 160th SOAR A (Special Operations Aviation Regiment, Airborne) was arriving from Fort Campbell, Kentucky. This included dozens of UH-60 utility, CH-47 cargo, and AH-64 attack helicopters, along with the pilots, crews, and maintainers needed to operate them. At dawn the next day, search, rescue, and recovery operations would commence for all employees within the remains of the Pentagon. They would be retrograded to the base community hospital, which was urgently being reconfigured to handle the influx of casualties from Washington.

After the Pentagon was secured, the 160th SOAR A would join the regional rescue and relief efforts being orchestrated by the Federal Emergency Management Agency and the national incident commander appointed by the president that morning. This would include a complex mix of military, police, medical, utility, and security elements from the federal, state, and local echelons of government as well as from the private sector. Initial relief efforts were slowed by still-clogged roadways, radioactive fallout, unreliable communications, and the gargantuan size of the task at hand. To help overcome ground transport challenges, the army activated flotillas of landing craft prepositioned at Fort Belvior and at Fort Eustis, Virginia. With its fleet of watercraft, the Coast Guard began offering similar water transport services.

The DOD was busy mobilizing assets for the potential defense of the Capitol against unknown aggressors. Navy destroyers, littoral combat ships, and submarines were reassigned to patrol the Atlantic coast. The Air Force repositioned reconnaissance satellites to monitor the eastern seaboard. The Army's First Infantry Division was deployed from Fort Drum, New York, to the Chancellorsville Civil War battlefield, about fifty miles southwest of Washington. From there, it could quickly mobilize to defend the capitol without interfering with on-going rescue and relief efforts.

***

The president re-entered the small bunker conference room at exactly 6:00 a.m., plunking his unopened Diet Coke on the tabletop and dropping heavily into his chair. His military aide trailed behind him and was shadowed by someone new: a White House speechwriter. With a silent point of his index finger, the president directed her to an unoccupied seat and motioned for the secret service guards to close the room's entry/exit door. Scowling with hands on both knees, he glanced at Commander Schiffman and dourly ordered, "Let's get this started."

"Good morning, Mr. President," Schiffman began solemnly, "as directed, there has been no change from yesterday's attendees, other than..." He trailed off, nodding towards the new arrival.

"Speechwriter," the president grumbled.

"Yes, sir," Schiffman replied. "The vice president is connected from Air Force Two. The Senate and House leadership are connected through the G-COOP. Also, as directed, discussion will be limited to the current speaker and the president. Time limits for each speaker will be monitored and enforced."

"By you?"

"Yes, sir."

"I want to hear from the CIA first," the president directed, and the deputy director stood to make her presentation."

"Good morning, Mr. President!" She began chipperly with a broad smile.

Fuck that, he thought, angrily interrupting. "We are here—in this shithole—he began while audibly jabbing a forefinger on the tabletop, because something bad, very, very, bad happened yesterday morning, and we need to fix it fast, right? I'll help you people get started. First off, there was nothing serious last night to respond to, other than yesterday's very sad disaster. Also, nobody has stepped forward to claim responsibility, which is not good. I am also told a dozen of the big cities are looking like they did during the Vietnam-era riots, so I have ordered martial law to help out those mayors and governors. I've also been told that I have legal authority to make a decision on our immediate way ahead, and I plan to do that before I finish this soda pop. Then, with a new speech, I'll update the country. For the next hour, I need each of you to keep your comments relevant and succinct—no happy 'good morning, mister president,' okay? Before you start yacking, restate my guidance from yesterday, and stick to your time limits, right? Now CIA," he said glancing up at the crest-fallen deputy director, "start over."

"Sir," she began briskly, "you wanted to know more about the Pentagon employee we were monitoring and you wanted more detail on the Iranian's involvement. Finally, you wanted additional information on the suspected Russian and Chinese citizens in the hospital."

"And?" the president asked impatiently.

"We began monitoring Michael Cappiello in 1991. His Iranian handler was Naghi Panahi, an Iranian Army lieutenant colonel that paid him almost two-hundred thousand dollars over a decade."

The president had obvious questions—and profane accusations—to hurl at the speaker, as did some of the others in the room, but all remained silent.

"Cappiello's relationship with the Iranians went dormant in 2003—meaning they had no contact with each other. We kept him in his same job, preventing promotions and transfers, hoping the Iranians would reactivate him. That happened in 2015 when he was paid one-point-one million over two years to assist with the purple smoke incidents and the bombing." Overnight, between the two meetings, the agency had decided not to provide the president with details of Conway and Loretta's interrogation of Mike. That information, they decided, would be best kept in-house.

With his head drooping to his chest in disbelief, the president resignedly inquired, "who was his 'handler' the second time? The same guy?"

"No, sir, it was Meysam Hedayati, a former colonel from the Iranian Air Force."

"Former?" the president mumbled, picking up on that key point.

"Retired, Mr. President."

“Is it a sure thing this second handler was working for the government of Iran, and not moonlighting for some terrorist outfit?” the president wondered, regaining his confidence.

“*Mister President!*” The unwelcome interjection came from the far end of the table. It was the JCS vice chairman again, barking in frustration at the obvious Iranian involvement being challenged.

Shut the fuck up! The president thought as he glared harshly at the interrupter. Struggling to project calm while churning within, he calmly repeated to the deputy director, “Can you prove this second handler was working for the Iranian government—or can’t you?”

“The same bank account was used in 1991 as in 2015. Also, other sleeper assets were being reactivated...” She watched as the president’s head jerked backward repeatedly, as if he were being electrocuted. His grimacing face was a shade of red. Never known for patience, restraint, or subtlety, he looked like he was about to explode. “No sir,” she quickly added, we do not have definitive proof that Meysam Hedayati was a current agent of the Iranian government.”

Trying to regain his calm, the president made a show of slowly opening the Diet Coke and taking a small sip. “Do you have proof that the Iranian government possesses a working atomic weapon?”

“We don’t, but the Russians and Chinese...” She was cut off by the president's raised palm, the last non-verbal warning she would receive that morning.

“Tell me about the two men in the army hospital you mentioned yesterday. Do you have it nailed down, for certain, that they are from Russia and China?”

She wanted to explain the two men's presence at the Penrose warehouse and inside the white van before the bomb ignited. The agency had photographs and reams of documentation in the form of agent reports. However, because the men carried no identification, and could not speak after being shot in the face, she simply replied with a mumbled, “No, Mr. President, not at this time.”

“Two minutes remaining,” CMDR Schiffman quietly intoned.

“So,” the president began rhetorically, speaking to the ceiling while reclining in his chair with legs crossed. “We don’t know *who* attacked us, other than this now-deceased, low-level Pentagon employee that was being monitored for almost three decades—and never stopped. We also don’t know *why* whoever did it felt compelled to nuke Washington.”

“Mr. President, I have to strongly disagree,” the JCS vice chairman verbally shot across the table.”

"In a minute, general." the president murmured in a neutral tone. "CIA, do you have anything else for us this morning?"

"There's a proven logic," she began defensively, "for monitoring subversive activity over a time period, Mr. President."

"It's your time—please explain."

"As we stated, the information Mr. Cappiello provided was non-actionable."

"I'd have to say you're phenomenally wrong about that, given what happened yesterday morning."

"He did not have accesses to critical information."

"That's stupid too," the president absentmindedly responded, picking at lint on his navy-blue jumpsuit.

"We track hundreds of military personnel, federal employees, and defense contractors that we suspect of being compromised. For most of them, our goal is to leave them in place so they can lead us to higher-value opposition targets."

"That," the president decided while sitting up in his chair, "is a debate for another time. Thank-you for your input, it was very helpful." Glancing to the deputy director's right as she sat down, he studied the deputy secretary of defense, who had yet to contribute to either meeting. "Do *you* have anything to add?" he wondered.

"Me, Mr. President?" The gray-bearded and bespectacled man meekly asked, unprepared to speak.

"You're the deputy secretary of defense, right? What are your thoughts this morning?"

"The department stands ready to implement your orders, Mr. President!" he replied.

A wallflower and a loser, the president thought, *the government was full of 'em. They would not last five minutes in the business world he came from.* His gaze and thoughts were directed toward Commander Schiffman.

The vice president is next, Mr. President—five minutes.

"I only have one thing to say, Mr. President," came the VP's former talk-radio host voice over the speakerphone.

Good, the president thought, replying with, "Let's hear it, Mike."

"Before we launch any military response, we need incontrovertible proof of another nation's guilt."

"Believe me, Mike, I agree," the president stalled, not sure of the meaning of 'incontrovertible.' "Do you have any examples?"

"It's just common sense, Mr. President. If we don't have transpicuous and unequivocable proof of Iranian, Russian or Chinese participation in the blast, then it would be foolish to attack any of those countries."

"Don't attack without surefire poof. If that's what you're saying, Mike, then I agree—it's just common sense," the president awkwardly responded to the black speaker phone while warily keeping an eye on the JCS vice chairman for another outburst."

"That's all I have, Mr. President."

"Thanks, Mike." *No use avoiding it, the president thought,* unenthusiastically adding "while we're on the phone, let's hear from the House and Senate—three minutes each."

"Good mawhnin', Mistuh President!" came the Brooklyn voice of the Senate leader. He seemed to always have reading glasses balanced on the tip of his nose. The president wondered if he wore them while jabbering on the phone. "The Speaker of the House and I would like to combine our time allotments into one block, if that is okay."

"Go ahead," the president grumbled.

"First, of course, and most importantly, our thoughts and prayers go out to everyone in Washington impacted by this cowardly terrorist attack." He paused, awaiting confirmation, but the phone remained silent. "We understand that evacuation efforts are underway and expanding in size with every hour. Secondly, the speaker and I want to assure you, Mr. President, that Congress will fully support whatever actions you approve today. Now is the time to work together and put aside our political differences."

An olive branch peace offering? "Is that it?" the president asked, ready to move on to the military hawks eager to brief him.

"Just a few other things, Mr. President."

Here it comes. He imagined the senator looking through his eyeglasses at a long list before him.

"The impact on the mid-Atlantic environment will be devasting, as will overall negative impact on global climate change. Who knows if we will ever return to the Washington area with the lingering radiation damage? The speaker and I are sponsoring a $10 trillion-dollar American Rescue Plan to support recovery operations and to begin planning for the future. Also, to ensure the safety and continuity of the federal government, we propose a new bicoastal American capital—half in New York City, and half in San Francisco. This will be enabled by modern technology and built by union labor with stringent diversity, equity, and inclusiveness goals in mind."

With his face buried in hands supported by tabletop elbows, the president decided it would be best to ignore the shameless and naked political power grab. "Okay," he sighed while reaching for his drink can, "let's hear from the joint chiefs."

The vice chairman stood slowly, with the solemn look of a pastor beginning a sermon on Revelations. "Mr. President," he began, "I'll speak for all three services and present a combined arms recommendation for your consideration." The president nodded his understanding, so he continued. "You asked for strategic nuclear and tactical non-nuclear scenarios, with a prohibition against ground forces."

"I did," the president concurred. "What have you got?"

"Sir, we agree with the vice president, that lacking incontrovertible proof of responsibility, a nuclear strike at this time is not recommended."

Relived to have that burden eliminated, the president wondered, "What do you recommend?"

"Sir, we are prepared, upon your orders, to execute three scenarios to demonstrate American supremacy and resolve to our enemies. To not quickly do so aggressively, and definitively, we believe, would be a grave mistake."

"Time, Commander Schiffman?" The president inquired, eager to pick up the pace and end the lecture from the generals.

"Twelve minutes remaining, sir" came Schiffman's blunt reply.

Annoyed at being rebuffed, the general continued, "We recommend using the X-37B OTV (Orbital Test Vehicle) to disable the Chinese Tiangong-2 Space Laboratory."

"What exactly does that entail?"

"The OTV will be maneuvered towards, then depressurize the Tiangong-2, forcing it to renter the Earth's atmosphere."

War in space, the president thought, *was probably inevitable, but not on my watch*. "What's the second scenario, general?"

"Cyber warfare, Mr. President. We recommend severing the undersea fiber optic cables that support Russia's access to the internet. This will disrupt vital computer systems and severely impact their military, industry, and overall economy."

"And the third?" the president asked.

"Iran appears to be the most culpable actor in yesterday's attack, so they should receive the harshest counterattack."

"Which would be?"

"The B-2 stealth bomber will drop the GBU-57 Massive Ordnance Penetrator on underground research reactors in Bonab, Ramsar and Tehran, Iran."

Of the three scenarios, the last one was the best, but it did not matter, because there would be no counterattacks—at least not right now. Maybe when more intelligence came in and they could prove someone's guilt, then he would let the military do what it was best at. It was almost seven o'clock. He needed to read and correct whatever the speechwriter was typing on her laptop. He also needed to practice delivering it a couple of times before the broadcast. He needed to end the meeting so he could clear the room. "Thank-you, general, that will be all for now."

Miffed by the president's dismissive attitude, the vice chairman demanded, "Sir, we need your guidance *now*!"

Here we go, the president thought, studying the admiral and general seated to either side of the vice chairman. They looked either embarrassed or concerned about their boss, who was still standing and glaring at the president. "My decision, general, is the same as it was yesterday. Military reprisals will have to wait until we have absolute proof. Until then, our priorities are as I laid them out at yesterday's meeting."

All eyes, even of the preoccupied speech writer, were on the vice chairman, wondering whether he would sit down and calm down—or possibly something else. Of all the odd events of the past several days, another was not unimaginable, and the Air Force general did not disappoint. As perceived in slow motion by all attendees, he somewhat mechanically removed his sidearm from its holster. A dull click accompanied the release of the safety mechanism as he pointed his loaded automatic at the President of the United States of America. What seems rational to a madman can never be known or understood. The changes or outcomes he envisioned, as his two fellow joint chiefs looked on in horror, will never be known.

The uninvited interlopers may have saved the president's life, or they may have just overreacted to a manageable situation. Exchanging quick and knowing glances, Col. Pawlowski shoved Maj. Elliott out of her chair and onto the thinly carpeted floor. Commander Schiffman watched in astonishment, as she tugged at her clothes and chest, as if on fire—then removed a miniature revolver. Reflexively, she assumed a prone firing stance on her elbows with feet spread far apart. Gripping the very small gun with both hands, she pulled back the hammer, took careful aim, and fired one round.

The others in the meeting would later remark, in shrouded secrecy, how it all happened so fast—just like a car accident. Still focused on the vice chairman, yet aware of movement along the wall seats, most of them thought the president was being shot when Elliott's derringer fired. Aiming carefully between multiple legs under the table, she hit the bottom of the room's door, alerting the Secret Service guards outside. They apprised the situation before the door fully opened. "Gun!" one of them screamed while launching himself horizontally to shield the president. Steadying himself against the doorframe, the other agent squeezed off a fatal three-round burst that knocked the startled vice chairman into the far wall. "Nobody move!" he screamed in a deep, commanding voice, a cordite haze blossoming around him. They all willingly complied.

Having tossed the derringer, Elliott wondered if she would be shot next. She laid perfectly flat and immobile on the floor, having just witnessed the president being tackled from his chair by a black-suited man. They both lay just a few feet away, the president red-faced and struggling to breathe with the agent atop him.

Chapter 27
Come What May

9:00 a.m., 1 June, 2017

Ahmed had the volume on the RV's radio turned down to low. The Emergency Alert System had been repeating the same information on fifteen-minute loops, and it was becoming annoying. As planned, his bodyguards had driven him to the moribund tourist trap on the North and South Carolina border. Arriving before the second action, the mall-sized parking lot had been nearly deserted. Now it overflowed with stranded travelers from the adjacent interstate highway. Ahmed was anxious to continue southwest towards the Smoky Mountains and escape the lavatory stench that was beginning to surround them.

At 9:00 a.m., he turned up the radio volume and reclined in his seat, eagerly anticipating a promised update from the president. Then the unmistakable voice of the famous man filled the interior of the luxury motor coach:

> Good morning, America.
>
> I have just completed two outstanding meetings with our country's highest military, congressional and administration leaders. The good news is—and believe me on this—there will be absolutely no more incidents like yesterday's terrible events in Washington.
>
> As I mentioned yesterday, General Darius Jackson is already making tremendous progress leading recovery operations in our nation's capital. The fabulously brave men and women of our armed

> Services, police, and fire departments and medical personnel are working arm-in-arm to recover and provide care for those impacted by yesterday's events.
>
> Also, General Lynn Shupbach is leading the effort to identify the source of this horrible, terrible thing. Currently, we do not know who is responsible or what may have motivated them. Believe me, when we do find out who the bad guys are; they will never, never challenge America again.
>
> What is tremendously important now, is that we all return to our normal lives as soon as possible. This will be easier for some than others and will require everyone's patience and adjustments. This afternoon, my wife and I will depart for Camp David, Maryland, where the provisional White House has been established. I will be returning to my job along with each of you.
>
> I have unbelievable faith that if Americans stand united, and work together, we can quickly recover from yesterday's events, and continue to accomplish extraordinary things.
>
> Thank-you; may God's protection be upon you and your family, and may He continue to bless the United States of America.

The driver's seat quietly hummed as an electric motor slowly elevated Ahmed to an upright position. Turning off the radio, he looked to his right at Mike, who was fully reclined and loudly snoring in the passenger's seat. Ahmed fondly recalled a fall afternoon spent with Mike and his dog at the University of Kansas. They had shared a few beers and, as usual, had friendly debates—probably about religion. Mike had been stubbornly independent and free-willed. At the time, Ahmed thought he was helping to broaden his friend's provincial mindset. It took decades for him to realize the opposite had happened. Unwittingly, Mike had planted seeds of doubt and awareness that slowly blossomed within Ahmed, helping him immensely in navigating from his youth to the present.

Grabbing a fleece blanket from an overhead bin, Ahmed gently placed it on Mike. "A friend in need is a friend indeed," he softly intoned. Ahmed had defied his billionaire brotherhood of co-conspirators by scheming with Arif to ensure Mike's safety. A key tenet of the plan was that the hired American would perish when the weapon detonated—thus eliminating a loose end that could potentially expose the perpetrators. Being an arms merchant required the ability to shoulder a heavy moral burden, but Ahmed found he could not sanction the death of his long-ago friend.

Conway and Loretta did find a man sleeping under Mike's desk in room 1D343. They also interrogated him in their secret basement SCIF, then remorselessly shoved him off the Pentagon rooftop. That man looked and acted like Mike Cappiello; he was even clothed in Mike's soiled shirt, pants, and shoes worn on the day of the first action, but he was an imposter. The two agents were sloppy and easily fooled; their reconnaissance had always been at a distance through telephoto lenses. They had never been face-to-face with Mike until that fateful night.

Mike's double was an out-of-work actor. His Broadway credits included being a background bookstore worker in *84 Charing Cross Road*. Then, in *Children of a Lesser God*, he was a deaf student who spoke with a guttural moan. During 736 performances of *Cats*, he convincingly licked the artificial fur covering his shoes and hands. He was also poor, single, and dying of colon cancer. Two million untaxed dollars convinced him to accept one final role. Then he hosted a huge party and gave it all away.

Unable to gain weight, the actor created fattening undergarments to look more like Mike. Hair coloring and a trip to Mike's barber to duplicate his cheap combover finished the transformation. He had never been inside the Pentagon, but a map and Mike's identification and CAC card were all he needed to make his way to room 1D343. He knew something would happen at 4:00 a.m., and he understood there would be no more sunrises for him. Instinctively, sheltering under Mike's desk felt more secure to him, so he hid there with a box of tissues. Being jarred awake by Conway's stabbing toe was never part of the plan. Before the final curtain came down, he willingly complied with the two agents and played the most interesting improvisational role of his life.

***

Their next stop was a commercial RV campground in Sevierville, Tennessee, almost 500 miles from Washington. Ahmed wanted to hide among the other tourists and monitor the situation before risking their final dash to Savannah, Georgia. After three cramped weeks of eating canned food and avoiding the few other campers around them, Ahmed, Mike, and the two bodyguards were ready to leave.

Ahmed had expected a post-9-11-type reaction to the bombing of the Pentagon. Americans would stay close to home and avoid traveling. School summer programs and college classes would probably be curtailed or cancelled. Business would be slow for airlines, hotels, and restaurants. At the macro level, home sales would decrease, stocks would fall when markets reopened, and there would probably be an uptick in the newly unemployed. After a month or two, the shock would subside, and things would slowly but eventually return to normal.

What happened was much worse. The entire country—and many foreigners—seemed to suffer from a collective case of post-traumatic stress disorder, with little sign of abatement. First, there had been the expected rioting, vandalism, and looting—but in thousands of towns, not just in the big cities. Then came the predictable hoarding of perishables and essentials like milk, bread, eggs, and toilet paper. It was as if the entire country was prepping for the same blizzard. The next stage was the ransacking of building supply, drug, liquor, gun, tobacco, and other stores by eagerly paying customers. The rumors were that once current supplies were sold, it was doubtful when the shelves would be restocked—and they were prescient.

Three weeks after the blast, airlines were still grounded, and the probability of anyone receiving working internet or telephone service was 50/50 at best. The National Guard was still deployed nationwide, and homeless shelters were overflowing. The reconstructed Department of Homeland Security was busy drafting rationing procedures for essential items like flour, sugar, coffee, gasoline, and home heating oil. The stock and commodity markets attempted to reopen multiple times, with trading halted by automatic stop-loss triggers after just a few minutes. Due to a lack of foreign buyers, the provisional Treasury Department abandoned a half-trillion-dollar American Recovery Bond sale. Maybe, the collective PTSD would eventually lessen, Washington would be rebuilt, and the economy would expand back to its previous robust levels. Maybe, but it would take years—possibly decades.

***

The motor coach was approaching Macon, Georgia, less than two hundred miles from Savannah and the refuge of Ahmed's waiting yacht. Mike was driving, having grown so accustomed to piloting the big RV that it felt like a much smaller truck gliding down the near-vacant highway. Squinting out the grimy windscreen, Ahmed searched an upcoming exit for signs of a truck stop that was not only open, but also had diesel fuel to sell. "We might be walking pretty soon," Mike lamented after glancing at the fuel gage.

At its core, the plan was basically to save America from itself. The mind-bending jolt of the atomic bombing of Washington would magically reverse the death spiral of political and social upheaval that was slowly, but surely, degrading the country's influence on the world stage. This would stymie expansion plans by nefarious dictators and despots eager to fill the power void left by the Americans. An unspoken stretch goal would have been mankind's recognition that it had outgrown the unwanted legacy of nuclear weapons developed by previous generations. If only it were that simple.

"Keep going," Ahmed murmured dispiritedly with a slight wave of his hand at the passing exit. "There's no fuel here."

After a few minutes of silence, Mike asked, "Do you think we'll get caught?" He sensed Ahmed developing a reply, so he waited a few more road miles for his answer.

"We are already caught, Mikel, not that it matters." Now Ahmed waited for a response from his surprised friend, which, Mike being Mike, did not come. "They know about you, and Arif and the two mercenaries. The blast forensics will tell them the source of the bomb's core. Eventually, one of my friends will say something stupid where he should not, and then the Americans will connect all the dots. I imagine that is a pretty high priority for them," he added off handedly.

"Where *did* that core come from?" Mike asked. "For that matter, where did you get the entire bomb?"

"Mikel," Ahmed sighed, "many things are best left unsaid."

Mike, drove, thought, and waited.

"They will never hold a news conference, pointing at enlarged bad pictures of us. It would be too embarrassing to admit such a big screw-up on their part. Eventually, they will quietly come to us for information, but we will never be locked up."

"So says you," Mike added skeptically, his gaze on the shimmering roadway. "What about the press, and private investigators? People don't just forget and move on, not for big things like that."

"You mean conspiracy nuts?"

"Yeah," Mike responded, "...like the aliens at Roswell...or JFK in Dallas."

"Marylyn Monroe, "Ahmed said, faking a swoon, "who died *alone* in her bedroom."

"Elvis lives!" Mike shouted triumphantly, thrusting a fist into the air.

They snorked enthusiastically, both secretly wondering when the misery they had unsheathed would inevitably ensnare them.

***

Look back over the past, with its changing
empires that rose and fell, and you can
foresee the future, too.
Marcus Aurelius, Roman Emperor, 121 to 180 A.D.

So, in war, the way is to avoid what is
strong, and strike at what is weak.
<u>The Art of War</u>, by Sun Tzu, around 500 B.C.

Let your plans be dark and impenetrable
as night, and when you move, fall like a thunderbolt.
<u>The Art of War</u>

Clearly, a civilization that feels guilty for
everything it is and does will lack the
energy and conviction to defend itself.
Jean-Francois Revel, French Philosopher, 1924-2006

Made in the USA
Columbia, SC
25 August 2024

41162697R00133